What Readers Are Saying about

Death of a Garage Sale Newbie:

"Fun and perceptive, intriguing and entertaining—*Death of a Garage Sale Newbie* is a mystery that demanded my attention from page one. Interesting characters with a passion for the "good deal" won my heart, and I loved tagging along on the hunt for the next great find *and* the next clue. Sharon Dunn is one of my all-time favorite authors, and I wasn't disappointed!"

TRICIA GOYER, award-winning author of
Generation NeXt Parenting and *Night Song*

"What a fun read! In *Death of a Garage Sale Newbie*, Sharon Dunn has concocted a lively mystery peopled with characters I'd love to spend time with."

CAROL COX, author of *Ticket to Tomorrow* and *Fair Game*

"*Death of a Garage Sale Newbie* is Sharon Dunn's latest triple-play homerun. She swirls together whimsy, faith, and mayhem into a delightful read. Thank you, Sharon!"

LYN COTE, author of *The Women of Ivy Manor*

"I love the members of the Bargain Hunters Network. Hats off to Sharon Dunn for a fun and intriguing read!"

MARLO SCHALESKY, author of *Veil of Fire*

"*Death of a Garage Sale Newbie* is more fun than a table full of underpriced gadgets at a yard sale! It's a clever mystery filled with engaging characters."

MINDY STARNS CLARK, author of the *Smart Chick Mysteries*

"How much trouble can four garage-saling, bargain-hunting friends get into? Plenty! Murder, danger, and excitement...but also some unexpected revelations about the power of love, friendship, and faith."

LORENA MCCOURTNEY, author of the *Ivy Malone Mysteries*

A Bargain Hunters
MYSTERY
Book One

Death
of a Garage Sale Newbie

A Novel

SHARON DUNN

Multnomah Books

DEATH OF A GARAGE SALE NEWBIE
Published by Multnomah Books
A division of Random House Inc.

© 2007 by Sharon Dunn

International Standard Book Number: 1-59052-689-9

Cover illustration by Krista Joy Johnson

Scripture quotations are from:

The Holy Bible, New International Version © 1973, 1984 by International Bible Society, used by permission of Zondervan Publishing House.

Multnomah is a trademark of Multnomah Publishers, and is registered in the U.S. Patent and Trademark Office. The colophon is a trademark of Multnomah Publishers.

Printed in the United States of America

For information:
MULTNOMAH BOOKS
12265 ORACLE BOULEVARD, SUITE 200
COLORADO SPRINGS, COLORADO 80921

Library of Congress Cataloging-in-Publication Data
Dunn, Sharon, 1965-
  Death of a garage sale newbie : a novel / Sharon Dunn.
    p. cm. — (A bargain hunters mystery ; bk. 1)
  ISBN 1-59052-689-9
  1. Garage sales–Fiction. I. Title.
PS3604.U57D43 2007
813'.6–dc22

2006031463

07 08 09 10 11 12—10 9 8 7 6 5 4 3 2 1 0

*To my mother, who saw the blue lights
and ran toward them.*

•••••••••••••••••••••••••••••••••

For I have learned to be content
whatever the circumstances.
I know what it is to be in need,
and I know what it is to have plenty.
I have learned the secret to being content
in any and every situation,
whether well fed or hungry,
whether living in plenty or in want.

PHILIPPIANS 4:11–12

The first ring of the phone vibrated in an empty house. Morning shone through open curtains. Breakfast dishes—two plates, two coffee mugs—hung drying in the rack. The second ring went unnoticed, but the third ring caused a gray cat with white toes to jump from her usual post on the counter by the microwave to the floor. The cat rolled on its back in a beam of sunlight, flexing its paws to the ceiling.

After the fourth ring, the answering machine clicked on and a crisp, mature female voice said: *"Hello, you've reached Ginger and Earl's place. Obviously, we're not here right now. Although Earl might be working on some contraption in his garage."*

In the background a male voice said, *"They're not contraptions. They're inventions."*

The female voice cleared her throat. *"In any case, he can't come to the phone. Please leave a message."*

The machine beeped, and a voice that rippled like sheets fluttering on a clothesline said, *"Ginger, Mary Margret here. I was hoping to catch you before you left. You'd be so proud of me. I've already hit four garage sales, and it's not even eight o'clock. I got the cutest little fishing pole for Jonathan and...well, you'll see. I can't wait to show you and the girls my finds. I have to pop over to some property to meet another agent from the office; then I can hit a few more sales. I'm so excited. I'll see you and Suzanne and Kindra at noon, my place. You have the key, so you can just go* inside if I'm not there yet." She laughed. *"I have a gift for you sitting on the counter."*

Three hours and twenty-seven minutes passed. The cat sauntered across the countertop, stopping to stick her nose in the butter dish before resuming her post. This was the feline's secret. When her people were home, she had to trade the smooth hardness of the countertop for the lumpy cat bed the old woman had sewn.

The phone rang again. On the first ring, the cat stood up and arched her back, spreading her toes to get the sleepiness out of them. On the second, she posed at the edge of the counter, and on the third ring, she leapt to the floor and stood at the door, expecting someone to open it. The phone rang a fourth time, and Ginger spoke her message again.

The cat tilted her head in the direction of the speaker as the machine beeped and the same rippling voice spoke—only more frantic this time.

"Ginger, Ginger are you there?" Heavy sigh. *"You're probably still out garage saling. I think I've discovered something, something terribly bad, illegal from the past. I don't know what to do. I can't think straight; I'm afraid. Please, if you do stop by your place after you're done garage saling, well I—I'm so shook up, I can't remember your cell number. I've gone and erased what I had programmed in."* She lowered her voice. *"I'm really afraid."*

The answering machine clicked off with a vibrating buzz.

One

Ginger Salinski gripped her box of garage sale treasures a little tighter. She slowed her pace up the stairs to Mary Margret's house. The door hung slightly open. Odd. Her friend was one of those tidy people who closed doors even if she was just running out to the mailbox.

"Hello...Mary Margret?" She shifted the bulky box in her arms and pushed the door open the rest of the way with her foot.

Sunlight flooded through the kitchen and splashed across a counter that separated the kitchen from the small living room.

A broken drinking glass glistened on the linoleum.

Ginger bent over and placed her box on the floor. Her hand fluttered to her neck. Alarm corseted her rib cage. So Mary Margret, the compulsive cleaner, had left a broken glass on the floor. No big deal.

The kitchen clock said it was exactly noon. The other bargain hunters, Suzanne Thomas and Kindra Hall, would be here any minute. Mary Margret should have been sitting with a tray of cookies and iced tea waiting for them. They always met at her house because it was centrally located to the good garage sale territories in Three Horses.

Ginger stepped toward the counter, pushing aside a gift basket that blocked her view to the living room. Folded clothes had been knocked off the coffee table to the floor.

Something was not right.

Mary Margret wouldn't leave clothes out. She certainly wouldn't leave them on the floor. Ginger gathered up the clothes, tossed them in the laundry basket, and trotted down the hall. "Mary Margret? It's me, Ginger."

Her friend was eight years older than her, but in good health. She pushed open the bedroom door and held her breath, expecting to see Mary on the floor unconscious or gasping for breath—or worse.

Her heartbeat increased. Broken glass and knocked-over clothes suggested some sort of struggle or a person in a hurry. But there was no blood, no reason to think...

She slammed her palm against her chest. Why couldn't she get a deep breath?

She ran to the attached garage. Mary's little blue Jetta was gone. She raced back to the kitchen. If her friend had run an unexpected errand, she would have left a note. Mary Margret always left a note.

She scanned the refrigerator and the bulletin board. No note. No note anywhere. When she raced outside to check for the blue Jetta, Kindra and Suzanne were coming up the sidewalk, holding their boxes of treasures. Suzanne's box rested on her bulging stomach. Kindra had a way of lilting up and down as she walked.

Their smiles, the sight of them, calmed her. She'd been alone, and she had allowed her imagination to run wild like a contestant on *The Price Is Right*. This was supposed to be a happy afternoon. Any moment now, Mary Margret would pull up and explain where she had gone off to in such a hurry.

Ginger took a deep breath and managed to smile back. Her friends were here. Together, they would decide what to do about the missing fourth member of the Bargain Hunters Network.

SHARON DUNN

Half an hour later, no amount of deep breathing could loosen the tension in Ginger's chest. The consensus had been to share the treasures and to wait for Mary Margret.

Ginger focused on the polka-dot skirt Kindra held up. "It's nice, kiddo." She massaged the tight spot in the middle of her chest. "You can wear it to classes in the fall."

The sight of the broken glass in the garbage had made the hairs on the back of Ginger's neck come to attention. Suzanne and Kindra weren't as worried as she was. Why couldn't she just follow their lead and relax? Because they hadn't spent five minutes calling Mary Margret's name in the empty house. Because they hadn't seen the messed-up laundry. Because they hadn't looked for the note that wasn't there.

Kindra's blond ponytail bobbed as she bounced three times. The kid's cheerleader syndrome was acting up again. She could not do anything important without bouncing three times first.

Kindra twirled with the skirt held up to her waist. "And I can wear it for work at the restaurant this summer. Isn't it just breezy and fresh? It's a LizSport. Fifty cents, ladies, fifty cents! And I don't think it's even been worn."

"I like it." Suzanne lowered herself onto the couch beside her box of garage sale finds. She rested one hand on her huge belly. Sweat glistened on her forehead. "I can't wait until I can wear cute stuff like that. I've worn this jumper through four pregnancies. I'm so sick of it I think I'll have a ceremonial burning after this one is born. Is that how you felt about your four pregnancies, Ginger? Ginger?"

Ginger shook her head. "Mary would have left a note if she had run out for some reason."

Kindra followed Ginger into the kitchen. "Maybe she saw a last-minute sale she couldn't pass up on the way home."

"The garage sale section of the newspaper is right here. So is her city map." After checking a city map, Mary had put numbers beside the garage sales to show the order she would hit each sale so she wouldn't backtrack and lose valuable time. Ginger fingered the map. *God bless her, just like I taught her.* "Did any of you see her while you were on your circuit?"

Both women shook their heads. "I worked the south side of town." Suzanne readjusted herself on the couch.

"Me, too," said Kindra.

Ginger glanced down at the torn newspaper listing the garage sales. Mary Margret had worked the north side.

"What say we give her another fifteen minutes?" Kindra adjusted her shirt collar. The diminutive nineteen-year-old looked smart in her navy shorts and sleeveless cotton blouse.

Ginger planted her hands on the countertop. "You're right. I'm sure there is a reasonable explanation." Short of Mary Margret being abducted by a UFO, she couldn't think of what that explanation would be. "Let's share what we bought. I promise I'll pay attention."

Think happy thoughts. Don't let your mind scurry to those anxious places.

"Suzanne, it's your turn to share." Kindra folded her skirt and wandered back into the living room.

Suzanne half bent and half rolled toward her own box. "I've got to show you this cute little toy I picked up for Allie. Got it in that subdivision off of Fourth Street. The lady wanted two dollars, but I talked her down to one."

Kindra sat in the leather easy chair kitty-corner from Suzanne. "I love that subdivision. There's like a bunch of skinny women who are shopaholics. Their husbands must make them garage sale stuff when the closets get too full. I find clothing with tags still on them."

Suzanne nodded. "I pick up lots of almost-new things for the kids there all the time." She pulled out a plastic multi-colored box with stars, ovals, and circles cut into it. "It plays music and comes with little rubber toys you can put through the holes and..."

Suzanne's words faded as Ginger's thoughts spider-webbed in a thousand worried directions. Where on earth could Mary Margret have gone? She hadn't dashed out to help a neighbor. Her car was not in the garage or on the street. She'd gone somewhere in her car...or been taken.

A crashing noise jerked Ginger out of her worry-fest.

Suzanne had tossed the toy back in her box. "Oh, forget it. Ginger, you're not listening to me."

Ginger gripped the countertop. She'd done it again. "Ladies, I'm sorry. I know we're supposed to be having fun, but some-thing is wrong here." Her eyes traveled to the gift basket Mary Margret had left on the counter. The little envelope read *To Ginger*. She removed the card from the envelope and read:

> Ginger, everything in this basket I got on clearance
> or at garage sales. Just like you taught me. And it is
> everything you love. Thank you for all your help in
> teaching me to balance my budget. MM.

Ginger touched her friend's precisely formed letters. They'd been acquaintances at church for years. But a year ago, they'd met at the clearance rack in JCPenney. Mary was newly widowed and learning the meaning of the term *budget*. Ginger's picture was in the dictionary beside the word *budget*. She and Earl had raised four kids on his phone company salary and done just fine, thank you very much. You meet the nicest people at clearance racks.

Mary had lined the basket in pink gingham. There were candles, tea, soap, bundles of fabric wrapped in ribbons, and seed packets. The scratched fishing pole, with its oversized reel that featured Mickey Mouse dancing, looked out of place. Ginger didn't fish and it was old and icky, not new like the other stuff. Maybe Mary had intended it for Earl as an afterthought.

"Earth to Ginger." Kindra's voice caused Ginger to jerk her hand away from the basket.

"Join us on this planet," Suzanne said. "You usually jump up and down when I show you stuff still in the box it came in. You didn't so much as bat an eyelash." Placing a fist on her hip, she scooted to the edge of the couch and narrowed her eyes. "Are you feeling okay?"

Ginger tugged at one of her brassy brown curls. She was closer to Mary than the other two were. That's why she was feeling this way. "Mary Margret would call if she was going to be late." She let go of the strand of hair. It sprang back to her head, resuming its sausage shape. "Have you ever known her *not* to leave a note about where she would be?"

Both women shook their heads.

"When I came in here, the door was unlocked. You saw me clean up the broken glass on the kitchen floor, and I refolded and put away the laundry that had fallen off the coffee table. You know what a neatnik Mary Margret is. If she had gone anywhere, she would have cleaned up first unless she had to leave in a hurry."

Both women nodded.

Suzanne performed her version of leaning forward to show interest, which involved bending her neck about ten degrees. "And her car is gone?"

Ginger nodded. Now they were tracking with her.

"I know." Kindra sprang to her feet and bounced three times. "What is the one thing that makes you change your habits and behave unpredictably?" She didn't wait for an answer. "Being in love. Mary Margret met a really hot guy, and she's taken off on a whirlwind romance."

Suzanne rolled her eyes. "Kindra dear, after age thirty, the word *hot* only comes into your vocabulary when you're talking about oven temperatures."

Sometimes Ginger had a hard time believing Kindra was a physics major. "Mary hasn't dated since her husband died. Her whole life is church, work, and learning how to spot a bargain. Besides, how many men do you see on the garage sale circuit, let alone hot ones?"

Kindra tossed her skirt into her box of garage sale treasures. "It was just a theory." The younger woman's shoulders drooped.

Ginger edged past the kitchen counter and wrapped an arm around Kindra, giving her shoulders a reassuring squeeze. "Theories are good, kiddo. They get you to thinking and coming up with ideas, right, Suzanne?"

"Maybe she got into a fender bender or something." Suzanne wiped sweat trickling past her temple. "We are obviously not going to have any fun today until we find Mary Margret."

"I don't have to work until tonight." Kindra pulled her scrunchie out of her hair and combed through the long blond strands with her fingers. "I can stay here in case she comes back."

"I'll stop at the real estate office where she works on the way home." The tightness in Ginger's chest subsided. Doing something to solve a problem always took care of her tension. Now the others understood the urgency she felt.

"I can swing by the church." Suzanne planted her palms behind her and pushed as if to get up.

Ginger and Kindra darted to the couch and held out hands for Suzanne to grasp. The pregnant woman only wobbled slightly when she straightened her knees. They stood holding hands.

Ginger uttered, "Lord, help us to find our friend. We're worried."

The other two women said "amen."

Kindra lifted Suzanne's box of garage sale stuff and placed it in her hands. "I'm sure she'll show up within the hour. Maybe we can all get together tomorrow after church to share what we bought."

"I can't after church." Suzanne waddled toward the door, breathing heavily, as if she had just run a marathon. "Ben has a baseball game."

Kindra tilted her head. "This is my favorite part of the week, sharing the good deals I found with you guys."

Ginger tucked a stray strand of Kindra's hair behind her ear. "We'll figure something out." She walked over to the counter and hooked her arm through the gift basket, then gathered her own box of stuff. "Whoever sees Mary first calls the other two." Ginger pointed to the cell phone pocket on her purse. "I'll keep checking messages."

"Deal," said Kindra.

Outside, Suzanne squeezed into the driver's seat of her little Honda and drove away. Ginger unlocked the trunk of her car, put the basket and the box in, then shut it.

The invisible press of a gaze caused her to turn suddenly. The only movement in the neighborhood was a child riding a tricycle down the sidewalk.

Shading her eyes from the noonday sun, Ginger looked at each parked car—a blue SUV, a beige compact, a white truck, two red cars, and a brown older-model something or other parked where the street curved.

SHARON DUNN

She studied each empty green lawn. A bald, potbellied man two houses down from Mary Margret's came around the side of his house holding a hose connected to an outdoor spigot. After flipping up his sunglasses, he leaned over to turn on the water and sprayed his flower bed, not even glancing at Ginger.

Nothing suspicious. Just a beautiful Montana summer day in a nice neighborhood. Mary Margret's neighborhood.

Ginger placed a flat hand on her chest and took a deep breath. Where on earth could that woman be?

Kindra came to the door waving her microscopic phone in the air. "Remember, message on the cell."

Ginger waved back. They were doing all they could. She got into her Pontiac and turned the ignition key. Her car started with a smooth hum. She said a prayer of thanks that Earl always kept the cars running so nice.

Almost as quickly as she had a clear positive thought, her head filled with cotton balls—tangled, anxious thoughts she could not shake. She pulled out onto the street, revved up the hill, came to a stop, and clicked on her blinker to pull out onto the main road.

The real estate office where Mary Margret worked was next to a convenience store and attached to doctor's and dentist's offices. Business was slow on Saturday, only five cars in the lot and none of them were Mary Margret's blue Volkswagen Jetta. She stopped in front of the glass door that said Jackson-Wheeler Real Estate. Inside, a heavyset woman pushed a vacuum across the carpet.

When Ginger pulled on the metal handle, the door didn't budge. She rapped on the glass. Her knuckles were hurting by the time the cleaning lady noticed her, clicked off her vacuum, and trudged to the door.

"Yes." The woman groaned rather than spoke her words, then pulled back her sleeve to check her watch.

Ginger recognized the crocheted sweater the woman was wearing as one that had been on the two-dollar table at Wal-Mart a week ago. The cleaning lady had close-set eyes, and the only makeup she wore was bright orange lipstick.

"I'm looking for someone who works here, Mary Margret Parker."

"I just clean the place on Saturday. I don't know anybody but the man who hired me, Mr. Jackson; he's a big fella."

"You haven't seen anybody, say in the last hour or so?"

"Only been here fifteen minutes. Place was locked when I got here."

"Can I look around?"

The woman rubbed the middle of her back and squinted. "You work here?"

"No, my friend does. If you're concerned about me taking anything, you can watch me."

The woman half nodded and then stepped to one side. "I guess that would be okay." She wandered back to her vacuum. "Long as you stay where I can see you." The vacuum clicked on with a shrill buzz.

The bulletin board just inside the door featured the top salespeople for the month. Mary Margret's bright face was noticeably absent. All the others on the board probably hadn't seen the far side of thirty yet.

Beside the board was a computer-generated list, complete with pictures, of the properties that had been sold that month and who had closed the deal. Jackson-Wheeler Real Estate sure sold a lot of houses, half of them vacation homes. Three Horses, Montana, had a fluctuating population of about thirty thousand. The town's main draw was a lake

　　　　　　　　　　SHARON DUNN

surrounded by mountains. Many of the citizens were part-timers who left when the white stuff fell out of the sky. In five months, the town would decrease by about five thousand, and the permanent residents would hunker down for winter, extending hospitality to the occasional out-of-state hunter.

She studied the sales board. None of the properties had Mary Margret's name by them.

With the shrill hum of the vacuum pressing on her ears, Ginger wandered to the back of the narrow office, where she found Mary Margret's desk. A snapshot of Jonathan, Mary's two-year-old grandson who lived in California, and a photo of Mary standing with Ginger, Kindra, and a much thinner Suzanne were the only personal items on the desk.

She picked up the picture of the Bargain Hunters Network, called BHN by the four members, that had been taken at their barbecue last summer at Ginger's house. Mary had her arms around Ginger and Kindra. Glints of sunlight shone in her silver-white hair. She beamed at the camera with that easy smile she had.

Still clutching the photo, Ginger turned a half circle in the office. That was that. Unless she was hiding in the paper clip drawer, Mary Margret was not here. After placing the photograph back on the desk, Ginger wandered past the cleaning woman's cart and pretended like her chest wasn't getting all tight again. One of the bottles on the cleaning cart caught her eye.

The woman shut off her vacuum, straightened her spine, and placed her hand on her ample hip. "Can I help you," she barked.

Ginger held up the bottle. "This will be on sale next week at the House of Spic and Span. I have a friend who works there. She always gives me the heads-up when a sale is coming."

For the first time, the cleaning woman smiled. "Thank you. I'll have to get down there."

A kind word turned away much wrath, and if the kind word mentioned a good deal, it worked even better. "Glad to be of help."

Helping people save money usually made her warm all over. But right now she was too worried about Mary Margret. Ginger left the office and got into her car. She checked her cell for messages. Suzanne had already phoned in to say that Mary was not at the church. After starting her car, Ginger shifted into reverse, turned around, shifted into first, then headed back to the main road.

She came to the edge of town where the mall, now twenty years old, buzzed with Saturday activity. She passed a boundary of the town, which was marked with a Welcome to Three Horses sign, a sculpture of three metal horses, and a man in a military uniform. The town had been settled over a hundred years ago as a fort and trading center with the local tribes. The town name was a reference to a good trade a military man had gotten. What the Native American had received out of the transaction never came up in the history books.

Main Street turned into the highway, and she pressed on the accelerator. After ten minutes, Ginger pulled onto the country road that led to her and Earl's house. She checked her rearview mirror.

A brown car was riding her bumper.

Two

The disclaimer on the side mirror of Ginger's car read: "Objects in mirror may be closer than they appear." If that were true, this nondescript gold, no-sort-of-brown car would be hooked to her bumper.

The dust cloud blowing through her open window had jerked her out of her preoccupation over Mary Margret. When she glanced in the side mirror, the visor covered most of the driver's face. The car slowed and drew farther away from her. Still, it continued to follow her.

The houses were far apart out here. Not good garage sale territory. She passed a trailer house with a huge red barn beside it. Cows grazed in rich green fields. She sped past a white Colonial framed by two large oaks. The car, about a hundred yards behind her and stirring up dust, still did not pull off. At the next opportunity, she took a sharp right turn onto another dirt road away from her house. The brownish car turned as well. This guy stuck like glue.

Ginger readjusted her sticky palms, loosening the death grip she had on the steering wheel. Her heart drummed away. Lifting her foot from the accelerator, she slowed to a snail's pace. Again, she checked the rearview mirror. The car hung back but continued to follow her. She slowed to the pace of a snail about to die. Why on earth would someone be after her?

Maybe it was just some kid with a new driver's license playing a game.

Ginger stared straight ahead and considered her options. If she turned back and tried to get home, she'd have five miles of open fields before she got to Earl and his shotgun. She glanced at her purse on the passenger seat. She could use her cell to alert Earl. The police were at least twenty minutes away in town, so no sense in calling them. Besides, this might be nothing.

The roar of an engine caused her to look out her side window. As a red Jeep zoomed by, rocks sprayed against the metal of her car, making pinging noises. The driver yelled indiscernible phrases and pointed at her. His compressed expression and pucker suggested he had just left a lemon-sucking party. Was he sitting on a porcupine? Poor man looked like he was in pain.

The silver bumper of the Jeep glinted in the sun as it turned onto a side road and disappeared behind a blanket of trees.

The brown car had slipped even farther back, but it was still there. Ginger hit the gas. She could see a house up ahead, a log cabin with a row of rosebushes on one side of it. But as she approached the house, she saw no cars, no sign of life anywhere. The brown car loomed behind her. She zoomed past the log cabin.

The landscape was flat enough that she could see a little yellow house with kids jumping on a trampoline about half a mile ahead. Ginger swallowed, trying to produce some moisture in her mouth.

The needle on her speedometer pointed to forty when she let up on the accelerator and turned left down the long driveway to the house. The children, a boy and a girl, slowed their jumping and gazed at her.

She killed the engine, took a deep breath, and opened her car door. Their bouncing stopped altogether when she set her sandaled foot on the ground and stepped out of the car. A light breeze rippled her cotton shirt and matching capri pants that she'd gotten on clearance at Macy's last August, 60 percent off. It paid to shop out of season.

The children, who didn't know her from Adam, stared.

She needed to get out and meet her neighbors anyway. This was a good excuse. "Kind of a windy day, isn't it?" She glanced up the road. No sign of the brown car.

The children continued to eyeball her, their mouths open. The girl, maybe six years old, was dressed in a floral one-piece swimsuit with a yellow ruffle around her belly. She placed a protective arm across her younger brother's back.

The boy twisted away and started to bounce again. "I can do a flip."

"Stop it, Johnny." The girl's body shook from the effect of her brother's jumping. She crossed her arms and wrinkled her forehead. "Are you looking for my mom?"

"I'm your neighbor, Ginger Salinski. I live up the road about five miles." The screen door creaked, and a woman holding an area rug came out the door. The woman, short auburn hair blowing in the breeze, flipped one end of the rug out and lifted her arms to shake it—then she noticed Ginger.

Still gripping the rug, she stepped down the stairs and approached Ginger. "May I help you?"

Ginger glanced back up the road, searching for her pursuer. A blue van rolled by. Maybe she should just explain about the brown car. No, that made her seem like one paranoid package. She resolved to stop watching those reruns of *The Rockford Files* with Earl. There was no reason someone would want to chase her. This thing with Mary Margret had her thinking crazy.

She said the first thing that popped into her head. "I'm sorry; I thought there was a garage sale here."

The woman turned slightly and pointed up the road. "That's north of here at the MacPhersons, way up the road." The woman assessed Ginger's feet, her knees, her stomach, and then her face. "They have all kinds of signs up. Anyone should be able to find it."

"Thanks so much." Feeling the heat rise in her cheeks, Ginger took several steps back. So much for getting to know the neighbors. This woman thought she was one slice short of a loaf.

The mom didn't take her eyes off Ginger. "No problem."

Ginger slipped behind the steering wheel as the two children returned to their bouncing. She turned the key in the ignition and glanced up at the mom, who continued to watch her. Ginger nodded and smiled. The woman didn't smile back. Instead, she gave her rug a flip and a hard shake.

After shifting into reverse, Ginger cranked the steering wheel and turned the car around. She headed up the long gravel driveway. When she glanced in her rearview mirror, the mom was still eyeballing her car, hands on her hips, eyes drawn into a squint. They probably thought she was one weird lady. Talk about making a poor first impression. One thing was for sure. They wouldn't be getting together anytime soon for a barbecue.

Ginger pulled back on the road, checking the rearview mirror again. Nothing. No brownish-gold car. She took in a full breath.

She turned onto the road that led home. The tires crunched under the gravel with an occasional spray of rocks against the side of her car.

A rock flew up and hit the windshield before deflecting off. Ginger flinched. The stone left a nick. "Earl's not going to be happy about that one." Golden fields of barley stretched in front of her without any houses in sight. Up ahead was a grove of trees and beyond that her home. It had been Earl's idea to move out to the country when he took early retirement. He wanted property with a big workshop.

Ginger inhaled deeply and relaxed her arm muscles.

Crunch! Metal rubbed against metal as her car lurched forward.

Before she could react, she felt a second bump. This time, the steering wheel jerked out of her hands. The car swerved toward the ditch.

Every ounce of oxygen vacated Ginger's lungs. Muscles in her arms and legs turned to stone. She gripped the steering wheel, struggling to keep the car on the road. With strength that surprised her, she straightened the tires, narrowly avoiding the ditch. She sped up.

Now she did have a reason to call Earl. This had gone way beyond a prank. Keeping her eyes on the road, she reached over to the passenger seat to grab her cell phone.

A glimpse of brown flashed in her rearview mirror. Again, the crunch of bumper against bumper. Her neck snapped back, but she held on to the steering wheel. Her purse rolled to the floor, out of reach.

Ginger's lower torso felt like it was being crammed into a corset. Her heart raced. She took in shallow breaths and punched the gas pedal. The old Pontiac lurched forward, engine roaring and rumbling as it gained speed.

She was a grandmother, for Pete's sake, not a character in a Steve McQueen film. Why was someone trying to run her off the road? This maniac wasn't going to prevent her from seeing all her grandchildren graduate from high school, by golly.

Topping out at sixty-five, she kept the car toward the center of the road, hoping the gravel wouldn't act like marbles under the tires and flip the vehicle. The brownish-gold car was ten feet behind her. Then twenty feet, then thirty. The open fields gave way to aspens and evergreens.

Ginger's whole body vibrated with adrenaline and fear. She slowed the car only slightly to turn into her driveway, the back tires catching air.

When she hit the brakes, the car swung around in a half circle. She waited for the dust to settle and her heart rate to slow down. She had never been so elated to see her cute blue house with the porch swing and the metal building that functioned as Earl's workshop.

She craned her neck and glanced up the road. Large evergreens partially blocked the view, but no car roared down their driveway.

She'd already opened the car door and planted her feet when Earl, welder's cap pushed back on his head, came running out of his shop. "What on earth, woman!" He furled his bushy eyebrows.

That was Earl, Mr. Sensitive. Heaven forbid that her near-death experience should interrupt his work. Her legs rubberized when she stood. "Oh Earl, someone—" She glanced back up the road. Every part of her body trembled. Her stomach clenched into a tiny ball. She took a single step forward and then got a really good view of the ground, each irregular stone, growing closer to her face.

Footsteps pounded across gravel.

Earl's strong arms pressed against her stomach and back as black dots consumed the view in front of her.

Three

Earl Salinski worried that his wife had suffered a head injury at the last door-buster sale she attended. She sat up in bed, blinking a hundred miles an hour. What had she said right before she fainted? That someone was chasing her? No one would want to run Ginger down, unless they were after her buy-one-get-one-free coupons. Some of those ladies could get pretty vicious when it came to saving money. Where did she get these crazy ideas? Maybe he shouldn't ask her to watch *The Rockford Files* with him anymore.

After tucking the covers around her, he touched her curls. "Now that's better, isn't it? You're not dizzy anymore?" Her hair hadn't always been that shade of metallic brown. He'd have to look at their wedding photo to remember what her original hair color was. That new perm made her look like a fiftysomething Shirley Temple.

She patted his hand. "Yes, dear, thank you."

He handed her the cup of tea he had placed on the nightstand.

She looked at him with those almond-shaped eyes he had fallen in love with nearly forty years ago. The eyes went from being soft and slanted to big and round.

She took in a sharp gasp of air. "Earl, I led him straight to our home." She shook her head. The teacup rattled on the saucer. "He knows where we live."

They should cut down on movies from his Steve McQueen collection, too. He wrapped his hand over hers, steadying the rattling teacup at the same time. "Ginger, please, I grant you that it's possible that some kid was playing games with you. But let's not assume you're being stalked."

He had examined the car after he'd gotten her into bed. A dent in the bumper did look new, but the old white Pontiac already had so many imperfections and scrapes, it was hard to tell.

She pulled her hand away and set the teacup on the nightstand. "Don't talk to me like I'm a child, Earl Salinski. I know what happened." Her voice skipped up half an octave, and tears rimmed her eyes. "It was terrifying. You don't believe me." Her thin lips pressed into a straight line.

"Ginger, I—" He swallowed hard to keep the irritation out of his voice. She'd been through so much today. Truth was, if someone had tried to hurt her, he was angry at himself for not being there to take care of her.

"I'm fifty-six years old." She sat up straighter in bed, tugging at the edge of the quilt. "I may have married young, but I've done a lot of living."

Earl sighed. He hated when they had to have the "you treat me like a child" fight, but they hadn't had it for several months. Obviously, she was upset about Mary Margret going AWOL, and it was coming out in this familiar fight.

Time to change the subject. Time for a fight they had never had before. Time for something that was bothering him. "You know what I'm tired of, Ginger? I'm tired of the way you don't support me in my dream of inventing something."

Ginger's mouth dropped open, and she studied him. "That's not true." She sounded like she was trying to convince herself.

"You call them contraptions. If you respected what I was doing, you'd call them what they are—" he paused for effect, not taking his eyes off her—"inventions." He pounded his fist into his palm. "Inventions, Ginger."

"Well, I—"

It was one of the few times in their long marriage he'd seen his wife speechless. "I know that you giggle with your girl-friends about the stuff I make. Inventing something that changes the world is my dream." Sure felt good to take a load off and say exactly what had been on his mind for so long. This speech had been building up in him since they'd moved out here. "Do you think working at the phone company for twenty-five years was my dream? Why do you think I took early retirement? Don't you have dreams, Ginger?"

He waited for her answer.

She cast her eyes downward, tracing the pattern in the quilt with her fingers. "I'm living my dream, Earl. Marry a good man. Raise kids. Love God. Love people. Buy stuff on sale."

His stiff posture softened. Poor thing. She looked really confused. Maybe he had dumped too much on her too quickly. But it was how he felt. He stepped toward the bed where she lay, sat beside her, and gathered her hands in his. "Help me to live my dream. I need a cheerleader in my corner."

She blinked twice, her lips drawn into a tight rosebud. "I'll try."

"Thank you." He patted her leg and rose to his feet. "I'm going back to work. You'll be okay?"

She touched her hand to her forehead. "I don't suppose anyone called about Mary Margret?"

He shrugged. "I've been in the workshop all day."

"I have a lot to do. What kind of tea was that anyway?"

"Chamomile, sweetie, chamomile. Maybe you should get a little rest." He stood in the doorway, watching her as she fluffed her pillow and turned on her side. She curled her petite frame into a C shape.

"Earl?"

"Yes."

"I'm worried about Mary Margret."

"I'm sure she is okay. She's probably on her way out here right now." He waited until she closed her eyes. She looked sweet resting under the covers.

"I need to call the girls." Her voice faded.

"It'll wait. Why don't you get a little nap?"

Just like their oldest son, Robert, who read all those self-help books, had said: Total honesty in a relationship was where it was at. Whistling, Earl stepped lightly through the house. Yep, it sure felt good.

Ginger listened to Earl's workman boots pounding on the wood floor of the hallway and through the linoleum of the kitchen. The screen door creaked as it swung open and then slammed against the door frame. Her eyes shot open. She sat up in bed. Even though she was exhausted, the last thing she wanted to do was sleep.

She felt horrible after what Earl had said to her. Was she really not supportive of him? Was that how he saw it? For the two years he had been retired, she always regarded what he did in his workshop as "piddling." And she had assumed that his view on the matter was the same. That's what retired people did; they piddled around. What kind of a man chases dreams when he's close to sixty? Just when she thought she knew everything there was to know about Earl Salinski, she found out something new.

Today of all days. He has to go and bring this up. The tingling numbness that signaled a migraine rushed through her arms

SHARON DUNN

and legs. Her vision blurred, and tension bunched up between her eyes. *No, not now.* She had so much to do. She pressed the heels of her hands against her lids, willing the pain to go away. The stress of the car chase had brought this on. And then Earl. The front of her head throbbed. *Please, not now.*

The phone hadn't rung since she'd regained consciousness. She needed to see if anyone had called on the landline. The tightening in her head intensified. She opened the drawer by her bed and pulled out her nausea medication. She could still lessen that side effect even if she hadn't taken the migraine medication in time. She placed the pill on her tongue and gulped some tea.

The curtains were drawn and the lights off. That helped. She closed her eyes and put the pillow over her head. As soon as this was over, she would check messages. But now, she simply had to endure the pain.

Even with her eyes closed, bright circles of light exploded across her lids. She took in slow, deep breaths, tried to ignore the pulsing of her brain, the sensation of a hatchet wedging between her eyes. Maybe Earl was right. There was no reason why someone would want to run her down. They certainly weren't rich. The Pontiac wasn't worth stealing. It was just some kid taking a prank too far.

She pressed the pillow harder against her face. She didn't have anything anyone would want.

Earl stepped out of the shop to catch a breath of fresh air and to think about what a neat thing total honesty was. He and Ginger were going to get close in the empty-nest years, just like he had prayed for. A few stars twinkled in the summer night sky.

Movement by Ginger's car caused him to turn slightly.

Earl took several steps to the center of the yard. With only one outdoor light, he couldn't see much. Had that been a shadow by Ginger's trunk? His skin prickled from some internal warning system.

"Who's out there?" Ginger's gray cat appeared on top of the car, and Earl let out the breath he had been holding. "Phoebe, what are you doing on Mama's car?"

He walked the short distance to the Pontiac. The cat padded to the edge of the car roof, and Earl gathered the bulky critter into his arms. She must weigh twenty pounds. The animal was some kind of genetic mutant. Phoebe was nearly two years old, and she just kept getting bigger.

He'd gotten Phoebe for Ginger when their youngest, Heidi, had left for the military. He had hoped the cat would soften the blow of dealing with an empty nest. Ginger spoiled the critter, feeding her from the table and taking her for rides in the car.

The animal yowled and wrestled free of his hold, plopping on the ground beside him and rubbing against his leg. A branch cracked in the forest beside their property. He spun around to look at the trees.

"Who's out there?" His heart pounded.

He surveyed the dark evergreens for signs of movement or more noise. Seconds ticked by. Still watching the trees, he rested his hand on the trunk. Nothing out there. This thing with Ginger just had him spooked. He shook his head and chuckled but couldn't unload that feeling of being watched.

As he turned to go back to the shop, he noticed scratches around the keyhole of the trunk. He traced several marks with his fingers. Even if she had forgotten her key, Ginger wouldn't do this kind of damage to her car.

He pulled his bulky key ring out of his pocket, filed through the keys, and shoved one in the slot. Earl popped the trunk lid and peered inside. Just a bunch of garage sale junk—

treasures, Ginger would say—and a spilled basket. He pulled the basket out. Maybe she'd gotten the Mickey Mouse pole for one of their grandkids. He needed to go inside for a cup a coffee anyway; might as well take the stuff in for his wife.

Phoebe stood on her back paws and dug her claws into Earl's jeans, preparing to use his leg as a scratching post.

"Git, Phoebes." He stepped forward, but she hung on. He kicked his leg out to the side and shook it until she gave up. "Like wrestling with a cougar." He was not looking forward to the day when Phoebe, instead of leaving a mouse or bird on the doorstep, would be dropping off livestock as a gift.

Lots of new things cluttered the trunk as well: towels with the tags on them, boxes of tea in plastic wrap, those stinky pink soaps women liked, candles and seed packets. Some old stuff too that she must have picked up garage saling: a vest, a photo album, and a box with shells on it. Not the usual stuff Ginger would buy. She usually tried to find almost new things at her sales.

He tossed a piece of pink-checked fabric into the basket and piled the rest of the stuff into the box, including the Mickey Mouse fishing pole. Ginger had to have been driving pretty wildly to spill all those things. He shut the trunk and checked to make sure it had locked. Later he'd put the car in the garage just to be on the safe side.

He gave one final glance to the forest. With the basket in one hand, the box tucked under the other arm, and Phoebe trailing behind him, Earl ambled toward the house. He shifted the load in his arms so he could reach the door handle. The screen door creaked as it swung open.

Leaning against the door frame with the box and basket growing heavy, he waited for Phoebe to saunter inside. "Take your sweet time." The cat lifted her furry chin to him and continued at the same leisurely pace, waving her question mark tail side to side.

He stepped into the kitchen, and the screen door slammed behind him. After checking the refrigerator for a potential late-night dinner and deciding on a sandwich, his gaze wandered to the phone on the wall.

The answering machine showed the number two. Hadn't Ginger said something about phone messages?

Four

Kindra Hall awoke with a start, jerking sideways. The heavy book that had been on her chest fell to the carpet with a muffled crash. She sat up, blinking in near darkness. Where was she?

As the fog of sleep drifted off her brain, the rough texture of Mary Margret's couch oriented her while her eyes adjusted to the blackness. The sequence of the evening came back to her in pieces. When Mary Margret hadn't shown up at four-thirty, Kindra had gotten a sub for work and gathered her study materials, including her monster size lit book, out of her car.

Kindra took in a deep breath and tried to remember where the nearest light switch was. She'd been dreaming about a department store sale where the BHN was allowed in before anybody else. But the dream wasn't what had awakened her. Had there been a noise?

She grappled to make the transition from confusion to coherence, sorting through which sensory information was real and which was a product of her dreams. The dream had been wonderful. She, Ginger, Suzanne, and Mary Margret had checked the price tags and pulled clothes off the rack without being pushed and bumped.

Kindra swung her feet to the floor, leaned over, and felt around the carpet for her lit book. She tossed the colossal textbook back on the couch. Summer school was a drag—less time and money for shopping and less time to hang out with the BHN—but it was the only way she would be able to finish when she was twenty-two.

It would take her three more pathetic years. Over and over, her parents reminded her of what a failure she was because her older brothers had finished undergrad work at sixteen. She came from a long line of scientists whose idea of a good time was to recite the periodic table. Achieve, achieve, achieve! Everything was a competition in her family, and she always felt like the loser.

Being with the BHN made all the pressure from Mom and Dad bearable. Ginger and the other ladies hugged her a lot and made her laugh. Her own family certainly wasn't big on hugs. In high school, though she had joined the squad to spite her parents, some of the other cheerleaders were her substitute family.

She rested her forehead against her palm, curling and uncurling her toes. At one point in her dream, Mary Margret had shaken her shoulder, holding a blouse in the other hand, and said, "Look at this. Such a deal." Or had she really been here and tried to wake her?

The worry she had felt when Mary Margret hadn't shown up at four-thirty returned tenfold. Ginger had been right. Mary wouldn't stay away this long without calling. Unless she *couldn't* call.

Rain pitter-pattered on the roof as she stumbled toward the kitchen, where she remembered seeing a light switch. Once the living room and kitchen were illuminated, Kindra felt like she had finally arrived in the land of the living.

Textbooks, notebooks, and highlighters cluttered the coffee table. Her box of garage sale goodies was on the easy chair.

SHARON DUNN

Kindra mostly bought designer clothes, paperbacks, and Beanie Babies. Ginger was the real pro when it came to garage saling. She had furnished and decorated her new home mostly with stuff she purchased at sales. It was a skill Kindra aspired to.

She had two goals. First of all, she wanted to be the best-dressed physicist in the world. She considered it her mission to dispel the assumption that if you were smart, you dressed like you shopped at "House of Dowdy."

And someday, she wanted to marry a cool Christian guy and stay home with her kids. Mom and Dad would have a cow if they knew that was her plan. She needed to learn to shop like Suzanne and Ginger if she was going to make that happen. She and Mary Margret were apprentices at best, newbies to the bargain hunting craft.

Kindra walked down the hallway, switching on lights. She leaned against the door frame to the master bedroom. The bedspread was so smooth it looked like a marine had made it. The room smelled like Mary Margret, gardenia.

A stack of folded shirts rested on the hope chest at the end of the bed. Those must be the clothes Ginger had found knocked off the coffee table. No Mary Margret or even a sign that she had been here.

Maybe she had dreamed that Mary shook her—a sort of wishful dreaming, her unconscious working through the anxiety she felt. It just wasn't like her friend to be gone this long without any word.

An eeking, squeaking noise came from the attached garage. Kindra trotted down the hallway and opened the door. Rain hitting the metal roof of the garage sharpened and intensified.

Her hope renewed, she started to speak Mary Margret's name just as the garage door creaked shut. She let out a huff of air. Something felt wrong...creepy.

A wedge of light became a sliver and then disappeared as the garage door shut completely. Kindra clicked on the light by the stairs. Mary Margret's little blue Jetta was parked on the concrete. A naked incandescent bulb created a circle of light over the vehicle.

Goose bumps formed on Kindra's bare arms. She ran to the driver's side. Empty. Someone, probably Mary Margret, had brought the car back. But why not just go through the door that led directly into the house? Kindra darted back up the three wooden stairs and into the hallway.

"Mary Margret? Is that you?" Her feet pounded across the hallway carpet then on the cool linoleum of the kitchen. She opened the front door and ran out into the cool, dark night. Rain drizzled from the sky. Drops spattered against her face.

She scanned up and down the quiet street. A car, its red taillights staring at her like angry eyeballs, edged toward the stop sign. Without coming to a full stop, the car pulled onto the main road and roared away.

Boy, he was in a hurry. Streetlights illuminated empty yards and dark windows. No one was out here. Not a soul. But someone had brought Mary Margret's car back. Concrete chilled Kindra's bare feet, and rain soaked her thin cotton shirt. Must be 2 or 3 a.m. by now.

She turned slowly back toward the house. Another car pulled off the main road into the subdivision. The flashing lights of the police vehicle caused white spots to jerk across her field of vision.

Ice entered her veins.

She wrapped her arms around herself and shivered as the police car came to a stop across from Mary Margret's. The officer got out and walked toward Kindra.

SHARON DUNN

Ginger sat at her kitchen table, resting her face in one of her hands. She gripped the answering machine tape with the other.

Mary Margret had been in danger.

Ginger shivered at the thought of the fear in Mary's second message. Earl had awakened her when he came in for his coffee break. Her migraine had subsided enough so she could function.

Her jaw tightened. Why hadn't she checked messages first thing? So what if that car had chased her. So what if she had a migraine. Something worse could be happening to Mary.

I'm a terrible friend.

Ginger lifted her head. The kitchen clock indicated that it was 2 a.m. Why? Why did she have to get a migraine and lose twelve hours of her life just like that? Phoebe lounged on the kitchen table surrounded by garage sale stuff and the gifts from Mary Margret. The feline, her paws tucked underneath her, narrowed her eyes at Ginger.

"'Something terrible, something from the past.'" Ginger repeated the panic-stricken words from her friend's message.

Resting her palms on the table, she rose to her feet and stared at the beat-up fishing pole. Everything must have shifted in the trunk when she was being chased. Three other items were not new and weren't anything she had gotten: a box with seashells on it, an old vest with lots of pockets, and a photo album. Mary Margret must have stuffed those items under the pink gingham in the gift basket. Odd.

She touched the frayed photo album. *All this stuff is from the past.*

Something had happened to Mary Margret. Now she did have a reason to call the police. Her hand touched the phone just as it rang.

Tossing the light comforter on her sleeping husband, Suzanne Thomas propped herself up on her elbows. Greg's snoring only bothered her when she couldn't sleep.

In her rational moments, she knew she was seeing everything through the lens of whacked-out hormones and her own fatigue, but tonight his snoring seemed to shake the bed. The nerve of him sawing logs when she couldn't even doze. She really wanted to yell in his ear so they could both be awake and miserable. Sweat trickled down her back. Even with the fan running and the window open, she was hot. She rolled sideways, struggled out of bed, and lumbered across the floor out into the hallway.

The baby was doing gymnastics in her womb by the time she made it to the bathroom and splashed cold water on her face. She ran a washcloth under the faucet and patted her neck and arms with it. A glimpse of herself in the mirror reminded her that every day was a bad hair day when you were the mother of three small children with another on the way.

Tonight she had been more restless than usual, but it had nothing to do with the heat or her pregnancy. Since she'd left the church, two trains of thought wrestled in her mind. Both the Saturday cleaning crew and the pastor had been there. No one had seen Mary Margret.

The thoughts doing battle inside her were not unfamiliar. Every time one of her kids disappeared in a department store, the same warring impulses raised their ugly heads. The first thought spoke with reassurance that her child had just wandered away and that within five minutes, he or she would be found.

The other notion appeared in half shadow shaking its head, nagging her about all the terrible things that can happen

SHARON DUNN

to children who are not watched closely. It allowed visions of horrible people who hurt children to enter her mind. Images of her and Greg on the news pleading for the life of their child flashed through her brain as she checked under every clothing rack and called her child's name, her chest getting tighter and tighter and her breathing shallower.

The same type of opposing scenarios rolled around her head when she thought about Mary Margret. One part of her said that by morning this whole thing would be cleared up. And the other more sinister thought made it hard to breathe.

Suzanne leaned on the sink and closed her eyes. Everything Ginger had pointed out about Mary Margret was true. She always left notes or called to let people know what her plans were. The woman was compulsive about it.

On the other hand, Mary was a real estate agent, a grandmother, and a churchgoer. She didn't have an enemy in the world. No one would want to hurt the oldest member of the Bargain Hunters Network.

Had her waking up in the night been prompted by God? Her knuckles turned white as she gripped the sink and prayed for Mary's safety. Shopping for a good deal had brought the four of them together, but the bond ran much deeper than gathering for a half price sale. Something beyond her senses told her that Mary Margret was not okay.

The phone in the kitchen rang. Suzanne tensed. She trudged down the hallway and through the living room. It had to be two or three in the morning. *Only drunks and people with bad news call at this hour.*

She picked up the phone on the fourth ring.

And I don't know any drunks.

Five

Ginger appreciated the way Earl clasped her trembling fingers in his big strong hand. She was grateful that the female police officer spoke so kindly to her and brought her hot cocoa.

After Kindra had phoned Ginger and Suzanne, they agreed to meet at the police station to get the details about Mary Margret together. They had gone up the stairs to the station house with arms wrapped around each other. She was thankful she didn't have to do this alone.

But none of it made her friend any more alive.

The officer who said her name was Tammy spoke softly. "We'll have to notify her next of kin."

"How did—how did she die?" Ginger knew she was talking, but the voice didn't sound like hers.

Tammy cleared her throat and shifted in her chair. "I didn't know if you wanted to hear the details."

Ginger closed her eyes. "Tell me. She was my friend."

"A hiker had found her in a forest not far out of town. She was lying in the grass with a head wound...and a hunting arrow sticking out of her back."

Earl gripped her hand tighter. Suzanne gasped.

Ginger twisted the top button of her blouse and stared at the off-white walls of interview room number two. *Hold it together. Focus on what you can deal with.* She swallowed. "She has

SHARON DUNN

a daughter in California, Mariah...and a grandson. Please let me make the call."

Her vision blurred. Kindra sobbed beside her, but all noises seemed to be coming through a filter that made everything sound far away. She reached out and patted Kindra's leg with numb fingers.

"So the last time you heard from Mary Margret was eleven or twelve on Saturday afternoon?" Tammy picked up her pen beside the legal notepad on the table.

"That's when she must have called." A chill blanketed Ginger's skin. "I had a migraine. I couldn't check messages until—until—later."

"Thank you for giving me the answering machine tape." Tammy kept her eyes on Ginger. "You said she sounded afraid on the message?"

Ginger nodded.

"Did she say where she was? Where she was going? Why was she out there in the forest at night?"

The barrage of questions made her thoughts tangle. This was too much. Ginger's hand curled into a fist. "If only I had checked those messages earlier, maybe—"

Kindra cupped Ginger's shoulder. Even the warm touch of someone who cared about her failed to shake her from the paralysis.

"I'm sorry to put you through all this." Tammy placed her pen delicately on the notepad in front of her. "But any time there is foul play—"

"That's an understatement." Suzanne's voice cracked.

"Could it have been an accident?" Kindra squared her shoulders and wiped a tear from the rim of her eye.

"It's possible someone was out there practicing for bow hunting season." Tammy tapped her pen on the table. "But it seems like they would have known, would have heard her. In light of the message on Mrs. Salinski's machine and that Mary Margret's car was gone and then put back, I think we need to look into this."

Tammy seemed like a real nice lady. Though her build was like one of those big German women who threw the shot put at the Olympics, she had a pretty face. Her light brown hair was pulled back into a tight bun, and she wore only lip gloss for makeup. But she had a sweet demeanor, more suited to a nurse or Sunday school teacher than a police officer. That's probably why she had been sent in to talk to them.

This had been the longest night of Ginger's fifty-six years on earth. If only she had listened to her messages earlier. If only she had been there to pick up the phone in the first place. Her temples throbbed. She'd make this right. Or as right as she could. She'd be a grandma to Jonathon and a mom to Mariah. She'd help the police find out who had done this.

The tingling numbness subsided, and she felt the warmth of a tear trickling down her face. Earl's thumb brushed her cheek, and she took a ragged breath of air.

Tammy laced her fingers together, resting elbows on the table. "This has been a difficult night for all of you. I know you're in shock. I've got your contact information. I may need to interview you more formally later. I'll need to know more about Mary Margret's habits, who might have reason to—"

"Nobody." Suzanne placed her arms on her bulging stomach. "Nobody wanted her dead. She was the nicest person on this planet."

Tammy rose to her feet with the notebook and pen in hand. "I'll be in touch with all of you. I am sorry for your loss." Tammy walked the few feet to the door of the interview room. "I'll escort you out."

As Ginger and the others stood, chair legs scraped abrasively on the floor. She winced. With the numbness subsiding, all of her senses had kicked into overdrive.

Mary Margret's words ricocheted in her head. *"Something terrible, something from the past."*

With Tammy following behind, the four of them walked through the police station, their feet padding softly on the carpet. At the lobby, they returned their visitor badges to the woman behind the glass window. Earl held the door for the women.

They made their way down the huge concrete steps. The rain had stopped hours ago. The air was heavy with that clean, after-rain smell. A gauzy gray with a hint of light to the east covered the sky. Sunday morning, the Lord's Day.

In a couple hours, I'll have to fix Earl his breakfast. They would go on with their day, finding safety in the same old routine. But the world had shifted. Ginger placed her palm on her chest. The heaviness was almost unbearable.

They stood at the bottom of the stairs. No one speaking and no one willing to leave. Maybe it was just the veiled light, but both Kindra and Suzanne looked tired and older. *All of us are getting older. Time's passing.*

Time's passing and my best friend is gone.

Six

Chills trickled over her skin when Tammy listened to the Parker woman on the message tape. She rubbed her eyes, then massaged the back of her neck. She'd have to get the tape turned in to the evidence clerk.

She typed the final sentence of her report on Mary Margret Parker, noting that the case was still open and that she intended to question the women further. She clicked on an icon to close the file. If she had known she was looking at a possible homicide, she would have interviewed them separately as procedure dictated. But she thought she would only be informing Mary Margret's friends about her death.

She usually worked property crimes. They didn't even have a full-time homicide detective. Maybe Captain Stenengarter would let her work this case.

Her Betty Boop watch told her it was eight o'clock in the morning. Time to go home to her other full-time job. Trevor, her teenage son, had called three times with problems that ranged from burning macaroni and cheese to his girlfriend breaking up with him.

Summers were hard for both of them. She had requested the midnight to eight shift so she could be with him during the day. In theory, Trevor was supposed to be sleeping while she worked. Her mom, who lived next door, checked in on him. Despite her planning, the kid always managed to enmesh himself in some kind of drama when he was supposed to be snoring under his bedspread.

Tammy took her last gulp of Chai tea and tossed the cup in the wastebasket beside her desk. Informing Mary Margret's three friends of her death had not been easy. Apparently, Captain Stenengarter thought that since she was the token female on the force, she was the best candidate to deal with the emotionally charged situation.

Hoping to clear the tightness in her shoulders, she took several deep breaths. The memory of those three women crying had haunted her all through her shift. Maybe a workout and a hot bath would shake the tension.

After dropping the tape off with the evidence clerk, Tammy clocked out, changed into jeans, and stopped by the coroner's office on her way out of the station house. A puffy, balding man in a white coat perched behind a desk. A single lamp angled over him. As always, the curtains were drawn.

"Hey, Deaver, what's the news on the Parker case?"

Bradley Deaver's skin appeared jaundiced under the dim light. "The news is it was an accident. There's a practice archery range just up the hill. One of our bow hunters got a little careless and whammo." Deaver continued to flip pages of his paperwork and write while he talked. "The arrow didn't actually kill her. The fall did. She hit her head on a rock. The arrow would have killed her eventually, but much more slowly."

Her stomach clenched. "But she left a panicked message on an answering machine. Her car was taken and returned."

Holding his precious paperwork in midair, he raised his eyebrows and leaned forward. "Nobody told me any of that."

"I just found it out from the Parker woman's friends." Her stomach tightened even more. "Other than what the college kid told me, I'm not sure how you would prove that the car had been taken out and put back after Parker was dead unless a forensic unit—"

"A full forensic team would need to come up from Missoula. All of that costs money." Deaver shrugged. "It was a busy night, Tams." He pushed his pile of papers to one side. "Rain caused a pileup on the interstate, and the drunks are out in full force on Saturday night. We had more than enough dead and predead to deal with. I was told not to dawdle."

"Who told you to rush it through?" Deaver was exaggerating to appear put-upon. This was Three Horses. It wasn't like the coroner's office was wall-to-wall with corpses.

"The muckety-mucks informed me that a full autopsy on the Parker woman wasn't necessary. All I had to do was determine the TOD, which, by the way, was in the evening." Deaver pushed a model car he had sitting on his desk back and forth, performing tight turns and wheelies.

Muckety-muck was a term Deaver used for anyone who was his superior, which was pretty much everyone in the department. He was the deputy coroner, not an MD, and most of his job was administrative. Rumor had it that Deaver had flunked out of med school.

"Which muckety-muck?"

"The order came out of Officer Vicher's mouth, but that doesn't mean it originated with him." He parked his car beside the penholder and returned to his stack of papers. "You know this place is a bureaucratic labyrinth. Who knows who gave the original order."

Tammy glanced at the two books he had on his desk. One was about Ruby Ridge, and the other was a thick reference guide to the Kennedy assassination. "It's not a labyrinth to everyone, Deaver."

He shrugged. "I know what I know." His voice held the same ominous tone of a kid around a campfire telling scary stories.

"So that's it. No more investigation?"

"Really, it was like they'd already determined the cause of death before I did the exam." He stared at the wall for a moment, then rubbed a mole on his cheek. "I just did what I was told. Talk to the bigwigs if you're not happy with the conclusions."

Tammy crossed her arms and leaned against the door frame. "I'm not upset." So she said. The pinching sensation that started at the back of her neck and worked its way down her spine was like a message from her subconscious. Was this the gut instinct senior members of the force always talked about? A lot about the Parker woman's death made her uneasy. No matter how hard she tried to talk herself out of it. Being raised in a Christian home had given her a strong sense of justice, and right now she didn't feel like she was getting it.

"It's just that what those women said made me think there was more to it. I don't understand why it's being shut down so fast."

"Sorry, Nancy Drew. If you want to get your teeth into some real crime, you should transfer to LA or Detroit." He moved a paper from one stack to another. A satisfied smile crossed his face. His chair squeaked when he straightened his spine. "Not much happens here in Mayberry."

"So the case is closed?"

"They are sending up a peon to try and match the arrow to whoever was at the practice range Saturday night. Rain washed away a lot of evidence. Only trace amounts of blood on the rock."

At least they were doing some investigation. That was hopeful. "How are they going to find out who was at the range?"

"Membership list. A club owns and maintains the range. We might get lucky if they have a sign-in sheet for each day. Don't ask me who would have been shooting off arrows at twilight."

Tammy nodded. She had already decided she would ask to be assigned to question the members of the archery club. Deaver cocked his head at her, not unlike an owl preparing to dive-bomb a mouse.

She rubbed her forehead and sighed. Thought of a few hours' sleep eased the fatigue. "You have a good day, Bradley."

Deaver's expression softened. He pushed back his chair and walked to the front of his desk. "My guess is that Captain Stenengarter was the one who wanted things expedited. We all know Officer Vicher is his lackey."

"Thanks." The information was Deaver's version of doing her a favor. He must have been responding to her exhaustion. He did have a human side.

Her shoes echoed down the linoleum corridor. She pushed open the door to exit the station house, took the stairs at a substantial pace, and strode toward her car. Morning sun shone through her window as she drove home to help her son deal with teenage angst and maybe get a little sleep. She hit her blinker and turned into a subdivision where all the houses were pastel colors.

Yeah, it would take more than a workout and a soak in the tub to shake the tightness gripping her shoulder blades.

Trevor and her mom came out to greet her when she pulled into the driveway. Trevor, hands shoved in his pockets and shoulders slumping, trudged toward her car.

Tammy gripped the steering wheel a little tighter. Why was she thinking about the Parker case so much? It wasn't like she didn't have enough problems on her plate already.

After the sunny faced teenager slapped some wobbling pink Jell-O onto Ginger's paper plate, a revelation formed in her brain. *Americans do death all wrong.* She had just buried her best friend. What on God's green earth made people think she wanted to partake of tuna casserole at a time like this? Those people in other countries who ripped their clothes and slapped their heads—now they understood mourning.

Suzanne and Kindra, along with Earl, little Jonathan, and Mariah, sat at a far table in the church basement. She shuffled past the table where Mr. Jackson, his business partner Mr. Wheeler, and the other people from Mary's real estate office sat eating from heaping plates. She recognized them from the pictures on the office wall.

She stared down at the food on her plate. The last thing she wanted to do was eat and be social. What she really needed was to curl up in bed and sleep for a week.

A hand touched her wrist. "All of us at the office are real sorry." A blond woman in a dark suit had gotten up from the table where Mary Margret's coworkers were seated. "I'm Dana Jones. If there is anything I can do..."

Ginger stared at the woman's plate of three bean salad and tapioca. "Thank you, Dana." This was grief counseling in America, bean salad and pudding.

Behind her, someone cleared his throat. Ginger turned around to face Mr. Jackson. Mr. Wheeler rose to his feet as well. The two men were a study in opposites. A tent-sized suit covered Mr. Jackson's pudgy form. His bouffant, wavy hair appeared to be held in place with a heavy coat of shellac. Mr. Wheeler was in good shape, wore jeans with a huge belt buckle, and his salt-and-pepper hair had no shine to it. Both men were probably around her age.

Mr. Jackson sucked in his bulbous lips and nodded. "Mary was a valued member of our team. I know her budget was kind of tight. Maybe we could help out with the cost of the funeral."

Ginger fixated on the bright colors of Mr. Jackson's tie. Looney Tunes had to breach some unwritten rule of etiquette. Was Yosemite Sam with his pants on fire a good choice for a funeral?

Wheeler stepped in front of his business partner. "Had she made arrangements to cover funeral expenses?"

Ginger opened her mouth to speak, but her throat went dry. Money, they were thinking about money right now. "It has all been taken care of, thank you." She fought to keep the tone of offense out of her voice.

People said really flippant things at funerals, thinking they were offering comfort. Ginger loved the Lord with all her heart, but if one more person quoted a Bible verse as though that would make the pain go away, she was going to lose it.

Mr. Jackson's doughy hand touched hers. "Keep us in mind."

It took some deliberate effort to turn the corners of her mouth up to form a smile, but Ginger managed. Satisfied, Mr. Wheeler returned to his chair and Mr. Jackson ambled back to the buffet table.

Dana shook her head. "She was a real sweet lady. She was the only one who helped me learn the ropes when I started. How did she die? The obituary didn't say."

"Her daughter didn't want the details of her death publicized. The police suspect foul play."

Dana's lips parted, and she leaned closer to Ginger. "I'm sure the police will figure out what happened."

SHARON DUNN

It seemed strange that the newspapers hadn't done an article on Mary Margret. Murder, or even suspected murder, should be a front-page story. Ginger stared at her murky reflection in the Jell-O. "I'm sure the police will take care of everything."

....

"Thanks for the offer, Welstad, but I've already sent Vicher to question the members of the archery club." Captain Paul Stenengarter ejected the magazine from his police issue Glock and shoved it into the side pocket of his shooting bag. Behind them at the indoor shooting range, four men practiced with their pistols. The squeaking of targets being cranked forward broke the rhythm of double taps and rapid fire.

Tammy crossed her arms. "What was the result of that questioning?" After four days of pushing Trevor kicking and screaming toward adulthood and her own long shifts, she'd finally had time and energy to track down Stenengarter, who always worked day shift.

He didn't make eye contact. "Don't you have some stolen vehicles to track down?"

"Yes sir, it's just that I was the one to break the news to the victim's friends. Some of the information they gave me was highly suspicious, so I filed a report." She summarized the details of the evidence so far. "I thought maybe I should do a formal interview and talk to each one separately."

"Did the message say she had been kidnapped or feared for her life?" The captain stared down at her through his rimless glasses. He straightened his spine so he was even taller, an authoritative stance designed to remind her that he was the one with the superior rank.

Tammy stared at her shoes. Maybe she should just drop this whole thing. But the police handbook said that a break in someone's habits was a red flag. Stenengarter hadn't gotten the captain's job because he was a great cop who worked his way up through the ranks. His father was a local politician. Stenengarter had a college degree and a gift for administrating. But she had good instincts and a need for justice.

She lifted her head and squared her shoulders. "There is no explanation why she was voluntarily wandering in those woods at night. Someone her age wouldn't go for a hike at night alone. She had to have been taken or dropped there."

"You need to let this go." His voice dropped an octave.

She was not letting this go. All her instincts told her something was up. "Did Vicher track down who the arrow belonged to?"

Stenengarter touched his chin. A line of perspiration glistened on his forehead. "It was a generic arrow." He zipped and unzipped several pouches on his shooting bag. "Could have belonged to anyone."

"Was I the only officer who talked to her friends?" She spoke more softly, her momentary boldness fading.

"Why don't you contact them and tell them the case is closed." He punctuated his point by slamming a box of ammunition on the table. When he lifted his head, he didn't look directly at her but off to the right. "I'll contact the newspaper. The official story is that a hiker found her and the cause of death was an accident."

The firmness of his tone told Tammy that she couldn't ask any more questions. She'd lost all the ground she had gained. "Thank you, sir. I'll do that."

"Yes, you will. 'Cause it's an order."

SHARON DUNN

Tammy walked the few steps to the firing range exit, opened the door, and stepped outside. Her feet crunched on the gravel on the way to her car. She could kick herself for turning into Miss Minnie Weak-Knees. Stenengarter had a way of doing that to her.

She needed this job. The best way to keep her job would be to follow orders and respect the captain's authority.

As a child, she'd had an uncle who taught her how to play poker, much to her parents' chagrin. Uncle Randy had explained that the most important thing was not the cards you had, but knowing how to read the people around the table. If you watched them close enough, people would give you "tells" that showed they were bluffing about their hand.

Tammy closed her eyes, trying to shut out the thoughts. She couldn't go against the department. She wasn't Stenengarter's favorite. He'd fire her. Trevor depended on her. Her mom depended on her. If she followed orders, she'd still have a paycheck to pick up.

Tammy touched the cold steel of her car door handle and added up no fewer then six tells in her conversation with Stenengarter.

• •

When Ginger turned into her driveway, the first thing she saw was the strange car parked by her house. The second thing she noticed was that Earl's truck was gone. Her heart beat a little faster. The memory of being chased by that car less than a week before flooded her brain, along with all the anxiety that went with it. She wiggled in her car seat. Her arm muscles hardened. The car that had chased her had been brownish-gold. This car was yellow and smaller. She relaxed.

"Now who do you suppose that is, Phoebes?" Ginger spoke to the huge mutant cat who sat beside her in a child's booster seat. She had picked it up at a garage sale so Phoebe could see out the window.

An attractive thirtysomething woman with mid–shoulder length brown hair stood by the back door. Phoebe placed her front paws on the dashboard and let out a plaintive meow.

Ginger opened the car door and stepped out. "Hello, can I help you?"

Phoebe scampered across the driver's seat and plopped down beside Ginger. The cat sat back on her haunches and raised her chin, a soldier at the ready.

The woman came toward them. "I'm so glad I caught you." She had on blue jeans and a pale pink Windbreaker.

It took a moment for Ginger to realize that the woman was Tammy, the police lady. "I'm sorry, what is this about?" She probably had good news about Mary Margret's investigation. It had only been a day since the funeral, and already the police had done something.

Tammy looked very different with her hair down. She wore pink lipstick and the full workup on her eyes. At the police station, Tammy had been nice but all business. Now she seemed less threatening, shorter, and not as muscled up. Could a uniform and tight bun do all that?

"I'm sorry, I should have called first. I wanted to talk to you in person before the story came out in the newspaper."

"Have you found out who killed my friend?"

Tammy's face paled. "They ruled it an accident." She broke eye contact. "There's an archery range just up the hill from where your friend was found."

"But the messages on my machine." Ginger gripped the car door. "Who ruled it an accident?"

"The decision was out of my control. I'm really sorry, I—"

Ginger's cheeks warmed. "You said you suspected foul play."

Tammy leaned toward her. "I was out of line. I didn't have the authority to make that kind of call."

"Mary Margret always left a note when she went somewhere." Ginger had the sensation of slipping down a mountain, grasping at pebbles. "Someone took her, kidnapped her in her own car, and then brought the car back."

"Yes, all of that is suspicious, but I—" Tammy shook her head several times. "I really am sorry."

Ginger clenched her teeth so tight her jaw hurt. "You'll have to excuse me." This woman was just the messenger. Honestly, she seemed like a kind person. Her tone suggested that she was trying to convince herself as much as Ginger. "I have groceries to get out of my car." She jerked open the back door, pulled the bags out, and skirted past the police lady.

She trotted toward the house without looking back.

The police didn't care. Obviously they were going to treat this whole thing like it didn't matter. Like Mary Margret didn't matter.

Ginger yanked the door open, and Phoebe followed her. She plopped the grocery bags on the table. Mary's garage sale stuff still sat in a box on the counter.

Ginger straightened her back as realization spread through her brain. She picked up the kids Mickey Mouse fishing pole. Her hand rested on the photo album.

Mary Margret did leave a note; she just didn't have time to write one.

Seven

Ladies, this is the note Mary Margret left for us. A tiger cannot change its stripes, and Mary Margret had to let us know something was up." Ginger swept her arm across the table with a flair Vanna White would have admired. She had spread out all four garage sale items Mary Margret had bought the morning she died.

"What kind of message was she leaving with garage sale stuff?" Dark circles framed Kindra's red eyes. It had been two days since the funeral.

Poor kid. Ginger cleared her throat and focused on the task at hand. "Everything got mixed up in the trunk, but I took out all the items I know I bought and the stuff that was new in the package. Mary left that Mickey Mouse fishing pole on the top as a way of letting me know something was up because it looked out of place. She hid the other three things underneath the gingham."

Kindra refilled Suzanne's steaming mug of herbal tea, then sauntered to the table and picked up each item. "An old photo album with half the pictures pulled out and a fisherman's vest and this." She held the box with shells on it, opening it and turning it over in her hands. "Why did she want this stuff anyway?"

Ginger shrugged. Sometimes Mary's idea of a garage sale treasure was a little off center. "Mary Margret was fine when she called me around eight and said she had already hit four garage sales. These items must have been what she bought. I think they have something to do with her death."

And she was beginning to think it hadn't been a teenager fooling around that Saturday. Somebody wanted one of these things, and they had chased her down in that car. Earl had told her that someone had even tried to break into the Pontiac's trunk. "When Mary's daughter and I were over there packing stuff up, I picked up the garage sale section of the newspaper that Mary marked up. She numbered all the sales she hit one, two, three, four."

Suzanne pushed herself off the counter she had been leaning against. "So we retrace her steps." She set her tea mug on Ginger's table. "We talk to the people she bought this stuff from and see if they give up anything."

Ginger patted her curls. "Correctamundo."

Kindra sat at the kitchen table and flipped through the photo album. "There is nothing overtly incriminating about any of this stuff. These are just a bunch of vacation photos. This guy with the white hair liked to stand in front of mounds of dirt a lot. And sometimes that skinny older lady is with him." She pulled one of the photos out of the album and read the back. "Their names are Arleta and David. No last name."

Suzanne peered over Kindra shoulder. "Maybe they're archaeologists."

"Maybe, but some of them are of old buildings and stuff, no people. This is downtown Three Horses." She pulled one of the photos out. "And look at this one; he's just standing among some trees." Kindra wiggled in her chair. "None of this says crime spree to me."

"I know. I've gone through it a hundred times," Ginger said. "The only thing I could figure out was that the vest with all the pockets and zippers must have come from the same place because the old guy is wearing it in some of the pictures."

Suzanne slumped down into a kitchen chair. "What if her death has nothing to do with this stuff?"

"It's a place to start." Ginger crossed her arms and paced the length of the kitchen table. Maybe it wasn't the smartest choice or the choice the police would have made if they believed that Mary had been killed, but she had to start somewhere. She stopped. "Mary Margret was our friend. What happened to her was not an accident. If the police aren't going to do anything, we will."

The other two women nodded.

"For Mary Margret," said Kindra.

Suzanne raised her tea mug. "For Mary Margret."

• •

Ginger sat in the passenger seat of Suzanne's minivan as they drove through a neighborhood with huge houses, groomed lawns, and wrought iron fences. Because it was a resort town close to two lakes, Three Horses was a mix of middle-class people who stayed year-round and a more affluent group who mostly came in the summer.

Ginger glanced at the list of addresses she had written down from the garage sale section of Mary Margret's newspaper. "Looks like 57 Bryant."

Suzanne made her way through the exclusive neighborhood. "I think that is just up here a ways?"

Ginger adjusted her purse in her lap. With everything that had gone on with Mary Margret, she hadn't had time to think about the disturbing thing Earl had said to her the night Mary disappeared. This was the first time she and Suzanne had been alone since their friend's death. Normally, she would have gone to Mary Margret about marriage issues. Ginger cleared her throat. "So, Earl says he wants me to be his cheerleader."

Suzanne touched her bulging belly pressing against the steering wheel. "I am growing so fast, I can't even fit in my Accord anymore." She turned the wheel as the street curved. "His cheerleader? You mean like with pom-poms and saddle shoes?"

Ginger giggled. "No, he says I'm not supportive of him, of his inventions."

"You do call them contraptions."

That was true. Attempting to fight off the rising guilt by fidgeting, Ginger folded and unfolded the piece of paper in her hand. "I thought I was being supportive. I cooked and cleaned for him all these years, made his lunch. I never complained when he disappeared during hunting and football season. I even made bean dip for him and all his football buddies." She was the queen of budget balancing. She kept her house clean and organized. Wasn't she being a good Christian wife?

"I'm just so confused, Suzanne. What else am I supposed to do? What does he mean, 'be his cheerleader'?"

The minivan rolled past a small grove of pine trees, planted in perfect rows. She shrugged. "Maybe he wants you to be more a part of his life, of what he does."

"He never wanted me to climb up the poles with him when he worked for the phone company."

"Climbing up poles probably wasn't his passion." As they curved up the road, a lake surrounded by forest and mountains came into view. Suzanne turned off the Christian music station they'd been listening to. "You know, one of the best things I ever did for our marriage was to get a sitter and go hunting with Greg." She shook her head and smiled. "You would have thought I gave him a Corvette for Christmas. I never shot anything. I just tromped around the forest with him in the little camouflage costume."

"I don't know why Earl's bringing this up. When I see what other couples go through, what they do to each other.... I just thought we had a good marriage." That was what bothered her more than anything, that Earl thought something was wrong with their marriage.

Ginger glanced down at the piece of paper. It was nearly in pieces from her creasing it. She didn't know what to do. She didn't look good in camouflage. "Guess I could stop calling his inventions contraptions."

"At least that's a place to start." Suzanne pressed the brakes. "You'll figure it out."

Ginger tore a corner of the paper. She wasn't so sure about that.

A brick mansion situated on a cul-de-sac stood to the left. The property was on a larger lot than the rest of the houses and featured old-growth ash and willow trees along with an abundance of yellow rosebushes. Solar panels covered part of the roof.

"I went to the sale at this place." Ginger stared out at the huge expanse of lawn. "Must have been around ten. I only remember it because it was such a weird sale."

"Weird, how?"

"It was run by two foreign ladies. They laughed a lot and said something about 'quaint American customs.' The stuff they had was nice and very new. I got a crystal dish for like a dollar."

"Some people are so wasteful." Suzanne blew a strand of hair out of her eyes.

"You gettin' tired?" Ginger patted Suzanne's leg.

"I could use a nap. My legs are starting to hurt." Suzanne rubbed the back of her neck. "I know this house. It belongs to that lawyer. He's in the newspaper a lot. I can't remember exactly what for, but I do remember seeing this colossal castle in the pictures. I think I saw an article just a couple weeks ago."

Suzanne leaned back against the headrest.

Ginger pushed open her door. "Why don't you wait here? I can do this. Then we'll take you home. Kindra can help me with the other addresses when she gets off work." She opened the back door and pulled out the box of garage sale stuff. The large box decorated with seashells was on top of the vest; the fishing pole and photo album rested beside them.

Cradling the box in her hands, Ginger walked up the steps to the porch and rang the doorbell. While she waited, she thought about the end-of-summer sale at JCPenney. She could stock up on outfits for the grandkids.

She pressed the doorbell again. Hmmm. The garage door was open, and a green sports car was parked in the driveway. She glanced back at Suzanne, who raised her arms in an "I don't know" motion.

Ginger descended the steps and stared up at the curtained windows.

Suzanne stuck her head out of the window. "Why don't we try later, Gin? Maybe we can go to the library sometime and find that article about him."

Ginger walked across the lawn to the car. "You're probably right." She leaned into the open passenger side window. "Let's take you home so you can get some rest." She opened the side door, placed the box on the seat, then stepped up into the passenger seat. Suzanne shifted into reverse and cranked the wheel.

Ginger craned her neck to stare at the second story window of the mansion. Had the curtain moved?

•••••••••••••••••••••••••••••••••

Keaton Lustrum's hand curled into a fist on his keyboard when the doorbell rang a second time. Curse that Renata for forgetting to put out the Do Not Disturb, Lawyer at Work sign again. If she was going to shop all day spending his money, the least she could do was remember to put out the sign.

Everyone in the neighborhood knew not to bother him. He stood up and glanced out the window as a woman who looked like her curls were made of brass walked back to the curb.

The woman held a box filled with junk. Keaton's heart beat faster, and he leaned closer to the window. A whirlwind of anxiety twisted around his torso. No it couldn't be. He could have sworn the woman was carrying his shell box. His special shell box. The one Renata's stupid sister, Gwen, had sold at the garage sale.

He was perspiring by the time the car with the "momof3" license plate pulled away.

Keaton ran to the hallway and yanked open the linen closet. Just as he had done last Saturday, he pulled out sheets, towels, and pillowcases and dumped them on the floor. Only this time he didn't expect to see the box. Wishful longing made him look.

He stared at the bare space on the shelf where the box belonged. Panic seeped through his arteries. Sweat trickled down his back. He stomped on the pile of towels. That stupid, stupid Gwen. He leaned over gasping for breath and clutching his chest. He had to get that box back.

Renata had failed the first time. This time he would have to do it.

Outside, Renata's Lexus, actually his Lexus, pulled into the driveway. Keaton ran back to the window, staring out at the manicured lawn. The momof3 van had already rounded the corner out of view.

His girlfriend opened the door, and her high heels click-click-clicked across the Italian tile. He raced down the stairs into the kitchen. Renata held a jar of salsa. Two bags of groceries rested on the counter.

"Keaton, you're as white as a, how you say, a ghost." Her accent sounded stronger than usual. It always returned when she visited with Gwen. Keaton vowed that he would find a way to ship Gwen back to France before the summer was over. She had too much influence on Renata.

"Renata, it's the box. That minivan you passed on the way up here. That woman has my box."

"Uhn, Keaaaaatooon." The salsa fell to the floor, splattering across tile and cupboards. "I am tired of hearing of the stupid box." She narrowed her gorgeous eyes. "Gwen did not know. I did not know. It look like junk. We try to get it back."

"And that was a big disaster, wasn't it?" He pointed a finger at her. "You could go to jail for what you did."

Renata flinched. "You put the pressure on me."

"I didn't ask you to break the law." Keaton squeezed his eyes shut. He wanted to be angry with Renata. He wanted to tell her to put that sister of hers on a boat, a plane, in a barrel. "I know the license plate of the minivan—momof3. I have a friend at the DMV." He rubbed his fingers together to indicate money. "You know, my friend. He can match it to an address."

He stepped through the salsa and grabbed her soft hands. Tomatoes stained his expensive shoes. It didn't matter. He'd walk through gallons of salsa to keep her, his jewel. "We'll get the box back."

Curly golden brown hair piled atop Renata's head revealed a long neck, which matched her long arms and legs. Everything about her was lovely and foreign and exciting.

She was the jewel in his crown of success.

He was twenty years her senior and required frequent workouts and hair transplants to maintain the illusion of youth. Despite all his pretense and money, he was just a ranch kid from eastern Montana who happened to make a good living as an environmental lawyer and speaker.

He had to get it back. If he didn't retrieve that box, he'd lose everything, including Renata and his livelihood.

Eight

Tammy had been down to the holding cells of the city jail a thousand times, but never to retrieve her son.

"He needs a positive male influence in his life, Tamela." Hannah Krinkland trailed behind her daughter as they made their ways up the justice center steps.

The sun shone down from a marble blue, clear sky. The temperature hung around seventy. Midsummer in Montana would be the most pleasant time of the year if she didn't have to spend it keeping her son out of trouble.

"The only men who want to mentor my son want to date me, Mother. I just think that complicates things."

"If only Larry—"

Tammy stopped abruptly halfway up the stairs. "Larry? I hardly think that's a realistic solution."

Ironically, her first exposure to the law hadn't been at the police academy. She had married Larry Welstad when she was seventeen and pregnant. Among other things, he had several narcotics and auto theft convictions. After three frightening years of marriage, Trevor's father had gotten into a car he borrowed from a friend and driven off the face of the earth.

The abandonment had been a blessing in disguise. Tammy completed her GED, started attending church again with her mother, and entered the police academy within a year of her husband leaving. She was pretty sure the outstanding warrants would keep dear Larry out of Montana, hopefully forever. The last thing she needed was Larry around to influence her fifteen-year-old son.

Mom touched her forehead. "I'm fishing at the bottom of the pool, sweetheart; I'm sorry. I'm starting to feel a level of desperation. If only Daniel were still alive."

At the mention of her father, Tammy sighed and headed up the remainder of the stairs. She wasn't sure what God was doing leaving two women to raise a boy alone, but she had to trust His wisdom.

"We can't live on 'if onlys,' Mother. We've got to deal with what we have to work with." Which was close to nothing. If her parenting resources had been a poker hand, she would have folded a long time ago. But that wasn't what motherhood was about. You played the game to the end even if it looked like you were going to lose. Trevor had said plenty of mean things to her, but the one thing she did not ever want him to say was, "You gave up on me, Mom. You bailed. You wrote me off."

Tammy opened the doors and turned left down the long hallway. The administrative-interview wing, where the officers spent most of their time, was at the opposite end of booking and holding.

"Tamela Jane, slow down. I can't keep up with you."

Her legs had been moving at the speed of her thoughts. Maybe lawlessness was genetic. Maybe Trevor was doomed to live his father's life. *Don't go there, Tams. Don't go there.* She slowed her pace. "Sorry, Mom."

Her mom had a short, turned-under hairstyle that she dyed chestnut brown. Like Tammy, she was tall and big boned. She dressed mostly in matching outfits she ordered off the shopping channel. Today she wore head-to-toe lavender peachskin.

"I'm not a young woman." Hannah lifted her chin and stroked her neck.

Tammy nudged her and winked. "You could pass for forty." At least she had Mom, and that was a true blessing.

"Ha. Forty? Maybe in a dark room filled with blind people."

"Come on, Mom. This way." They opened the door that led to the jail. The processing room was a counter with a bay of video screens behind it. Tammy recognized Ryan Vicher, an officer who had moved up from Wyoming. He was the one who had told Bradley Deaver to push the work on the Parker woman through and the one Captain Stenengarter had sent up to question the archery range members. Tammy clenched her teeth. Why was her mind always returning to that case? It was over and done with. She needed to let it go.

Vicher nodded. "He's down the hall." He held up the police report. "This can disappear if you want."

"Trevor doesn't get breaks because he's a cop's kid."

Her mother stood beside her. "We agreed he had to suffer the consequences of his actions."

"He'll have to appear before a judge, probably pay restitution." Vicher placed the police report in a manila folder.

"What did he steal?"

Vicher glanced at the report. "Little miniature tool kit. Some wheels. Under fifty bucks' worth, so it's a misdemeanor."

"Wheels?" What on earth was he going to do with stuff like that?

"Little ones." He made a circle with his fingers. His fair features suggested Scandinavian heritage. "You want me to bring him out?"

Tammy and her mom nodded in unison. Vicher pressed a button and spoke into a microphone. "Trevor Welstad's mother is here."

Her eyes went to the video monitors. An officer appeared at the corner of the screen ambling past the first two cells. He leaned into the third cell, which Tammy noticed had not been locked. Trevor had opted to meet her at the jail, rather than at the store where he'd been caught, probably because it was too embarrassing.

Watching her kid be escorted by a police officer was like pouring salt in a gash. She looked away from the monitors. She needed to focus on something else...anything but this. "You remember about a week ago? The night the Parker woman was brought in?"

Vicher looked up from his paperwork and blinked several times. He shook his head. Apparently, the case hadn't made an impression on him like it had on her.

Tammy touched her back. "Arrow."

"Oh yeah, yeah."

She had hoped Vicher would give up the information without her having to pry. He struck her as a consummate people pleaser, desperate to get off desk work and patrol.

Tammy stared at the video screen. The other officer led a hunched-over Trevor up the hallway. She averted her eyes from the monitor and kept her tone casual. "You told Deaver to rush the postmortem. No need for a full autopsy?"

"Captain asked me to. It was obviously an accident." Vicher squared his shoulders. "Didn't you think?" He tapped a pen on the counter.

Tammy nodded. "Captain said you weren't able to trace the arrow back to a specific user—too generic."

Vicher stopped tapping his pen. His face paled. "The captain said that?"

"That's what he told me."

Vicher touched the side of his nose and then patted his buzz cut.

Nervous little Nellie, aren't you?

"The captain must have meant a different officer."

Tammy leaned a little closer to him. "I'm pretty sure he said you." Vicher was obviously not the mastermind behind the coverup. In an effort to please Stenengarter, the young officer had been turned into a patsy.

The security panel buzzed. "Looks like your son is here." The tone of triumph in Vicher's voice was a little over the top. He hit a button. The click of metal releasing from metal echoed in the empty admin room. The large steel door opened, and a red-eyed Trevor escorted by an older officer stepped into the room.

Sudden fatigue seeped into Tammy's body. She was tired of the constant psychological pummeling raising a teenager required. She gazed at her boy. He wasn't a big kid. The over-sized T-shirt and pants he wore made him look even smaller. His hair was the same shade of brown as her own, but wavy, like his dad's. He stared at the floor.

"Trevor, where are your glasses?" Mom took a step toward her grandson.

The fifteen-year-old looked everywhere but at his mother. "I lost them, Grandma."

Tammy lifted her arms and then let them fall at her side. She really wanted to hug her son. Even though she was parenting by the seat of her pants, instinct told her this had to be a tough love moment. "You'll have to earn the money to pay for them and for any court costs." She attempted to use the same emotionless tone she adopted when she stopped speeding motorists, but her voice cracked.

Mom gave her a sidelong glance but said nothing. If her mom thought she was making a poor parenting choice, she would tell her later in private. Right now, they were a united front in the battle to push Trevor into adulthood.

Tammy's fist hit the counter. Vicher flinched. "Why, Trevor? Why?" Now her voice was nothing but emotion.

He seemed transfixed by the pattern in the linoleum. "Me and Kevin found this really rad little motor just lying on the side of the road. We were going to put it on my skateboard." He lifted his head and gazed at his mother. "We just needed some things." His eyes steeled and his lips tightened. "So there!"

Whatever regret Trevor had had about his life of crime had been replaced by rebellion. Inwardly, Tammy shuddered. She knew that look—the cold, unwavering eyes and the expression that was like a mask of concrete. She'd seen it on a thousand faces right before the handcuffs went on...and she'd seen it in Larry.

Panic stretched and compressed her stomach like Silly Putty. A memory of two-year-old Trevor running through a field of dandelions, the light playing on his curly hair, flashed through her head. Tammy squared her shoulders.

I will not lose this kid.

She placed her feet shoulder-width apart and tilted her head. She was still two or three inches taller than him. *Two can play this game, Trevor.* "I think we better go home." The ominous tone in her voice implied that she had a medieval torture chamber in her basement that she wasn't afraid to use.

Trevor's shoulders drooped. Though his jaw remained tense, the coldness in his eyes melted. He fiddled with the zipper of his sweat jacket.

"The car is in the side lot. I suggest you hustle."

Trevor scowled at her and shoved his hands in his pockets, but he made his way past the counter and out into the hall.

"He looks half starved to death." Her mother readjusted her purse on her arm. "I'll make him soup when we get home."

"Mom, he's only been in jail for four hours."

Her mother waved her hand in the air. "I am his grandmother. It's my job to feed him."

Tammy took a deep breath. "You're right. That is your job." *And my job is to find Trev a mentor who doesn't think dating me is part of the deal.*

As they left short-term lockup, Tammy glanced back at Vicher, who tapped the keyboard at a furious pace. Even though she gazed at him for some time, he didn't make eye contact or even look up from the computer.

· ·

Ginger had never seen a man's eyes turn quite as big and round as the man named Frank's did. That phrase "eyes like saucers" really did have some truth to it. She waited for spirals to appear in his eyes like they did in the cartoons.

Frank shook his head. His cheeks and forehead reddened, making him look like a giant strawberry in a T-shirt. "I can't believe Beth did that." He tugged on the waistband of his green and black checkered shorts. "I just can't believe it." Frank picked up the Mickey Mouse fishing pole and set it back down in the box with the other garage sale stuff.

"So the pole is yours?" Kindra cocked her head and crossed her arms. Her eyes veered subtly toward Ginger in an "aha" expression. Frank was probably too busy turning red and clenching his fists to notice Kindra signaling Ginger.

They had laid out the box of four items on the hood of Frank's truck, the door of which said The Housewife's Helper in solid, manly letters. There was a lawn mower, toolbox, and floor buffer in the bed of the truck. Ginger shifted her weight to the balls of her feet. This was only their second stop on Mary Margret's chronological list, and already they had scored.

Frank was a fortysomething man with a head full of black hair. His skin, when it wasn't red with anger, was rich dark brown, probably from the outdoor work he did. His tan stopped midforehead. A white strip of skin jutted up against dark bangs. Ginger pictured a baseball hat with a reference to a sports team or beer on his head. Pasty skin was also evident on his upper arms. A large stomach caused his shorts to droop.

"This is my lucky fishing pole." His index finger jabbed toward the reel that sported Mickey Mouse dancing with an elated Pluto. "It's got the extra large reel, and the rod collapses in on itself so you can fit it in a small space." Frank shook his head again. "Beth!" His feet pounded on the concrete driveway as he lumbered toward the open garage. "Beth!"

A woman's high-pitched voice drifted out of a window. "What?"

Frank stomped out of the garage and stood beneath the open window. "I need to talk to you."

"I'm right in the middle of a batch of pineapple rhubarb, Frank."

"Did you sell my lucky Mickey Mouse fishing pole?" He tilted his head, glaring at the window.

No answer came from inside the house.

Something about the unfolding drama made Ginger think of Earl. He could be really rough around the edges, and sometimes he just pretended to be excited about things she bought on sale. But at least he pretended for her and never spoke to her like Frank was talking to Beth.

A moment later, the front door burst open and a woman who must be Beth stood wiping her hands on a dish towel.

A pastel scarf framed her round face. "What's going on here?" She glanced at Ginger and Kindra.

Frank strutted back over to the truck and snatched the fishing pole off the hood. "Did you sell this at a garage sale? You know this is my lucky fishing pole."

Beth raised her chin. "It's a piece of junk, Frank."

Poor Beth, she had probably thought she'd seen the last of Frank's silly fishing pole. And now it had come back to bite her.

"What else did you sell? Did you sell my antlers?" He strutted toward the garage and opened storage cabinets. "Where is my stuffed antelope head?"

Beth placed her hand on her hip and tilted her head back while she spoke. "No, I did not sell your stupid antlers."

"What about my bobblehead collection?"

Beth dropped her gaze to the sidewalk, then lifted her chin and crossed her arms. "Holy cow, Frank. Half of them were broken from the kids dropping them."

"You did sell them. You did." He dashed through the garage to the sidewalk and stood nose to nose with his wife.

"I didn't sell them. I threw them out. They're not worth anything."

Ginger pretended to be busy arranging the other garage sale stuff. Beth didn't know her junk from her treasures. Bobbleheads brought good money to the right collector.

Ginger caught a glimpse of Kindra in her peripheral vision. Something about that pixie face and blond hair always made her think of *Alice's Adventures in Wonderland*, which she used to read to her kids. A faint smile crossed Kindra's face. Was she thinking that life as a single person was pretty good? Kindra had a very large collection of Beanie Babies, which were not in any danger of being sold or thrown out.

"You threw them out." Frank performed an odd dance in the driveway. The choreography involved clenching his fists, bending at the waist, and turning a half circle one way and then reversing. "You threw them out."

Beth twisted and untwisted the towel around her wrist and hand. "I thought we were gonna dejunk our lives. We agreed." She fisted a hand on her hip.

"I noticed you're not getting rid of any of your stuff. What about all those ceramic roosters you got around the house?"

"They give the decor unity. We have rooster wallpaper."

"They collect dust, too."

Beth's gaze darted from Frank to the two strangers standing in her driveway. She softened her tone. "I have gotten rid of some of my things. I hauled away two bags of clothes last week."

Frank stopped dancing long enough to stare at them.

Ginger gathered up the garage sale stuff. "Maybe this is a bad time."

"Now my jam is ruined." Beth dashed back into the house, slamming the door behind her.

Frank chased after Ginger and Kindra. "Wait, can I buy that fishing pole back from you?"

Ginger turned and cleared her throat. Other than their misdemeanors against each other, Frank and Beth seemed like ordinary people, not those who would try to run her off the road or put an arrow through Mary Margret. Ginger fingered the fishing pole. Still, it might be important.

"Whatever your friend paid." He leaned toward Ginger. She detected the scent of Old Spice. "I'll pay you double to get it back." His expression communicated desperation. Poor guy had lost his bobbleheads.

Beth's voice drifted out of the window. "Let it go, Frank."

He hung his head and spoke in almost a whisper. "I really loved that pole. Took my son fishing with it." His voice gradually grew louder, and he directed his comment toward the window. "It's not like you form attachments to a pantsuit."

Beth's voice was singsongy. "I can hear you." Pots and pans continued to clang inside, and a faucet was turned on.

Frank moved his lips, mocking his wife. Watching Frank and Beth fight made Ginger feel like she had just drunk a vinegar soda. Showing respect for Earl's dream, at the very least, would begin with not calling his inventions contraptions anymore.

Frank turned back toward Ginger and Kindra. "Please, I just want my lucky fishing pole."

Ginger raised her eyebrows at Kindra, who nodded. She handed a smiling Frank the three-foot fishing pole. "You don't have to pay us anything."

He retreated to his garage. With Kindra in the passenger seat, Ginger drove her Pontiac out of Frank's neighborhood. Her thoughts whirred like bananas in a blender. What made people talk to each other like that? Sometimes she threw away stuff of Earl's without asking him. In an effort to run an uncluttered house, she had totally disregarded his feelings. Ginger pressed her lips together. *That has to stop.*

Last year, she had sold Earl's favorite tool kit at her own garage sale. They just looked so dirty and beat-up. How was she supposed to know they were his favorite? Still, she should have asked. Selling his tools certainly wasn't supportive. It wasn't the cheerleader thing to do.

"Ginger? You're doing it again."

"Sorry, did you say something?"

"Hello from this planet." Kindra held the piece of torn paper in her hand. "Mary Margret only marked two more sales that took place before eight."

"Let's do those two tomorrow. I just suddenly realized I need to get home to my husband."

Boy oh boy, do I need to get home to my Earl.

SHARON DUNN

Ginger placed a heaping pile of beef stroganoff on the plate alongside the fresh salad with Earl's favorite dressing: ranch. She cut a piece of chocolate cake and arranged it on a separate serving dish. Finally she poured milk into a plastic cup and snapped a lid on it so it wouldn't spill. The entire meal went into a plastic sectioned transporter with a cover, a handy little device she'd picked up when the Tupperware lady in their old neighborhood had a going-out-of-business sale.

The sky was a soft shade of gray as Ginger made her way across the gravel to Earl's workshop. She tapped lightly on the door. No answer. She knocked louder. Nothing.

Holding the tray with one hand and pressing it into her tummy, she twisted the doorknob and stepped inside Earl Salinski's strange world. She hadn't entered his workshop since they moved to this house. The last time she visited, it had been concrete floor and tin walls and bare counter space. Now, she couldn't even see the counters. Clutter, clutter everywhere.

The air smelled like oil and burned rubber with just a hint of barbecue potato chips. In fact, she noticed about twelve bags of opened potato chips scattered among the twisted metal and strange machines. Did Earl actually get a new bag without finishing the old one? She made a mental note to bring some bag clippies from the house so the chips wouldn't grow stale and be wasted.

She squinted. Blue haze hung in the air.

In the corner of the workshop, a creature in a leather apron and welder's hat perched atop the Bobcat Earl plowed snow and dug holes with. Sparks flew off the machine like firecrackers. The bug-eyed creature skipped over the top of the Bobcat and leapt to the floor, welding rod in hand. He tilted his head from side to side.

A pocket of air caught in Ginger's throat. She had no idea Earl could move with such flexibility and energy. She'd only seen him move that fast once before. He had been racing to get the remote before she did because she suggested that they watch the shopping channel on a Monday night. She had momentarily forgotten it was football season. That night, her dear husband ended up crashing headfirst into the TV trays.

She'd glared down at him, hands on her hips. "For Pete's sake, Earl. You didn't have to do a Mary Lou Retton impersonation. All you had to do was remind me that it was the big game."

Earl had wiped creamed corn off his face and righted the TV tray. "I just got worried, that's all." He rose to his feet with the remote pressed against his tummy.

This time though, Earl had done his gymnastic routine on the Bobcat without a hitch. A perfect ten. It was like watching a different person. Was the agile man in the corner even Earl, or had her sixty-year-old husband hired a much younger man to be his assistant? The creature flipped up his mask. Ah, there was the familiar square face and brown eyes of her husband.

But then his features scrunched up. "What are you doing out here?"

What was she doing out here? She was being his cheerleader. She was honoring his request. Couldn't he see that? "I—I—" She lifted the tray a little higher. "I brought you dinner."

Earl put down his welding rod. "But I always come in the house for dinner."

"I thought we would do it different tonight." Ginger searched for bare counter space to set the dinner tray on, of which there was none. The place was filthy. Maybe she could show her support by helping him organize his workshop. She could alphabetize his tools once she learned the names of them all.

"Oh." After taking off his welder's cap and wiping his brow, he ambled toward her. "Why?"

Earl's confusion confused her. Hadn't he asked her to be more supportive? Couldn't he see that was what she was doing? *Read my mind, Earl. Read my mind.*

"Well, I brought you dinner." Again, she looked around for a place to set the tray. Again, to no avail. She shoved the tray toward him. Let him find a place to put it.

He took the tray, closed the lid on a toolbox, and set it on top of that. "Did you bring your dinner out?"

Ginger's toes curled inside the leather flats she'd gotten half price when Harman's had closed their shoe department. Her jaw clenched. This was not going how she had hoped. Why was he being so uncooperative? "I already ate my dinner. It's close to nine, Earl. Most people had dinner hours ago."

"Why are you getting so upset?"

"I'm—I'm not getting upset." Tears warmed the corner of her eyes. "I made your favorite: Stroganoff, salad with ranch dressing, and chocolate cake." Her words became squeakier as she talked. Couldn't he see how hard she was trying?

His expression softened. "Oh, honey." Earl darted toward her, arms held out to hug her. His hand swept over the top of the toolbox and knocked the food tray off. It hit the floor with a muffled clatter.

Ginger threw her hands up. "Now it's all ruined."

Earl scrambled to pick up the tray. "No, it's okay. You got this nifty protective cover on here." He lifted the lid. The chocolate cake had ranch dressing and lettuce on it. Gravy covered most of the salad. Earl stared down at the disaster and shifted his weight from one foot to the other. Finally, he held the cup up triumphantly. "The milk is still good."

Ginger's heart sank into the cushioned insoles of her half price designer shoes. Earl was trying so hard. She was trying so hard. Why was this going so badly? "Maybe this was not a good idea. Maybe you should just come in and eat dinner like you always do."

He nodded.

"I'll toss that. I have more in the house." Again, the waterworks started in the corners of her eyes. "I'll put it in the containers just like I always do so you can warm it up in the microwave."

Earl's smile never quite reached his eyes. "Just like you always do."

"Course I'll be asleep when you come in." Maybe being a part of his world wasn't such a good idea.

He handed Ginger the tray with the demolished food. She really needed to get out of this workshop. The clutter was making her thoughts tangle like the mess of wire Earl had in the corner. How on earth could he even work in here? Shoulders slumping, she took the tray and trudged back to the house.

Twenty minutes later, Ginger lay in bed staring at the ceiling. She heard Earl open the outside door and speak affectionately to Phoebe. She listened while the microwave buzzed and dinged. Then Earl stomped into the family room, turned on the television, and talked to the FOX News commentators while he ate his late-night meal.

SHARON DUNN

Earl had been like a different man in the workshop, jumping around the Bobcat like a twenty-year-old. His actions seemed inspired, so enthusiastic. What was Earl thinking about that made him so excited? She wanted to get to know that man...but she had no idea how.

If Mary Margret were here, she would have good advice. She missed her friend more than ever. The white dots that were a precursor to her migraines crossed Ginger's field of vision.

Not again.

She closed her eyes and put the pillow over her head. To separate herself from the rising pain, she focused on her breathing.

In the next room, the television buzzed while Earl had a one-sided conversation with the television.

How was it possible for two people to be in the same house and live such separate lives?

....

In the darkness of her bedroom, Arleta McQuire stubbed her toe on the leg of the headboard. She yowled and stumbled toward the light switch. Illumination from a covered incandescent bulb on the ceiling filled the room. After clunking her revolver on the bureau by the door, she peered down at a bloody, pulsating big toe.

"That was no good." She placed a hand on her slender hip. Arleta paced the carpet, favoring the foot with the injured toe. For the life of her, she just couldn't get this self-defense drill right.

What had her firearms instructor told her? *Think, Arleta, think.* She could do this. Her seventy-five-year-old mind worked just fine. First, get the flashlight, then the revolver, grab the speed loader, find a hiding place. Sit with the flashlight off until the intruder is in the room. Switch it on long enough to locate the intruder. Give your warning in a loud, confident voice.

Arleta practiced her warning. "I have a gun, and I know how to use it. " Her instructor, an ex-policeman with muscles like Arnold Schwarzenegger, had said that the warning was often enough to scare an intruder away. She sure hoped so because she wasn't good at the rest of the drill.

She plunked down on her unslept-in bed and placed her face in her hands. Twice, she had grabbed her mascara out of her nightstand instead of the flashlight. Maybe if she dumped everything out of the drawer except for the flashlight and the speed loader, then it might work. She kept the gun and the bullets separate just like the instructor had advised.

In a way, she was grateful to have something to do in the wee hours besides watch bad television. In the fifteen years since her husband, David, had died, Arleta hadn't slept through the night. For the last month, she'd been practicing the drill instead of watching TV. It was a step forward. At least she was being productive when she couldn't sleep.

The neighborhood was changing. When she and David had moved here forty years ago, they had been surrounded by families. Now almost all the homes were rentals—mostly to temporary college students. Some of them drank alcohol and did who knows what all night. Partygoers thought her lawn was a good place to turn their cars around on.

The final straw was when she had listened to a fight between two men. The shouting started across the street, but eventually it ended up right outside her bedroom window. She stayed in bed, paralyzed and sweating, for close to twenty minutes while the men exchanged blows and threatened a thousand other ways they would do damage to each other. At some point, one of their bodies slammed against the side of the house. The next morning, she signed up for the self-defense class and drove to the sporting goods store.

David, an archaeology professor, had worked with college students. She had liked his students, liked having them over for dinner. But students these days were different—scarier. Not respectful.

She reached over to the nightstand, pulled out the drawer, and dumped the contents on the carpet. She'd try it with just the speed loader and the flashlight. An empty pewter frame caught her eye. She should have put that in the garage sale when she sold those other things a week ago. Just old stuff.

The money from garage sales helped pay for her class. She'd sold some of her antiques to pay for the gun. She'd gotten rid of David's vest, the one he wore on digs, and his old photo album. The nice woman who bought the stuff seemed so happy. Selling most of David's things had given her a stronger sense of closure. She'd been working on this closure thing for almost fifteen years.

Arleta could not afford to move, but even if she could, she was not about to be driven out of her home by a bunch of spoiled teenagers. One twelve Fremont was her home. She had no intention of leaving.

She placed the loader and flashlight at the edge of the drawer, closed her eyes, and practiced feeling for them. She wasn't a vigilante. She wouldn't shoot people who drove on her lawn. If the parties got too loud, she could call the police. The events just made her feel less safe.

Then a few nights after her last garage sale, she had heard someone walking outside her open bedroom window. Just yesterday, a tall, well-dressed man with snowy white hair had parked his brown car across the street and watched her house. The whole incident had given her the heebie-jeebies.

But she was not about to sit worrying and fretting like some helpless old lady. She had traipsed all over the world with David on his digs. She was a woman of action, not a whiner.

With renewed energy, she retrieved her revolver from the bureau and put it in the box under her bed. The man in the sporting goods store had said that women liked the Model 34 kit gun because it was light and very accurate. Revolvers didn't jam, and she had to pull back the hammer each time she fired a shot, so there was no danger of misfire.

For a month now, she had been in a class filled with single moms and widows staring at fluorescent orange targets and learning to squeeze not jerk the trigger. Although she hadn't told any of the other ladies in class, she gave her Smith & Wesson a real name. She called the gun Annie, after Annie Oakley.

With the revolver snug in the box, Arleta turned off the light and felt her way to the bed. She lay on top of the bedspread, closed her eyes, and pretended to sleep just like she would if an intruder showed up.

Even in the brief hours when she did sleep at night, it was a light sleep. She heard every noise, every creak of the old house. Each passing year without David, the noises got louder and more frequent.

Her arm fell across the other side of the bed. David's side. For a brief moment, she imagined herself as hollow with the wind blowing right through. Her heart ached. David had been her life. David and his work. They hadn't had any children. That hadn't bothered her when David was alive, but now she was alone. Arleta squeezed her eyes shut, taking deep breaths.

I am not a quitter. I've got plenty of life left in these old bones, and I intend to live it.

Arleta took one last deep breath and steeled herself for the practice drill. She rehearsed the steps in her mind. Reach for Annie, grab flashlight and speed loader, crawl to the closet, drop loader into gun...and wait. Wait.

••••••••••••••••••••••••••••••••

The air in the police records room smelled of sweat and old paper. For the sixth time, Tammy shuffled through the file drawers thinking, hoping, that the report on Mary Margret Parker had been misfiled. Since catching Vicher in a lie, she'd gone digging for the report she did the night she interviewed Mary Margret's friends. She could find no record of the report on the computer or in hard copy. These files in the basement storage room were the inactive files.

Her throat went dry. The steel of the file cabinet was colder than usual against her hands.

"Looking for something, Welstad?" Tammy jumped. Captain Stenengarter suddenly materialized at the door. The guy was quiet.

"I um—I um was just looking for an old stolen vehicle report." She straightened her spine and pulled a random file out of the cabinet and waved it. "And I found it."

Stenengarter took three steps into the room. His soft-soled shoes were silent on the concrete. "Must have been misfiled, huh?" He sauntered toward her and stood closer than what she would have considered to be polite social distance. "'Cause you were looking in the homicide-suicide cabinet."

Somewhere in the huge records room a fan whirred and a lightbulb sputtered. The reflections off of Stenengarter's rimless glasses gave the effect of a veil covering his eyes. The muscle in his left cheek twitched.

"Yes, that's it." She swallowed trying to produce some moisture in her mouth. "It must have been in the wrong cabinet."

The captain stared at her way beyond the etiquette time limit. Tammy's heart pounded.

"Well—" his Adam's apple moved up and down on his skinny neck—"if it's an old file, we shouldn't be bothering with it. We have enough active files to deal with; we have to let those old cases go, don't we, Welstad?"

She forced out a, "Yes, sir."

"So why don't you put that file back and go do your job."

Tammy slowly turned away from the captain, clicked open the file cabinet, and slid the file back in place. The press of Stenengarter's gaze was almost palpable on her neck and back.

"Do you like working property crimes?" He pulled the keys out of his pocket, twirling them, making tinkling metal noises.

"Yes, I do. I like the variety. I like the brain work involved."

"Good, I would hate to see you busted back down to patrol." Without another word, he walked out of the room.

Tammy pushed the drawer shut and stared up at the sputtering light. *Oh, God, I need this job.* She closed her eyes. She'd worked hard to get promoted to property crimes. But even as she thought about being demoted or fired, she knew what she had to do.

Do the right thing, and God will take care of the rest, her father had always said.

Somebody, probably Stenengarter, was making the Parker case disappear. She needed one more confirmation. As she stood alone in the records room, she decided then she would wait until she was off shift and check to see if there was anything left of the Parker case in the evidence storage room.

Stenengarter couldn't get on her case for that. She would be doing it on her time, not the department's. Even if the case was closed, anything gathered from it should have been in storage for at least a year.

At 8 a.m. when her shift ended, Tammy checked her cell phone to make sure she hadn't missed any calls from Trevor or her mom. She stood in the long hallway of the justice building holding her breath while she clicked buttons until the words *no messages* came up on the tiny screen.

So far, so good. Trevor had stayed close to home since his jailhouse experience. There had been only one small disaster. He had stolen and taken apart one of the neighbor kid's robot cats without asking.

On her way to evidence, she darted down the hallway passing Deputy Coroner Bradley Deaver, who held a sandwich in his hand. "Where ya headed in such an all-fired hurry?"

Maybe it was just the intense lighting in the hallway, but Deaver was looking more like a turtle than usual. Tammy couldn't decide what gave him his reptilelike quality—the large flat jowls, the high forehead, or the beady eyes that were more pupil than iris. She kept waiting for his tongue to flick out of his mouth. "I'm just taking care of some stuff."

He glanced at the doorway that led downstairs. "You going down to evidence?"

What a busybody. "Why does it matter where I'm going?"

Deaver moved toward her. "Aren't you off shift?"

"Don't you have a book to read about Waco or something?"

The remark must have hurt his feelings. His forehead wrinkled and his lips bundled up into a pout. He crossed his arms and stared at her for a long time. "We're the two people in this department who don't fit in. You know that don't you, Welstad? We're the outsiders."

What an odd thing to say. Tammy shook her head.

"So you are headed to evidence to check on the Parker case?" His tone was not accusatory.

Deaver's cryptic remark suddenly made sense. For whatever reason, Stenengarter wanted the Parker case to vaporize. He had used Vicher to see to it that that happened. Since she had asked to interview the members of the archery range, the captain had shown up four times on her shift, something he had never done before. And he had followed her into the records room making veiled threats about demotion.

Stenengarter might have other lackeys besides Vicher, but one thing was for sure. Deaver wasn't one of them. Tammy's irritation melted. If there was one safe person to talk to about this, it was Deaver. He was the most disenfranchised, unconnected person in the department.

"I just think more effort should have been put into it. I interviewed her friends. Something was up. All the paperwork on the case has disappeared." She realized now how isolated she had felt since she'd first had an inkling that the department was not on the up-and-up. "I'm not trying to be an outsider, Deaver."

He tore off a corner of his sandwich and shoved it in his mouth. "It's not something you choose. Believe me." A tiny bulb of mayonnaise clung to the corner of his mouth.

"I am headed down to evidence."

"You won't find anything." He wiped the mayo off his face with his knuckles.

"How do you know?"

"You were right. This thing felt funny from the beginning." Deaver rubbed his hands together to get the crumbs off. "Aside from the odd female lawyer or clerk who needs to straighten her panty hose, you are the only person in the women's locker room.

SHARON DUNN

The men's locker room, however, is just filled with outright gossip and mumbling. Being invisible has its advantages. I hear everything. I already checked the evidence room. Anything that was collected has been expedited through the system, and it has turned to dust."

The news caused the tension to return to Tammy's shoulder blades. That meant the phone message tape and the arrow were gone. What kind of corruption was she facing and why? "Bradley, do you know what this means?"

He shook his head.

"I hate to admit it, but I think we have a genuine conspiracy on our hands." How many people it involved beyond Vicher and Stenengarter, she couldn't begin to guess.

Deaver grinned. "So what's our first step?"

"You keep your ear close to the gossip. Be careful. Neither of us needs to lose our jobs. On the outside chance that I am wrong about this, I don't want to point fingers until I am sure."

A uniformed officer sauntered down the hallway and passed them. Tammy lowered her voice and leaned a little closer to Deaver. "And I need to get in touch with the Parker woman's friends. I made a terrible mistake telling them the case was closed."

Ten

Kindra clutched an autobiography of Einstein and leaned close to Ginger. "Is that librarian giving us the hairy eyeball, or what?"

Ginger glanced up from the newspaper she had been flipping through and studied the tall rows of books. "I don't see any librarian, and I don't know what the hairy eyeball is."

The last two days had been frustrating. They'd gone to the third address on Mary Margret's list, only to find that the people there had had a moving sale. The house was empty with a For Sale sign on the lawn. They had three items left and only one address they hadn't visited: 112 Fremont.

On top of everything, she and Earl seemed to be drifting even further apart. They weren't fighting. They just weren't talking. He was spending more and more time in his work-shop. When he wasn't working on an invention, he was read-ing the self-help books their son Robert gave him.

One night after Earl had gone out to the shop, she had glanced through the stack of books. Most of them were about mar-riage, and one of them said that women were from another planet. She knew what that book was really about. If Earl thought their marriage was in trouble, why wasn't he talking to her about it?

Ginger exhaled and closed the newspaper. "I don't think we're going to find anything in here about the lawyer in that big house."

Suzanne pulled another local newspaper off the rack. "I know I saw an article about him. It was just a little bit ago. They had a photo of him standing in front of his mansion. I remember the yellow roses in the background."

Kindra placed her thick book on the table, stepping forward and back so she could survey several bookshelves. "I'm sure she's been following me around the library."

Suzanne flipped a page of her newspaper, sucking on the insides of her cheeks like she always did when she was concentrating. "Maybe she's just putting books away." She pounded her fist lightly on the table and bent closer to the newspaper. "Oh darn, the Kid's Closet had a sale on children's clothes and I missed it."

"Suzanne, there are more important things than sales." Ginger's voice had a sharp bite to it that surprised her. *More important things like your marriage falling apart, like your best friend's murder being swept under the carpet and your not being able to do anything about it.*

Kindra and Suzanne stared at Ginger, eyes narrowed, pensive.

"Do you have a fever?" Kindra touched Ginger's forehead with her cool hand. "'Cause I thought you just said that their sales were nothing to get excited about."

"Of course, some things matter more than getting a good deal." Suzanne reached for Ginger's hand.

Both of the women gazed at her, waiting, her cue to explain why she had snapped at them. She couldn't put words to the chasm she felt growing between her and Earl. All she could think was that she was a lot like the mustard-colored coat on the clearance rack that no one would ever buy no matter how big the markdown. Just hanging there all sad and lonely.

It wasn't like they were fighting or anything. Even talking about it scared her. Ginger tensed, her frustration returning tenfold. "I just don't know if all we've been doing is getting us any closer to figuring out who killed Mary Margret."

Kindra shifted her weight and tucked a strand of blond hair behind her ear. "What else can we do?"

"I'm not Perry Mason and you're not Miss Marple." Ginger shoved the newspaper aside. "We don't know what we're doing."

"Nobody but us cares about what happened. We have to do this for Mary Margret," Kindra said.

Suzanne nodded.

Ginger shook her head. "It just feels like we are not getting anywhere."

Kindra elbowed Ginger. "I am way too young to be compared to Miss Marple."

"Maybe a private detective would do a better job." Ginger crossed her arms.

"Do you know what those guys charge?" Suzanne said. "I don't think they would do anything different than what we've been doing."

Spending thousands of dollars on something she could do herself didn't sit well with Ginger. "Okay, we'll find out who this lawyer guy is and go back to his house. Then we'll go to the last address on the list. If sparks aren't flying by then, we'll have to shop around for a cheap detective. Maybe there's one who gives out coupons for his services."

Kindra placed another newspaper in front of Ginger. "Start looking. Suzanne thought she saw it in the Features section."

The women flipped silently through the newspapers for several minutes until Suzanne asked, "Wouldn't a hairy eyeball hurt? I mean, when you closed it?"

"I think it would get stuck if you shut your eyes." Ginger mimed trying to pry open a hairy eyeball.

SHARON DUNN

Kindra stared at the ceiling and blew out a gust of air. "It's just an expression my father used, okay? It meant someone was staring at you like they suspected you of something. Can we get back to work please?"

All three women giggled while they scanned the newspapers.

"Here it is." Suzanne pointed. "I knew I had seen it."

Ginger stepped toward Suzanne. The story had a picture of the lawyer, whose name was Keaton Lustrum, standing outside his house, arms crossed, mountains and lake in the background. An attractive woman leaned close to him, an arm wrapped possessively across his back. The photograph had been taken from a low angle, which made Mr. Lustrum look that much more domineering. The headline read "Lawyer Seeks Ban on Motorized Vehicles."

Kindra leaned close. "Oh yeah, I remember. He's the guy who represents those environmental groups. He did a guest lecture at the college."

Ginger scanned the article. "Looks like he doesn't want any motorcycles or four-wheelers on the National Forest land." She tapped her finger on the woman in the picture. "That was the lady who had the garage sale, along with a lady who looked like her."

Kindra cleared her throat. "Don't look now, but the hairy eyeball is rounding the corner."

The librarian was as tall as she was wide. She walked like she had Velcro on the bottom of her shoes, each step taking substantial effort. Ginger was only five foot five, and she had to look down on her.

"Please, I hope you don't think I'm rude. But I've seen you in here before." She directed her comment to Kindra. "You're friends with Mary Margret, the lady who died?"

"Yes."

"Such a nice lady." The librarian used her stack of books to point at Kindra. "You helped Mary Margret at our used book fund-raiser. It took me a while to place you."

Kindra let out a faint, "Oh."

Ginger rested a hand on Kindra's shoulder. Now that the mystery of the hairy eyeball was solved, Kindra seemed a little embarrassed.

The woman arched her back to counterbalance the weight of the books. "You know, she was in here the day she died."

Ginger's heart skipped a beat. "She was in the library the Saturday she died?"

The short woman nodded. "I remember it because she seemed upset. She was waiting at the door when I came to open the library at ten."

"What was she upset about?"

The woman shrugged. "She never said. She just wanted to look at the newspapers from twenty years ago. They are downstairs on microfiche."

"Did she say what she was looking for?"

"No, but at one point, she came upstairs and wanted to know if we had the minutes from old city commission meetings." The woman adjusted the three books she had in her arms. "I told her that kind of thing was probably at the courthouse. They're not open on Saturday. Terrible thing that happened to her, that accident."

"It wasn't an accident." This news only confirmed her suspicions. Mary Margret had figured out something, and it had gotten her killed. Maybe she was Miss Marple. Better yet, Jessica Fletcher. Ginger thanked the librarian.

After the librarian disappeared around a bookshelf, Suzanne wiped the sweat from her forehead and tugged her shirt over her bulging tummy. "I can go to the courthouse and see if I can figure out what Mary Margret was looking for. When we get together tonight for midnight shopping, I'll let you know if I find anything."

"Sounds like a plan." Ginger looped her arm through Kindra's elbow. "Come on, kiddo; you and I are going to 112 Fremont for starters." Ginger headed toward the door. Renewed hope put an extra spring in her step.

•••••••••••••••••••••••••••••••••••

Earl stood in the driveway between his workshop and the house. He cocked his head to one side and rubbed his chin. He had closed the door to the house and yet, there it stood, open. He made his way across the gravel and up the front stairs. He examined the knob and keyhole area. A person wouldn't have to break in. He never locked the door when he went out to the shop. Shrugging off his suspicions, he stepped into the kitchen.

He found the Tupperware container of food Ginger had labeled and put in the fridge for him and placed it in the microwave. She had left earlier in the day to go to the library, taking Phoebe with her. The image of Phoebe perched in the booster seat made him smile. Whoever heard of a cat that liked riding in a car? He knew Ginger was gone because she had tacked a note for him on the fridge. They seemed to be leaving notes for each other a lot.

He noticed the number one blinking on the answering machine and pushed the button. A woman said, "Hi, Ginger; this is Officer Tammy Welstad. I have some news about your friend, but I need to tell you in person. I will come by your place after I work out; I should be there a little after eight tonight. If I don't hear from you, I'll assume that will be okay. I know you might still be upset at me, but this is important." The woman left her number and then hung up. Would Ginger even want to talk to Officer Welstad?

The microwave dinged, and he pulled the steaming lasagna out. The aroma of Italian spices swirled around the kitchen. He and Ginger weren't even having meals together much anymore. He was eating at weird times. He'd get so wrapped up in his project that he'd forget to come into the house until the growling of his stomach got louder than his power tools.

He needed to make an effort to come in at mealtimes. Maybe that was what she had been trying to say to him when she brought his meal to the shop the other night. Women were funny. They never came right out and said what they wanted, and yet they expected a guy to know. Early in their marriage, Earl had realized that almost everything Ginger said to him would be in some kind of code. After all these years, he still hadn't broken the code.

Earl grabbed a fork and wandered into the family room.

He still couldn't shake the eerie feeling that someone had been in the house. Furniture wasn't overturned. No drawers hung open. No catalogs cluttered the floor. It was more a sense that things seemed slightly askew. Ginger was an extremely organized and tidy person. The bills were spread across the desk, not in her usual neat pile. The couch cushion as well looked like it had been pulled out and pushed back in a hurry.

Earl shook his head and dismissed the thought. What did they have that would be worth stealing? He sat in his easy chair and clicked on the TV so he could give the FOX News commentators his two cents' worth.

He glanced down at the stack of self-help books he'd borrowed from Robert. The one that said women were from another planet he'd grabbed by mistake, thinking it was a science fiction book. The others, though, Robert had handpicked from his shelf. None of them had been much help. He was looking for a chart or a table that explained when a woman does X, it means Y.

He had spent nearly forty years with Ginger, he loved her more than anything, and yet sometimes he felt like she was speaking Russian. Maybe it was just the loss of Mary Margret, but honestly, the speaking a foreign language thing seemed to be intensifying.

Like the other night when she had come into his workshop. That made no sense. He had been glad to see her, a little surprised, but glad. And then she started looking around, those two vertical lines between her eyes deepening, and he was sure she was thinking about tidying up the place and alphabetizing his tools. That made him afraid. He had that shop just the way he wanted it. It was his space. She got to keep the house the way she wanted it.

Earl turned the volume down on the TV and sat forward in his recliner. In the corner of the room, his other stack of books—science fiction and invention reference books—were knocked completely over. He scanned the room again, unable to totally pinpoint why he felt a sense of invasion. His skin prickled; he gripped the lasagna container a little tighter.

Somebody *had* been in their house.

• •

"'Scuse us?" Ginger shaded her eyes and stared up at the tall, slender woman on the roof of 112 Fremont. Kindra stood beside her with her arms crossed over her chest, rubbing her bare arms. With the sun lowering on the horizon, a slight chill hung in the summer air.

The woman on the roof wore a large brimmed hat with a hot pink sash. Ginger couldn't see her face. She grabbed another shingle out of a box and lifted her hammer. Judging from the way she moved, she must be quite young.

Ginger shouted above the hammering. "Excuse me, ma'am." Oblivious, the woman pounded away.

Kindra gave Ginger a shrug and bolted up the ladder. She crawled to the top while Ginger held the bottom.

When she saw Kindra, the woman stopped hammering midswing. "Sorry, I didn't hear you. Got to get these shingles replaced before fall." She looked at Kindra and then down at Ginger "And who might you two be?"

"Can't you pay someone to do that?" Kindra asked.

"Fixed income. 'Sides I've always done the repairs on the house. My late husband, David, was busy with his work, so I learned how to do the plumbing and change the oil in the car." She tore off her hat. "How can I help you ladies?"

Ginger was momentarily speechless as she tilted her head. The woman under the hat had to be at least seventy. Her steel gray hair was pulled into a bun, and intense blue eyes were surrounded by skin that looked like crinkled tissue paper. She wore a man's wool shirt that Ginger recognized as being from the Pendleton catalog, maybe twenty years ago.

"We need to talk to you about a garage sale you had two Saturdays ago."

"Why don't you ladies come up here? My name is Arleta McQuire, by the way. I've got some lemonade in a thermos. I'm not asking you to live dangerously. There's a little balcony up here where I take my breaks."

It seemed an odd invitation to offer a stranger, but Kindra climbed over the ladder and onto the balcony, so Ginger followed.

The balcony was a six-by-six flat spot with a railing snuggled between dormer windows. There was a small bistro table with two matching chairs. French doors led into the upper floor of the house. Arleta slapped her forehead. "What was I thinking? I only have the one cup."

"I'm okay," said Kindra. "I'm not thirsty."

"You sure?" Arleta unscrewed the cap. "I could go inside and get us some glasses." Kindra shook her head. Arleta poured some lemonade into the cup she had on the table, handed it to Ginger, and then poured herself some in the cap of the thermos. She invited Ginger to take one of the chairs.

"Now which garage sale are you talking about? I had three of them."

"Two Saturdays ago, July 15." Ginger sipped the lemonade, which was homemade. Who had the time to squeeze dozens of lemons? She allowed the sweet-sour liquid to linger on her tongue. What a treat. "Did you sell a vest, a box covered in shells, or a photo album at any of your sales?" This woman seemed so friendly, but she might have something to do with Mary Margret's death.

Arleta nodded. "I sold my husband's vest and his old photo album. I took the pictures out that mattered to me. Don't recall selling a shell box. But there was a lot of junk I sat out in boxes, and people sorted through and took what they wanted."

"Do you remember the woman who bought them?" The woman was sharing the information without hesitation. Not a sign of someone with something to hide. "She had white hair, a real bubbly personality. A little taller than me."

Arleta perched in the other chair on the balcony. Kindra remained standing. "Oh yes, I remember her. We had a nice visit. She said she sold real estate. She gave me her business card. I don't remember where I put it."

Kindra said, "Mary Margret was like that. She gave everyone her business card."

Arleta took a sip of lemonade. "She was going to use the vest to go fishing with her grandson, said something about buying a fishing pole at another sale. My husband wore that vest when he went on his digs. He liked it because of all the pockets."

"What about the photo album?" Kindra crossed her arms, visibly shivering.

"She said she liked it because it had pictures of Three Horses before all the development and subdivisions went in. My husband was an amateur photographer with an interest in architecture. I remember she remarked about the black-and-white photos of the downtown buildings."

The older woman smiled. Light glinted in her clear eyes. What a sweet lady. There was nothing sinister or guilty acting about her. Despair inched its way into Ginger's thoughts. This had all been a wild goose chase.

"Why do you want to know about the stuff I sold?" The woman held out her hands palms up. "I'm not taking any of it back. It took me three sales to get the clutter out of this house."

"We won't make you take them back." Kindra kept her arms crossed and added stomping to her dance routine. The temperature hadn't dropped that much. The kid needed some meat on her bones. "The woman you sold that stuff to was murdered later that day."

"Murdered?" Arleta sat her glass on the little table. "Didn't the paper say it was an accident?"

"Long story," Ginger said.

"I would be happy to look at the stuff, if you have it with you, and see if I can remember if she said anything else." Arleta tapped her temple. "The memory is not totally gone

SHARON DUNN

yet." She stood up next to Kindra. "Besides, this poor thing is going to catch her death if we don't get inside."

Ginger was doubtful that Arleta would be able to help them, but she found herself saying okay because the look of hopeful expectation on the older woman's face tugged at her heart.

Arleta clapped her hands together. "Well, that's just peachy." She gripped Ginger's hand firmly.

Five minutes later, Kindra and Ginger were in Arleta's house sitting at her kitchen table, drinking more lemonade and eating peanut butter cookies. "I used to make cookies for David's students all the time. It's just a habit I can't seem to break. It's nice to have someone to share them with. I usually just throw them away." Arleta flipped through the photo album while Kindra zipped and unzipped all the pockets in the vest.

Ginger leaned over Arleta's shoulder. Most of the photos were of brick buildings or grain silos or of David and Arleta on digs.

"What is that one?" Ginger pointed to the photo of David in his vest surrounded by pine trees. One side of the photo revealed houses and a radio tower, indicating that the dig was not far from a town. The photo stood out from the others because no digging or excavation was taking place, and it wasn't architecture.

Arleta bent closer to the album. "I don't remember taking that one. Not at all. One of David's students must have snapped it." She tore the photo off and gazed at the back. "David wrote the year. 1986."

"Hey, look what I found in one the pockets." Kindra placed a piece of paper with six numbers written on it on the table. "It's not Mary Margret's writing."

Arleta picked up the paper. "No, no, that is my David's writing." She rubbed the paper with her thumb, a faint smile crossing her face. "This was probably written somewhere around the time of his last dig. I don't know what it means. Maybe the call number for a library book."

"License plates can have six numbers after the county designation," Kindra offered.

Arleta ran her hands over the vest. "He wore this old thing all the time."

"You must have loved your husband very much." Ginger touched the older woman's fingers.

Arleta nodded and sighed. "That I did. It was a good marriage. We were soul mates."

Soul mates? Ginger gazed around the room filled with pictures of Arleta and David. Standing with Stonehenge in the background. Digging into the side of a mountain. Working together painting their house. Arleta had found a way to be a part of David's world.

The photos Ginger had in her house were of the whole family at Disneyland and camping, Earl standing with their two sons and the buck they had shot, Ginger with Krissy and Heidi and the quilt they made together. She couldn't think of a single photo that had just her and Earl in it doing something together. They had been busy bees buzzing around in separate worlds, coming together to do stuff with the kids.

"Soul mates," Ginger whispered. She flipped through the photo album. There was nothing here, nothing suspicious. Arleta certainly wasn't a criminal. That only left the shell box and Keaton Lustrum.

Kindra took her last gulp of lemonade, then checked her watch. "We should go."

Arleta rose to her feet. "So soon? At least let me box up some cookies for you. I'll just throw them away otherwise."

"I have to get back to the dorm and shower and do some homework before midnight shopping." Kindra hopped to her feet.

"Midnight shopping?" Arleta pulled a container out of the cupboard where rubber storage bowls were neatly stacked. The spices as well stood in tidy rows. Ginger pictured Arleta alone in the house arranging and organizing and reorganizing, hour after hour.

All of the photos were of Arleta and her husband. No children, no girlfriends. "Arleta, do you have any relatives?"

She placed the cookies carefully in the container. "I have a sister in England. I see her twice a year." Arleta put several more cookies in, then pressed the lid on.

This sure was a lot of kindness to show a stranger. "Would you like to go shopping with us? They open the doors of the mall at midnight, and the discounts are incredible."

"Oh, I—" Arleta leaned across the table and handed the container to Ginger. "I hadn't thought about it." She touched the back of her head and released a nervous cough.

Mild tension slipped into the room. Moments passed as Arleta ran a dishrag under the faucet and wiped the crumbs off the counter.

Kindra sidled over to Ginger and tapped her finger on the rubber container. "Thanks for the cookies."

"Oh, you are welcome, dear. You are the kind of student David would have loved."

Mentally, Ginger kicked herself. She hadn't meant to make Arleta uncomfortable or call attention to her loneliness. "If you change your mind, we'll be at the south entrance when the doors open at midnight." Ginger's voice sounded forced, too singsongy.

"Thank you. I've still got a lot of home repair to get done."

After Kindra gathered up the vest and photo album, she followed Ginger out the door.

Ginger drove her Pontiac through the older neighborhood unable to shake the picture of Arleta alone in her house. Such a nice lady. Maybe God would allow their paths to cross again.

Kindra's cell rang. She took the call. Her "Hi, Suzanne" was followed by a series of "un-huhs" and "okays."

Ginger glanced in the rearview mirror. Phoebe sat in the backseat perched in her booster.

Kindra tucked her cell back in her purse. "As if you can't figure it out, that was Suzanne. She said there was so much going on at city commission meetings twenty years ago, she has no idea what Mary Margret might have been looking for. She did talk to the records clerk, who said that Mary Margret left a message on Saturday. She called saying she wanted to look at the records first thing Monday when the office opened. Suzanne is headed home to get her kids dinner and take a nap. She'll meet us at the mall at ten to midnight."

"We are no further ahead than we were earlier today. Arleta is not a criminal."

"Sure we are. We know Mary Margret went to the library and that something about the city commission twenty years ago interested her."

Ginger gripped the steering wheel a little tighter. "We're missing something here. Someone killed Mary Margret. Somehow she ended up in that forest outside of town with an arrow through her."

"So if her death is not connected to the garage sale stuff, what could 'something terrible, something from the past' be?" Kindra traced the seams on David's old vest with her fingers.

"It has to be something she found or saw between the first and second phone call, between eight o'clock and a little before noon, when we were supposed to get together at her house."

"We can assume that someone made her drive her car out to the place where she died, and we can assume that same person brought the car back."

Ginger yanked on one of her curls. "Was Keaton Lustrum even around twenty years ago?"

Kindra shrugged. "He looks forty or fifty in that picture."

Anybody over twenty-five looked forty or fifty to Kindra. "Mary said something on her message about popping over to see another agent about some property. Maybe we can swing by her old office and find out which agent it was and if Mary was upset when she saw that person."

"Maybe. And we need to talk to Keaton Lustrum." Kindra made clicking sounds with her tongue as she tapped the glass of the car window. "All of this detective work is exhausting. Forward one step and back two." She slumped down in her seat. "Sometimes when you're not thinking about something directly, that's when the answers come to you. I'm looking forward to midnight shopping to get my mind off of all this."

Ginger turned onto the street that led to Kindra's college dorm. "Me, too, kiddo. Me, too."

Eleven

Tammy had just bent her arm, bringing the barbell up to her shoulder, when she saw her mother's reflection in the floor-to-ceiling mirror. Hannah Krinkland's lime green capris and summer sweater with flamingos on it looked out of place in the athletic club weight room. But it was her expression, a combination of fear and weariness, that made Tammy grip the metal weight even tighter. Mom's eyes were dull and her mouth hung slightly open. Her finger rubbed up and down her purse strap.

Tammy's bicep tensed. She closed her eyes. Mom was not in the habit of hunting her down while she worked out to ask what she wanted for dinner. "Mom?" her voice came out in almost a croak.

"Trevor left. I went to the church to help fold the bulletins. When I got home, he was gone. No note."

Tammy held on to the barbell, but her arm went limp. She stared at the ceiling. Why did this have to be so hard? Couldn't Trevor see that she was trying to protect him?

"You had to know this was going to happen." Mom stepped toward her and touched her arm lightly. "You can't keep a fifteen-year-old under house arrest."

"Mom, he shoplifted." The last thing she needed was a sermon from her mother. "Today it's shoplifting, and tomorrow it could be selling and doing drugs. I know the pattern. It's never an improvement in behavior."

Though her impulse was to throw the weight across the room, Tammy placed it carefully in the stand. She took several deep breaths filled with wordless prayer before standing up straight. Losing control wouldn't help anything. But it sure would be nice to scream into a pillow right now. "I just don't want him to get into something that could—"

Mom pursed her lips.

Tammy appreciated her mother's restraint. She shook her head and grabbed her workout towel. While she patted the sweat off her neck, she pulled herself together and strategized. Back into the parenting fray. "Okay, list the most likely places you think he might have gone."

"Skateboard park, arcade, Joe's house, mall, Kevin's house. Some of his other friends, I'm not clear on their names."

Tammy shook her head again then glanced at her watch, eight o'clock already. "I had stuff I wanted to get done. I was going to tell that Ginger lady that I think something bad did happen to her friend. I wanted to tell her in person."

Her mom's fingers fluttered to her mouth and her forehead wrinkled. "You could be back on patrol...or worse."

"Keep your voice down. Cops work out here." Tammy glanced from one treadmill to another and then to the StairMaster. She didn't recognize anyone from the department. All the same, she leaned closer to her mother and whispered, "Didn't you and Dad teach me to do the right thing, no matter what it cost?"

Mom nodded. "That we did."

"Something is going on, and I intend to get to the bottom of it." Tammy sauntered into the locker room with her mother trailing behind her. She grabbed her gym bag off a bench. No time for a shower. She'd just have to call Ginger and see if she could come by later. She wasn't going to put this off another day. She slipped sweats over her workout suit. "I'll take his friends' houses and the skateboard park."

"I'll take the arcade and the mall and then head home to see if Trevor returned." Her mom folded Tammy's workout towel and handed it to her.

Only her mom would take the time to fold a dirty towel. Tammy unzipped her gym bag and set it on top of her street clothes. "When you get close to a phone, call me with a progress report." Mom was probably the only person over twelve in America who didn't own a cell phone.

The women left the locker room and headed toward the club exit. Tammy stood at the glass door. At this hour, the sky had only the faint hint of gray. Evening light waned. Already the tension had crept into the muscles between her shoulders. "One of us may have to go out to Kevin's house. If we just call him on the phone, he'll lie about Trevor being there. I don't know about his other friends."

On the sidewalk outside, a woman pushed a baby carriage past them. Tammy's shoulders slumped. She closed her eyes and tried to picture Trevor as a baby. He'd been so beautiful. And she had been so hopeful, imagining a bright future for her boy, a college education, a good-paying job, a pretty girl to marry, and a love for the Savior to guide him. With the exception of the recovery of her faith, she had managed very little of that for herself. What silly notion had made her think it was possible for Trevor?

The woman stopped pushing the carriage, bent over, and gathered a bald baby into her arms. As though she'd been punched in the gut, Tammy felt herself crumpling from emotional overload.

Her mom touched her shoulders. "Tamela, dear, you have to stop trying to do this alone." The older woman rubbed her back like she'd done when Tammy was little and couldn't sleep. "He's a boy. An old lady and an overworked mother can't turn him into a man."

Tammy took a deep breath. "You know, Mom, my brain just feels so hammered. I can only focus on the next thing I have to do, which is find my son, make sure he's breathing and not on the way to the police station again."

....

The clock in Ginger's kitchen said that it was nine-thirty. "What time did that police lady say she was coming by?"

She sat at the table pushing her mashed potatoes around her plate while Earl ate his late dinner. She'd noticed the lasagna in the container was gone, but Earl had not argued with her when she suggested she warm him up something. It had been ages since they'd eaten together. Here she was knocking the word *soul mates* around her head, and they couldn't even manage to have a meal together.

"She said she'd come by a little after eight." Earl made a crater in his mashed potatoes and poured gravy into it.

They sat at either end of the table. Phoebe perched on the chair between them, the chair that had been their son Patrick's. Ginger had put a pillow on it so Phoebe could see better. The cat's huge head was just visible above the table.

Ginger unfolded her napkin by flipping it outward. "I'm not going to wait all night for her." She really wasn't interested in hearing more bad news from the police department. She placed her napkin on her lap. That poor Tammy woman seemed to be their official bringer of bad news.

"Aren't you just going to bed?" He tore open his roll and slathered butter on it.

"The girls and I are going midnight shopping. I told you that." Or at least she had put it in a note for him somewhere. "I have some other errands I want to run before that, and I told Kindra I would pick her up."

"It might be a good idea to talk to the police." His knife scraped the plate as he cut up the roast beef. "I got this strange feeling this afternoon that someone had been in the family room. The door was open, and some stuff was knocked around."

Ginger glanced at the garage sale stuff she had brought in from the car. The room felt suddenly colder. "Someone was looking for something in our place?"

"It's not like the room was torn to pieces, but my stack of books was knocked over, and your bills were spread out all over the desk."

Ginger's neck muscles pinched. "I always put the bills in a pile."

Earl took a bite of his roll. "I know. From now on, I'm locking the house when I go out to the garage."

She willed herself not to think about someone being in their house. Earl knew her habits. She knew his. But they didn't know each other, not really. Not like Arleta had known David. She scooped up a forkful of mashed potatoes. It tasted like sawdust. From his chewing to the tinkling of silverware, every sound Earl made was almost deafening.

She took another bite of sawdust, chewing slowly. "Earl, do you remember any time that we did stuff together?"

"Sure, we went to the kids' games and recitals and baptisms." He stabbed the green beans with his fork.

Exactly, everything centered around the kids. "No, I mean really do something together, like go on an archaeological dig."

Earl set his fork down. The creases in his forehead multiplied and became more distinct. "Go on an archaeological dig?"

SHARON DUNN

What was she trying to say? "That's just an example. What I'm trying to say is—" What she was trying to say was that if she had to live in a house where the only noise was the smacking chewing sounds he made, she would go insane.

On the drive home, Ginger had gone through the catalog of everything they had done together, every conversation she could remember. They must have talked about something besides the kids. Was the depth of their communication limited to how they would weatherize the house before winter hit? She hadn't known that his dream was to invent something that changed the world. All this efficient, functional talking couldn't be what soul mates said to each other.

Earl's blank expression caused all the coherent thoughts to leave her head. All she could think about was the bulb of gravy on his upper lip. She pushed his napkin toward him, hoping he would get the hint. Earl bent his head back and narrowed his eyes at the napkin, like it was a neon lizard crawling across the table, but he didn't pick it up.

Ginger traced the flower pattern in her tablecloth. Why wasn't he following her? He was the one who suggested that their marriage lacked something in the first place. He was the one reading all those books.

"Do you remember the night Mary Margret disappeared?" Gathering courage, Ginger pushed her chair back and stood up. It was now or never. She put her hands on her hips and straightened her back. "What did you mean when you said I wasn't supportive of you, that you needed a cheerleader?" There, she couldn't be any more direct than that.

Earl wiggled in his chair and took two more bites of roast beef. He spoke slowly as though he were pulling each word up from the underside of his toenails. "I just meant that sometimes you say things that hurt my feelings."

Phoebe yowled.

"Hush, Phoebes, Mama's having a talk." She had cooked and cleaned for this man for over thirty years. She kept his sock drawer organized. Not an easy job. Why didn't he say thank you? Her feelings were hurt, too. "Earl, I don't want to live in a house this quiet. What's happening to us? Don't we have anything to talk about?"

"It doesn't have to be this quiet." Finally, he picked up the napkin and wiped the gravy off his lips. "This is the next chapter of our lives. We should live a little, do something adventurous."

"Something adventurous?" It was her turn to have a blank look on her face. The way Earl changed his tune every ten minutes was likely to give her emotional whiplash. First, it was that she wasn't supportive, and now he wanted to have an adventure. Why couldn't he just make up his mind?

"I just think now is the time for us to chase our dreams. I'm going to invent something big. I am." Earl rose to his feet and grabbed Ginger's arm just above the elbow. "We could buy a Harley and tour the United States."

Ginger gasped. Becoming a motorcycle mama had never been on her to-do list.

His shoulders slumped a little. "That's just an example. All I am saying is we should do things we haven't done before. Can't you think of something you've never done before that you have always wanted to do? That you couldn't do because we were busy raising the kids?"

Ginger shook her head. She had always believed she'd missed something by marrying so young. Now that she thought about it, she didn't know what she would have done different. Did she have dreams beyond alphabetized spice racks and balanced budgets?

SHARON DUNN

Earl grabbed his milk off the table and took a gulp. "I know. Go out tonight and pay full price for a dress." He slammed the empty glass on the table. "That would be daring for you."

Her vision clouded. She blinked fast five times. "Full price?" The words sounded foreign on her tongue. Her chest felt tight. She slumped back down in her chair. Full price? Was she having a heart attack? Her voice was a squeaky whisper. "I have never paid full price for anything in my life."

Earl seemed energized by the idea. His eyes kept getting bigger and rounder. "That's why it would be daring...for you. We don't need to get motorcycles. That's for later. We'll take baby steps."

Now he paced back and forth in the kitchen like he was center stage at the Met. "When we had four kids and money was tight, I appreciated that you found a way to make sure everyone had warm coats and winter boots."

Ginger calmed a bit. He had noticed. "I buy out of season. That's my secret." She raised her chin.

"The thing is, Ginger, money isn't tight anymore. God has blessed us. You could go out right now and pay full price for a new dress and buy matching shoes. It won't break us."

Full price. Full price. Why couldn't he have asked her to do something easier, like climb Mount Everest or something? She tossed her napkin on the table and jumped to her feet. "You don't want me to buy what's on sale?"

Earl nodded, pressing his lips together. "Don't even look at the price tag."

Her rib cage squeezed tight. All the air left her lungs. White dots floated into her field of vision. She really needed to sit down and catch her breath. "Not even look at the price tag?" she wheezed. If he kept talking this way, he'd be phoning 911 before the night was over. Such crazy talk.

He threw his hands up. "Live dangerously. I'm not talking about doing anything wrong or sinful. I just think we need to have adventures. That's what this time of our lives is about."

Ginger studied Earl for a long moment. Who was this man in front of her? Where had Mr. Predictable, nine to five, fall-asleep-in-front-of-the-TV gone? Not that the man standing in front of her was unappealing. She liked his energy, his enthusiasm. She just wasn't sure if she could keep up with him. "Maybe we should just buy a Harley instead."

"Go tonight and buy yourself the dress you want, not the one that's on sale. Sometimes I think you just buy something because it's on sale, not because you really want it. Like that time you said you were going to get a winter coat for yourself, and you came home with that prom dress."

"It was an evening gown, and it was 75 percent off."

"But you needed a coat."

She almost pointed out that she couldn't find a coat on sale. Ginger closed her eyes. Okay, so Earl was right. She had some kind of weird condition. "I just don't see how this will help." How would this turn them into soul mates? How would this make the house less silent? Earl was going off the deep end, and she wasn't sure she could go there with him...especially on a Harley.

Earl gathered Ginger's hands into his. "You know when a man buys a woman a diamond necklace and they go out together and she wears it? That makes the man feel good. 'Cause the money he earned paid for the necklace."

"Now you want me to get a diamond necklace?" Ginger pulled free of Earl's grasp and rested her head in her hands.

"What I'm saying is, when you keep buying stuff at those cut-rate prices, it's like you're saying I don't make enough money for you to get what you really want, to splurge once in a while. Like all my years of working for the phone company don't mean anything. Like my work wasn't good enough."

"That's not what I'm saying at all, Earl. I'm saying that I got stuff on sale." Splurge smurge. A memory that had been vaulted away escaped. "My mother used to splurge." She shuddered. "She used to buy me the prettiest dresses, never even looking at the price tags."

"Didn't it feel good to wear those dresses?"

"Yes, until I found out she used the grocery money for clothes and we had to eat bread and jam for a week." She hadn't thought about that awful, empty feeling of curling up in bed with her stomach growling in years. She waved her hands in front of her. "I don't want to talk about this."

"I didn't mean to upset you, hon. I knew your mother was flaky, but you never told me you went hungry because of her."

She'd never told anyone that. Her own childhood had made her vow that her children would never have growling stomachs because of her spending habits.

"I just want you to treat yourself." Earl's thumb brushed over her cheek.

The warmth of his touch communicated safety, but she still didn't see what he was driving at. "I am not going to run up huge credit card debt."

"Just buy something you really want, and not just because the price is right. That will be the beginning of our adventure, the beginning of our new life."

"Earl, things will be 50 to 75 percent off tonight. It doesn't make sense to pay full price." She'd been as direct as she could with him. He'd given her a confusing answer and stirred up memories she would rather forget. Really, it was the memory of taffeta, buckle shoes, and an empty stomach that upset her.

Earl couldn't understand what she was asking for. He couldn't hear her. And despite his best effort, she couldn't understand him. How had they managed to hold a marriage together for so long when they didn't even speak the same language?

"I can't wait for that police lady any longer. I'm going midnight shopping with my friends." *And taking advantage of the discounts.*

She grabbed her purse and dashed out the door. When she pulled out of the driveway, she could see Earl in the rearview mirror headed toward his shop. Phoebe loped behind him.

She pulled out onto the road. Sadness made her stomach tight.

•••••••••••••••••••••••••••••••••

Tammy stopped her car by the skateboard park and pulled her cell out of her purse. She rolled down her window to allow the cool evening breeze to relax her. Boy, did she need to unwind. She'd been to four places on her mental checklist and still no sign of Trevor.

Mom had returned home to wait for him there after checking several places. The sound of young men encouraging and harassing each other, of wheels rolling over concrete, floated through the window. The rest of the park was empty.

Her Betty Boop watch said it was after ten. She dialed Ginger's phone number. It rang three times, and then the message machine clicked on. Tammy hung up. She needed to get out there before her shift started at midnight. The clock was ticking. Evidence was disappearing. She couldn't wait another day.

Tammy closed her eyes and rested her head against the back of the seat. She'd spent the evening fighting off fear that

SHARON DUNN

something had happened to Trevor. She had been the first on the scene to a full repertoire of horrible things that teenagers did to themselves and others.

No matter how hard she tried, those ugly pictures pushed their way into her consciousness. Fear had made it nearly impossible to breathe, as if her entire body was wrapped tight in duct tape. *God, it would be nice if You'd give me just one small sign that everything is going to be okay.* Just a small sign. That was all she needed.

She opened her door and walked past the swings and merry-go-round toward the skateboard park. Two streetlights stood at either end of the skate park. About half a dozen boys, some of them standing, others riding the ramps or sailing into and out of the curved bowl, populated the concrete park. None of them were Trevor. She recognized two of the boys, though the last time she'd seen them they were in handcuffs.

She shivered. *Just one little sign, God. Please.*

One of the young men, a shirtless skinny guy with a bandanna on his head, seemed to be the informal coach. He shouted, "That's it, Bobby. Looking good, Dave. Did your mama teach you that move, Jason?"

The other boys responded with expletives, groans, and a generous sprinkling of the word *dude.* As they skated under the light, she could see their faces. Their skin took on a warm, translucent quality. So young, so full of promise.

The coach jumped on his own board, bent his knees, and sailed expertly into the pit and back up the other side to stand beside Tammy. He was a little older than the others, maybe college age. A dragon tattoo decorated his arms and angled over his back.

"I know you." He rubbed his flat stomach. "You're Trevor's mom. The cop." He wasn't a good-looking kid. Close-set eyes made his long face appear even narrower. But there was a softness in his expression.

"Guess that makes Trev really unpopular, to have a mom who's a police officer."

The kid shrugged. "My dad is a cop down in LA. Nothing wrong with cops. They're just trying to do their jobs." He flipped his board up with his foot and spun it around in his hands while he talked.

"Have you seen my son?" The words nearly stuck in her throat.

Coach yelled out to the other boys. "Steve? Dave? Trev W. Seen him?"

A bleached blond with low-slung shorts stopped his board and yelled across the concrete. "He was here a couple hours ago. Said something about going out to The Park."

Coach turned toward her. "You know that abandoned amusement park by the lake?"

Tammy nodded. She knew it well, knew that there were gates and No Trespassing signs posted. None of which seemed to stop teenagers from making it their hangout.

Coach set his skateboard down and jumped on top of it, sliding back and forth. "Trev's a good kid. He'll be all right. He's got a mom who loves him." His gaze was unwavering.

He turned on his board and skated back down into the pit, but not before Tammy saw the tattoo on his back. Right beneath the dragon's stream of fire were the words: *Jesus Rocks*.

· ·

Arleta lay on her bed, on top of the covers. Her hands rested on her stomach. The light from her nightstand lamp created a circle of illumination on her ceiling. The white numbers on her bedside clock

SHARON DUNN

glowed 10:45. The room was so quiet she could hear the numbers flipping over on the clock. Oh, to be able to go right to sleep.

Ginger and Kindra had seemed like really nice ladies. She should have swallowed her pride and taken them up on the offer to go shopping. The invitation had embarrassed her. They saw how alone she was.

Funny how all her friends had slowly fallen away after David died. Some had died, some had moved to a warmer climate, and some just didn't call anymore. She had tried to make friends after David died, but the people at the senior center just complained about body aches. Not her idea of a good time. She liked to do things, not just sit around.

The other ladies in her self-defense class were nice. They all seemed busy with children and grandchildren though. How had she let this happen? How had she become so unconnected to the world?

Arleta flicked off the lamp and closed her eyes. Sleep. She needed to sleep. She counted to a hundred in Spanish. *Uno, dos, tres...*

A sort of pounding squeak reverberated in the living room and floated down the hall. Arleta sat up straight. The silence was heady. She listened. Her heart beat faster. The digit on the clock flipped. Only quiet came from the living room. She exhaled a slow stream of air.

Batty old lady. Now, she was just hearing things. Maybe she should look into getting a roommate or rent out the spare bedroom to a college student. That Kindra had seemed nice. Respectful. There were still some nice college students left in the world. She lay back down and listened a moment longer, willing her eyelids to become heavy.

Satisfied, she turned over on her side. Just as the room went dark, she heard the crash of glass.

Twelve

Tammy parked her car outside the chain-link fence that was supposed to keep trespassers out of the abandoned amusement park.

About ten years ago, the park had gone bankrupt. The rides were too outdated to have any resale value, and the owners too broke to pay to haul them away. Far as she knew, the owners continued to pay the taxes on the land, waiting for the day when some real estate developer would see it as a high return investment and make an offer. Now the place was just a big pain for law enforcement. Despite constant building and rebuilding of security fences, teens considered the park a cool hangout.

Betty Boop told her it was eleven. She had an hour before she had to be on shift, and she still needed to get out to Ginger's. She'd phoned into the station and left a message with the administrative clerk that she might be a little late. She hadn't ever been late for a shift. When Trevor was born, her mother had advised her that schedules and plans would become meaningless. Mom had been thinking of sickness and soiled diapers, but the rule applied even more to teenagers.

After grabbing the flashlight out of her jockey box, she opened the door and stepped onto the gravel. Water from the lake lapped against the shore. The breeze was soft and cool, baby fingers touching her cheek. She shone her light toward the pier. Too cold for late-night swimming.

It took her only a few minutes of skirting the fence to find the place where it had been cut open. Stars twinkled in the night sky.

She stepped clear of piles of twisted metal and walked past chairs for a Ferris wheel. A washed-out metal sign advertising the bearded lady banged in the wind. Up ahead, several circles of light bounced, dimmed, disappeared, and came back on in a different location. Thirty feet away, water surged against the shore in a repetitive rhythm. This was the less-developed section of the lake. Vacation homes and quaint little overpriced shops were across the water.

Someone shouted a single indiscernible word. Again, the scenarios of all the destructive things teenagers found to amuse themselves with flashed through her head.

Drugs, sex, setting things on fire. She took a deep breath. *Jesus rocks. Jesus rocks.* Not all these kids were a bad influence on her son.

As she drew a little closer, the voices became more distinct. Her light flashed on Trevor's plaid shirt, the one he wore all the time. She sighed. He was still alive. Four bodies huddled over something by the roller coaster. So intent were they on what they were doing that they didn't even look up.

Tension corseted around her rib cage. She shortened her stride. *Oh please, God. Let it not be drugs.* Her foot crushed plastic.

One of the boys raised his head from the huddle. "Cop!"

How did they know even when she wasn't in uniform? Some sort of special radar teenagers must have. Or did they all just know that Trevor's mom was a police officer?

Three of the boys scattered. Their footsteps pounded on dirt, and one of them banged against something and groaned. Then they were absorbed by darkness. Trevor with his distinctive curly hair continued to bend over whatever was holding his attention.

"Hi, Mom, you found me."

She stared at his back, frozen by the dread of seeing needles or a stash of pot or whatever it was the other boys had left for Trevor to take the rap for. "Yeah, I found you. Do you know how worried Grandma and I were?"

She willed herself to take the last few steps. Two emotions tore her in opposite directions. Part of her wanted to grab Trevor by the ear, drag him back to the car, and revoke every privilege he had until he was thirty. The other part of her wanted to grab her little boy and hug him, touch his soft hair, and tell him that it was okay, that she was just glad he was still breathing. They would work through whatever mess he had gotten himself into. The right reaction was somewhere in between those two.

Trevor straightened his back. She saw what had been holding his attention: tools. He had lined up several wrenches and screwdrivers on his skateboard. Her steps felt suddenly lighter. No drugs. No drugs.

"Trevor, what are you...?" She shone the light on his face, his beautiful, sweet face. Like a rope untwisting, the tension left her body.

"Me and my buds were going to get the roller coaster running so we could go for a ride." He pointed at a motor that must belong to the roller coaster. Trevor rose to his feet and shoved his hands in the pockets of his baggy pants. "Until you scared them all away."

"Oh, Trevor, I am so glad you're not taking drugs." She pulled him toward her and hugged him.

"Mom, stop." He wiggled free of her hug, crossed his arms, and rested his chin on his chest. "Drugs? What are you talking about? I'm not stupid. You been telling me scary stories about what you saw on patrol since I could talk."

Tammy touched his cheek. He turned his head sideways. She had let other voices rule her perceptions, the voices that said single moms always raised messed-up kids. She wasn't a statistic and neither was Trevor.

It took substantial effort for her not to smile. But warm fuzzy moments wouldn't make him take responsibility for his actions. Her voice was calm and even. "You were supposed to stay at the house. That was your punishment for shoplifting. There'll be an additional punishment for this little stunt."

Trevor rolled his eyes.

Back to the same old same old. "Don't argue with me. You know all the bad things that can happen to kids out at night, all the trouble they get themselves into." This was their rehearsed script. This time though, it was easier to say her lines.

"I know. I know. But I'm not one of those kids."

He wasn't one of those kids. She saw that now. But they weren't out of the woods yet. Shoplifting was not a minor thing, and neither was this. But at least it wasn't drugs. "You are not immortal, Trevor Welstad. I tell you those stories for a reason. Now go to the car."

Trevor tilted his head heavenward, but after picking up his skateboard, he trudged forward. Tammy walked behind him. "I have an errand to run before I go on shift."

"Mom, I'm tired. I want to go home."

"I don't have time to take you home and then come back out this way. You'll just have to come with me." Any way she looked at it, she was going to be late for work. It would be the first time in the twelve years she'd been on the force, and it might give Stenengarter the excuse he needed to reprimand her. She didn't care. The right thing was the right thing.

Trevor slowed. "March, young man." She really wanted to hug him again.

They got into the car. Tammy shifted into reverse, turned around, then headed toward the road that led to the Salinski house.

In the car, Trevor crossed his arms and stared at the roof.

"Shoplifting and trespassing." She gave him a sidelong glance. "What's next, Trevor?"

His jaw jutted out. "You embarrassed me in front of my buds."

"That's not all I'm going to do."

"You can't make me stay in that house. I feel like a prisoner."

Why did they have to have the same discussion over and over? "I'm trying to protect you and get through that thick skull. I've dragged dead teenagers out of rivers. Do you understand?"

"That's not going to be me."

"Not if I have anything to say about it." He was right about one thing. She couldn't just keep him under house arrest until he was eighteen, as appealing as it sounded. She had to find something constructive to keep him busy so he didn't think trespassing was a good way to kill time.

Trevor slammed the back of his head against the headrest of the passenger seat. "I'm so bored."

....

In the darkness of her room, Arleta squeezed her eyes shut. She had never really believed in God. But for some reason, she said what she was pretty sure was a prayer. *Oh, please. Let that just be my imagination. Just let it be the wind because I left a window open. Oh, please. Oh, please. Oh, please.*

She waited for what seemed like a thousand years. As her heart pounded, mentally she went through her drill, tried to

SHARON DUNN

remember where she had put the speed loader and the flashlight, visualized the exact placement of each item in her drawer. Slowly, she swung her feet to the floor. Listening. Waiting. The clock flipped over another number, and she nearly jumped out of her slippers.

She turned her head slightly. Was that a footstep? Maybe. *And maybe I am just a lonely old lady with an overactive imagination.* She swung her legs back on the bed and lay down.

And then she heard the noise.

The squeaky desk drawer being closed, followed by a muffled footstep.

Arleta leaned over her bed, pulled out the shoe box, and grabbed Annie. She jumped to her feet, tiptoed across the floor, and opened the nightstand drawer. Her senses kicked up a notch. Adrenaline rushed through her system.

She stuck the flashlight in her teeth and shoved the speed loader into her revolver. She jumped over the top of the bed and positioned herself in her hiding place. If she had a phone in her room, she could have called the police. The only phone in the house was in the living room.

All her perceptions sharpened. The gun felt cold and hard in her hand. She could smell the faint scent of the vanilla candle she had burned earlier.

She heard another noise. Maybe papers being moved. Time slogged forward. The weight of the gun caused her hand to shake.

In her head, Arleta practiced her warning. *I have a gun, and I know how to use it. I have a gun, and I've been trained to use it.* She readjusted her grip on the revolver and reminded herself that she needed to squeeze not pull the trigger.

She clicked her flashlight on and off. Was the guy redecorating? What was taking him so long? She clenched her dentures.

Either this guy needed to leave her house or come into the room.

Her heart beat slowed. She set the gun on the bedspread and twisted her wrist around to get out the soreness. This was not going like she expected. She thought it would be a little more exciting, action packed. Someone was in her house shuffling around, looking for something, messing up her stuff.

This was boring. Was she even going to get to use any of the techniques she learned in class?

The instructor said she was the second best shot in the class, right after the single mom who used to be a marine. More noise from the kitchen, something hitting the floor.

That was it. She made up her mind. She was going to break one of the rules of her class. The instructor had said not to be a vigilante, not to go looking for trouble. She could hear his deep, gravelly voice in her head. "Ladies, there is a reason this class is called self-defense, not self-offense. We don't go out firing our guns just because we're in the throes of PMS."

The last time she had been in the throes of PMS, Ronald Reagan was president. She needed to get some sleep, and this guy was keeping her awake. She clicked on the flashlight and checked the path in front of her. After shoving the flashlight in the pocket of her bathrobe, she took a deep breath, picked up her gun, and darted through her doorway and down the dark hall, gun gripped in both hands, ready to fire.

Arleta cleared her throat. "I have a gun, and I know how to use it." Her voice was barely above a whisper. Darn it, she needed to sound stronger, more in control.

Near her china cabinet, a tiny pinpoint of light bounced and disappeared.

She pressed her back against the wall and moved a few steps closer to the living room and kitchen area.

A shadow passed by the window. Light from outside provided a momentary glimpse of snowy white hair.

Again, the adrenaline kicked in. Her heart was going a mile a minute. *Yes, that's what I am talking about.* The gun became part of her hand. Her finger slipped inside the trigger guard. Her own inhaling and exhaling created a rhythm that helped her focus.

"I have a gun, and I know how to use it."

Yes, that was it. Strong, commanding. Arleta stood at the end of the hallway that led to the living room and kitchen area. She listened. Nothing.

"You need to get out of my house. I have to get some sleep."

She didn't hear noises so much as she sensed that someone was in the room. He or she was standing very still, but Arleta knew she wasn't imagining things. It was the same feeling as when you knew someone was staring at you, even before you turned and looked. In the dark, someone watched her.

"I have a gun, and I know how to use it." This time she sounded a little less forceful. *Don't let him sense your fear, Arleta.* Again, she waited. Only this time she wasn't resting behind her bed, she was standing...and her bunions were starting to hurt.

What a time waster.

"I have a gun, and I've been trained to use it." *And I will use it.* With the gun pointed at the ceiling, she squeezed, not pulled, the trigger. The thunder of the shot nearly broke her eardrums. Something above her cracked. Plaster dust sprinkled on her head.

Footsteps pounded across floorboards. An outside door swung open and slammed shut. Arleta counted the intake and outtake of air...twenty-three, twenty-four, twenty-five. A car started up and sped away.

For what felt like a millennium, she stood in her dark living room blinking plaster out of her eyes. Arm relaxed, gun resting at her side, she was motionless enough to pass for a statue. Her pulsed drummed in her ears, creating that muffled feeling like wearing headphones. Arleta didn't remember thinking that she should turn on the light, only that she found herself at the light switch pushing it up.

She turned a half circle in her living room and kitchen. The place was much less messy than she had expected for the amount of time the man had been in her house, but there was clear evidence that someone had been here. A photograph turned facedown. A china cup on the floor, unbroken.

She walked slowly to the desk that had been David's. That's where she had seen the tiny light. She opened a drawer. She always paper clipped related papers together. Now they were one unorganized heap. The intruder hadn't been sloppy, but she would have known even if she had slept through the noise. When you lived alone, it was easy to tell when someone else had messed with your stuff. The intruder had focused his search around David's old desk.

Arleta ejected the bullets from her revolver and set it on the desk. An unexpected wave of nausea overtook her and she bent over. All the fear she hadn't allowed herself to feel rushed through her with the strength of a gale force wind. She slumped down in the chair by the desk.

The police. She needed to call the police and tell them what had happened. Her stomach churned like an old-fashioned washing machine. After the police, there would be no one else to call. Every person she could think of was an acquaintance at best. Not someone she felt comfortable calling in the middle of the night. Not someone who would talk to her and calm her down. Now that was sad.

SHARON DUNN

Yes, she could take care of herself, but she was tired of being alone. Her new life was starting tonight. No more living in the past, longing for David.

The clock in the living room said it was eleven-thirty. *Take note, Arleta. That was the exact time you decided to live again.* She still had time to meet those nice ladies for midnight shopping. But first, she had to call the police.

....

Keaton Lustrum thought Renata looked especially delicious in black. The dark turtleneck made her skin seem even milkier. The black knit cap that covered her silky hair made her features stand out that much more. Exquisite.

Outside the home that belonged to the momof3 license plate, Renata sat in the passenger seat of Keaton's Lexus trying to bite the tag off a knit cap she had bought for him. It had been Renata's idea that they dress in black for their little "heist." She got most of her ideas from television. In fact, Keaton had never seen her read a book, in French or in English. He read his speeches and briefs out loud to her. She nodded like she understood.

He gazed at Renata again as she continued to struggle with the tag on the hat. Who would have thought a nerdy ranch kid from eastern Montana would end up with a statuesque beauty like Renata. She was the jewel in his crown of success.

Her attachment to him and her willingness to help almost made it possible for him to forgive her for the first time she'd tried to get the box back and made such a mess of things.

He wasn't stupid. She didn't love him. She liked his money and the fact that photographers showed up from time to time to take her picture. That was why it was so important he get the shell box back. He had to keep taking the kind of law cases that made money.

A French expletive escaped Renata's lips. "Uh, I cannot get this tag off."

"It's okay. I'll just wear it the way it is." He put the cap on and wobbled his head back and forth with his face scrunched. "Look at me. I am a fashion magnet," he said in a whiny voice.

Her laughter made his toes melt in his black leather sneakers.

"Okay, here's the plan. We go in, look for the box, and take it."

"*Bon*." Renata's voice had a lilting quality. "If we do not find it right away, we go. If the door is locked, we go."

"Good girl." She had memorized his instructions. How flattering. Boost to his ego. He pressed the button that lighted his watch. Nearly midnight. Except for the pregnant lady leaving at a little after eleven, the house had been completely dark and inactive. For the life of him, he couldn't think where a pregnant lady was headed at this hour. Some new hot spot for expectant mothers, like a milk bar where people tie your shoes for you when they got untied?

The woman he'd seen carrying the box, the one with the brassy curls, must be the pregnant lady's mom or something.

"All right, let's go in." Keaton opened the door and dashed toward a bush close to the sidewalk. Renata was right behind him.

Thirteen

Trevor blew a strand of hair out of his eyes and stared at the ceiling of the car. "How much longer are you going to watch me like a baby?"

Tammy clicked her signal and turned into Ginger's gravel driveway. "I'm just trying to get you to eighteen alive, Trevor."

"Why are you signaling? Nobody's behind us."

"Who's doing the driving here?" Her fingers tensed around the steering wheel. He had grumbled the entire way out here, completely destroying the positive feelings she had about him not doing drugs. She was seriously tempted to make him walk home. "Doesn't matter who's watching. The law is the law."

Trevor crossed his arms and rested his chin on his chest. "I'm dying of boredom."

Tammy pressed the brakes. "Better boredom than something else." The lights were on in Ginger's cute blue house and in the shop next to it. Maybe Ginger was a night owl. She had been so torn up about the department calling Mary Margret's death an accident. Certainly, she'd be happy to hear that someone was on her side...no matter what the hour.

Trevor let out a loud huff of air. Loud on purpose, designed to get a reaction from his mom.

She didn't fall for it. "Look, I don't want to identify your body in a morgue, okay? That's why I do this. You have wasted half my night, and I'm going to be late for work, so I suggest you quit whining. Wait here."

She walked up the flower-lined stone walkway and knocked on Ginger's door. What was she going to do with that kid?

A low mechanical roar resonated from the evergreens that surrounded Ginger's property. She turned again to the house and peered through the window. Inside, a huge gray cat with white toes sauntered across the counter, stopping to lick the butter dish before jumping to the floor. The noise in the forest grew louder. Maybe someone was bulldozing property on the other side of the trees.

Trevor got out of the car and stared at the evergreens. "Do you hear that, Mom?"

"Probably just some construction."

"At this time of night? What a racket." He shook his head. "It's wild, man."

The mechanical grinding and humming ratcheted up a notch. Tree branches cracked. Tammy trotted down the path and stood by her son. "I don't think Mrs. Salinski is home." She raised her voice above the noise. "We should probably get going."

Trevor planted his feet. "I want to see what it is. It's coming this way."

The noise was almost oppressive. More branches broke. A hole opened up in the forest, and a Bobcat emerged from the trees. Or at least Tammy thought it was a Bobcat.

Trevor raised his fist to the air. "Way cool, dude!"

The machine lumbered toward the tin building. The contraption looked like something out of a science fiction movie. Mechanical armlike things jutted out of the back and front. It didn't look like anything you could buy at the equipment supply place.

Trevor stepped toward the metal garage. "Dude, it looks like a giant Swiss army knife. Awesome."

Tammy placed her hand on his shoulder. "Careful, Trev."

"Mom." He wiggled free of her.

The motor sounds slowed to a putt-putt-putt and then stopped. A man pushed himself out of the Bobcat seat and leapt to the ground. Gray hair stuck out from underneath his straw cowboy hat with a peacock feather in it. It took her only a moment to register who it was. Earl Salinski sauntered with a level of enthusiasm that was impressive. Very different from the night she had met him in the police station.

He walked toward Tammy and her son. "Can I help you?"

She opened her mouth to speak, but Trevor interrupted her, curling his fingers into fists and stepping side to side. "Did you build that thing?"

Earl smiled and nodded. "Just the attachments."

"Way cool." Trevor raced across the lot and circled the Bobcat.

"Trevor, be careful."

"Ah, he's all right. The boy is just excited. My wife and I raised four of them, two boys, two girls, with the Lord's help."

Four kids? She'd gotten the impression that night in the police station that Ginger and her husband were good, decent people...and believers. "I'm here to see your wife. I called earlier."

The man tilted his hat by pushing on the brim with his thumb. Recognition spread over his face. "You're the police officer who told us about Mary Margret. You look really different."

"I get that a lot."

"Ginger went midnight shopping at the mall. Must be close to twelve by now. What happened? I thought you were coming a little after eight."

Tammy glued her gaze on Trevor as he danced around the Bobcat. "I had to track down my son."

Earl craned his neck in the direction of the Bobcat. "Seems like a nice boy. He likes to build things?"

Tammy played a mental game of connect the dots. A skateboard with a motor, taking apart the neighbor's robotic cat, and the roller coaster. Duh. She nodded. "Yes, he likes to build things."

Was she thickheaded, or had her job made her pessimistic about teenagers? Ginger's husband had hit the nail on the head within seconds of meeting Trevor. All her negative experiences with teenagers had blocked the truth about her own son.

Earl took his hat off and ran his fingers around the rim while he twirled it. "I got to tell you; Ginger didn't seem real interested in talking to you."

"Actually, I think she will want to talk to me. When do you expect her home?"

Earl shrugged and stared at his boots. "I don't know. We haven't been communicating real well."

"Midnight shopping, huh?" She was late for work anyway. Might as well see this thing to the end.

Trevor trotted across the gravel. "Did you really make that?"

Ginger's husband grinned. "Yup, I'm an inventor."

"Cool, what else have you made?" As if by magic, Trevor had transformed from a grumbling teenager to someone capable of conversation.

Earl almost glowed. "Ah, just little things. I'll show you them sometime."

"How about now?" Trevor blurted out.

"Trev, I have to—" She'd never seen her son so animated. He was looking Earl in the eye, admiration evident in his

SHARON DUNN

expression. What a change. The kid spent most of his day talking to his shoes. "Mr. Salinski, would it be okay if I left Trevor here while I ran out to the mall to find your wife?" It was the most impulsive thing she'd ever said. And somehow, she had a feeling it was the most right thing.

"A little company would be nice." Earl nodded. "I'll show your son the ropes."

....

An officer knocked on Arleta's door within five minutes of her calling the station. She bolted down the hallway. After fretting for ten minutes before making the call, she had barely had time to hide Annie in the drawer.

"Oh my, Officer—" her eyes fell to the policeman's name tag—"Vicher. I didn't expect you to get here so quickly." The officer had light skin, a blond buzz cut, and a blank look on his face.

Vicher peered over Arleta's shoulder, surveying her living room. "We were in the neighborhood."

What did he mean by "we"? Did he have a mouse in his pocket? And what was so blasted interesting in her house that he looked past her like she was invisible? "Yes, it does seem like there are more reasons to call the police in this neighborhood." The officer didn't respond to her comment.

Instead, Vicher stepped inside and wandered around Arleta's kitchen. What a rude young man. He hadn't even waited to be invited in. Of course, she didn't expect she would be serving him tea and crumpets. But one did expect a minimum of manners, especially from a police officer.

Vicher shoved his thumbs in his police belt, which contained all sorts of scary looking doodads. "So you had a break-in?"

"Yes, someone was in my house looking through my things."

"Your things?"

"He was here for quite some time." She ambled into the living room. "My papers in this desk are all messed up."

"Did he take anything?" The officer cocked his head sideways. His hand brushed over the gun holster on his belt and then the flashlight.

She knew from her class that the gun was a 9mm. Arleta opened and closed the drawer, shivering involuntarily. "Not that I can tell." Why wasn't Officer Vicher writing all this down? He hadn't even asked what her last name was. Certainly, he was going to make a report or something.

"How do you think the intruder got in?" Again, he started pacing through her kitchen and living room.

What a nosy body. "I don't know. I suppose that side door by the back of the kitchen." Arleta pointed.

Odd, the officer was already headed in that direction before she even pointed. This was starting to feel way too much like those awful movies she used to watch late at night when she couldn't sleep. Maybe this guy wasn't even really a policeman. Maybe he killed a police officer and stole his uniform. Maybe he was the guy who had actually broken in. But she had seen a flash of white hair on the intruder. This guy had a blond buzz cut. What if he was some kind of alien who wanted to suck her brains out? That always happened in those movies. Arleta tugged the collar of her cotton pajamas.

The so-called police officer opened the door and looked at the outside of it. He took a flashlight out of his belt and examined the lock. "No sign of a break-in."

"I would have heard if he had come in the front door." She always locked the front door, but sometimes she forgot about the side door. "Maybe he just opened it."

"You didn't lock it?" The officer moved toward her, and Arleta suddenly wished she hadn't put Annie back in the drawer. Her heart beat a little faster.

Okay, so he probably wasn't going to turn into a giant brain-sucking alien spider. But he still made her uncomfortable. She hadn't had that much experience with policemen, but she was pretty sure they were supposed to be a little more polite. And not snoop around your house like they were lord of the manor.

He squared his shoulders and narrowed his eyes, challenging.

"Somebody was in this house." What kind of game was this guy playing? His nostrils flared as he inhaled and exhaled. He crossed his arms. "I lay in my bed and listened to him rifle through my things for close to half an hour." Arleta chose her words deliberately and kept her voice level. The last thing she wanted was to be dismissed because she was a "crazy old lady." Her mind was as sharp as any twenty-year-old's. "This neighborhood is not safe."

Officer Vicher kept his eyes on her and stepped toward her. He did kind of look like a spider.

Arleta took a ministep back and made a mental note not to watch anything but the weather channel at night when she couldn't sleep.

Plaster dust sprinkled the officer's head. He blinked rapidly. "What the—" He tilted his head toward the hole Arleta had blown in the ceiling.

Her cheeks were on fire. "I did that."

"You did that?"

"With my...my gun."

"With your gun?"

Arleta crossed her arms. This guy was a bully. "It is a legal, registered firearm. I am taking a self-defense class." She left out the part about not following the procedure her instructor had given. "I have to protect myself." If all policemen were like this man, it really was up to her.

The officer flattened his lips as though he were debating something in his head. The seconds ticked by. "Ma'am, I don't think there has been a crime here. If something does turn up missing, we might be able to file a burglary report."

"Oh, fine." *Guess I have to do everything myself. Annie and I will defend the neighborhood.* She checked her watch. "You know, Officer, I'm meeting some friends at the mall." It felt good to say that. "I'll let you know if anything comes up missing." She strutted toward the door and opened it. "Good night."

"You're going out at midnight?"

"I'm meeting friends." She lifted her chin. *That's right, Officer. Even helpless old ladies like me have social lives.* She watched him make his way down her stairs and across the street to his patrol car. It sure looked like a real police car.

She waited until he pulled away from the curb. Arleta raced to her bedroom to change out of her pajamas.

Time to go shopping.

· ·

Renata came up behind Keaton while he crouched in the bushes outside the pregnant lady's house. She touched his back with her cold fingers and giggled. His palms were sweating, his heart felt like it was going to burst out of his chest, and she was laughing. This "heist" had been her idea. How had he allowed her to have this much influence over him? He was the one paying the bills.

They snuck around to the back of the house. Somewhere in the neighborhood a dog yelped, setting off a chain reaction

SHARON DUNN

of other dogs barking. All of which made Keaton's heart pound even faster and the sweat flow like Niagara Falls. Still crouching, he turned the knob of the screen door and eased it open.

Renata let out a gleeful but muffled cry.

She thought this was fun. He was too old for this. All this crouching and crawling made his knees feel like they had been beaten with a hammer.

The screen door creaked. He cringed. He waited a moment before reaching for the doorknob. His hand trembled. He twisted the knob and opened the door.

"Oui," whispered Renata, triumph coloring her voice.

They were breaking into somebody's house. She didn't seem to be a bit afraid. Was everything a movie to her? Didn't she understand the legal ramifications of this? She couldn't be that dumb, could she?

He had a brief moment of thinking they should just get back in the car. No. They'd come this far. He needed that box.

He pushed the door open wider, and they crawled inside on hands and knees. Sharp objects poked into his legs. A hundred tiny needles stabbed through his kneecap. He suppressed a cry and patted around the floor for the cause of his pain. Something plastic and rectangular with little bumps on it.

He clicked on his miniflashlight. A Lego? A Lego made him wish he could cut his leg off? So much for governments developing weapons of mass destruction. All the army had to do was spread a bunch of these puppies out on the ground. Disable a whole platoon in no time.

He shone the light around the little room. Hundreds of different size shoes, sweat jackets, various assorted clothing items, and sports equipment littered the room. He turned off the light and continued to crawl across the floor. The floor changed from tile to carpet. If the box was anywhere in the open, it would probably be here in the living room.

Without a word, both he and Renata clicked on their tiny flashlights, rose to their feet, and checked every flat area for the box, which was no easy task. Papers, mail, catalogs, and toys occupied all the surfaces.

He felt a tug at his leg, turned slightly, jumping and gasping in the same movement. Below him stood a child with a flourish of blond hair. Keaton's entire body compressed. His stomach and lungs folded over his intestines, and his toes tensed. The reality of what he was doing plowed over him like a mob of angry protestors. The kid was going to scream. His desperation to get the box back had made him blind.

The child opened her mouth. Keaton's breath caught in his throat, a tiny bubble of panic. Time stood still.

The creature opened her mouth even wider. *Oh no. Oh no.*

"I havfoo go potty," the girl whined.

A gurgle that was something like "oh" fell out of Keaton's mouth.

"I havfoo go poooooooteeeee." This time a bizarre dance that involved lifting alternating feet and swinging from side to side accompanied her plea.

Renata came up behind Keaton. "Go on now. Go back to bed, little girl."

"Do you want to talk to my daddy?"

"No," Renata and Keaton spoke in unison.

Keaton got down on his knees. "Why don't you just go use the toilet and go back to bed and pretend like you didn't even see us."

"Issa secret?" The child leaned close to him, her breath hot on his cheek.

"Exactly, it's a secret." *Maybe this kid could prove to be an asset.* "Does your mom have a box with shells on it?"

The little girl shook her head. "Ginger has that. It's pretty. "

"Ginger?"

"Mama's friend."

"What's Ginger's last name?"

"Ginger." She cocked her head to one side. "Ginger Ginger."

"No, her last name." He fought to keep the impatience out of his voice. "Does Ginger have curly hair?" He mimed ringlets around his own head.

The girl nodded.

"Does she live here?"

The little girl shook her head. She stuck a finger in her mouth and stared at Keaton. "I know my phone number." She planted her feet, preparing for her minirecitation. "Five-five-six—"

Keaton leaned close to Renata and whispered, "The box isn't here. We've got to find out who this Ginger woman is and where she lives."

"I think I should go get my daddy." The girl turned quickly and dashed out of sight. Tiny feet padded on hardwood.

Keaton's heart ripped into overdrive. "Oh no." He turned a half circle and bolted toward the front door. He stepped on something with wheels that caused his foot to slide out without the benefit of the rest of his body going with it. His groin stretched. Again, he had to stuff down a cry of pain.

Down the hallway, the little girl said something in her chirpy voice followed by the sleepy moans of an adult male.

Keaton took another step toward the front door. His leg banged against something hard and metal. A bicycle? This whole place was a death trap, a giant toy land mine field. The entire lower half of his body screamed in anguish. Sweat drenched the upper half of his body. It was only ten feet to the front door, and he wasn't sure if he would make it there alive.

A male voice said, "Emily, just go to bed."

The little girl said something indiscernible. And then Keaton heard footsteps, heavy footsteps coming down the hallway...toward him. He inhaled several shallow, desperate breaths and took a big step toward the door. By the door, he hit something else solid, only this something barked.

The footsteps grew louder, more insistent. Keaton's hand touched the door. The dog let out a sharp yelp. He bolted down the stairs and raced across the lawn toward his car.

He was safely behind the wheel and had started the car when he thought of Renata. He stared at the door of the house. A porch light went on. Where was she? Had she opted to go out the back door? Was she hiding somewhere in the house waiting to slip out once things calmed down?

A man came out of the house and stood beneath the porch light. Keaton clicked off his motor and slumped down in the seat. Fortunately, he hadn't turned on his headlights yet. The man stood for some time with his hands on his hips. Keaton could have negotiated a speaking fee in the time that passed. Finally, the man went back inside. A few moments later, the porch light went off.

Should he drive away or wait for Renata? All of this had been her nutty idea. He placed a flat hand against his chest, where his erratically thudding heart threatened a coronary.

If he could just figure out who this Ginger person was and offer her money for the box.... He could say it was a family heirloom and that it had been sold by accident. That would be partially true. He had no idea how he would find out Ginger's last name.

SHARON DUNN

Keaton's chest hurt. Who was he kidding? He was too old to be crawling around a house in the dark. Why did he allow Renata to talk him into these things?

She was the one who thought a garage sale would be fun. If her stupid sister hadn't sold that box, his career wouldn't be slipping through his fingers.

This was all her fault.

Renata had really messed up the first time she tried to get the box back, and now she'd talked him into breaking and entering. Maybe he should just drive away and leave her.

Before he could finish mulling over the thought, she was suddenly in the passenger seat, sitting beside him laughing. "Voilà, it is me." She was breathing heavily and tilted her head back. "Oh, that was fun. So exciting."

"Fun?" Amusement park rides were fun. Breaking and entering was risky. He'd nearly had a heart attack, and she thought this was fun. He saw Renata for who she was—a nut job from France. Albeit a beautiful nut job. "Renata, we are not in a movie. Do you understand that?"

"Oh, Keaton." She reached over and slapped his leg. Hard enough that it hurt.

He drew his leg away protectively. "What took you so long?"

"I hid," she said gleefully. "I wait until the big man go to bed."

"We still have to get that box back. I need to find out who this Ginger person is." He started the car and clicked on the lights.

"Oui, we don't want people to know you are a heep-pie creet."

"The word is *hypocrite*, Renata. Hypocrite." Her remarkable inability to learn English was starting to annoy him.

The evening had garnered one revelation. Breaking and entering was too high a price to pay just to have a pretty girlfriend.

He was pretty sure that as long as he had the dirt on her about that Mary Margret woman, she wouldn't reveal the secret of his box. He could always find another safer Renata.

True. She was the jewel in his crown, but jewels could be replaced.

Fourteen

A crowd of maybe a hundred people gathered at the south side of the mall outside the Macy's entrance. Electricity, created by the anticipation of a good deal, hung in the air. People huddled together in clusters, their laughter and animated chatter filled the summer night.

Ginger stood with her hands shoved in the pockets of her Windbreaker. The clock above the store entrance said it was 11:57. She sighed and bent her head back to stare at the dark sky and soft beautiful moon, so far away. Midnight shopping used to be fun, but now it felt empty. Her best friend was dead. Nobody was going to do anything about it. Other than hunting down Keaton Lustrum, she was out of brilliant ideas of what to do next. The fight with Earl had been the purchase that put her over the limit.

Kindra and Suzanne pressed closer on either side of Ginger as the crowd size and noise level increased.

"I heard they were going to have Cole Haans and Clarks marked down." Kindra's shoulders rose in an excited jerk. She took a sip of her steaming latte.

"I need to get Greg some work pants." Suzanne said, doing the pregnant lady version of standing on tiptoe to peer over the top of the crowd. The movement involved a great deal of neck stretching and very little lifting of heels.

Both women looked at Ginger. She knew the routine. It was her turn to say what she was going to look at first, what she wanted to get a good deal on. Instead, she just hung her head. She couldn't remember why she had even come. Why bother? With Mary Margret gone, what was the point?

Kindra wrapped her arms through Ginger's. "Don't be sad."

Ginger managed a smile and stroked Kindra's cheek. For this kid and Suzanne she would make an effort at being pleasant, even if she didn't feel like it. "Earl wants me to pay full price for a dress tonight."

Kindra's jaw dropped. "Is he breathing funny fumes in that garage of his?"

"Have aliens abducted him and replaced him with a clone?" Suzanne tugged on her shirttail. "I thought you said he wanted you to be his cheerleader. What does that have to do with buying a dress at full price?"

"He changes his mind every ten minutes. Now he says I hurt his feelings when I buy things on sale. He says it would be the start of an adventure if I would pay full price." Ginger leaned a little closer to her friends. "You know, he's reading that book that says women are from another planet."

"I'm going to write a book about relationships someday." Kindra swayed from side to side to see around the crowd.

Suzanne crossed her arms, resting them on her stomach. "And what are you going to call it?"

Kindra took another sip of her latte. "I'm going to call it *Women Are from Neiman Marcus, Men Are from Kmart.*"

"I know that book isn't really about women being from another planet." Ginger's throat tightened. "It's about relationships that don't work."

Suzanne leaned against her shoulder. "Actually, it's about fixing relationships."

SHARON DUNN

That was where the roadblock was for Ginger. Admitting that the marriage needed to be fixed felt too much like the last thirty-eight years meant nothing. At the same time, she longed for something more than her and Earl trapped in separate little busy bubbles. Twenty years of that would make her crazy.

Inside Macy's, the lights made everything warm, soft-focus, and glowing. Salespeople raced around clothing racks, sorting and adjusting.

Suzanne placed her palms on her lower back. "I still don't understand why he wants you to pay full price."

"You know when a man buys a woman a diamond necklace?" Ginger adjusted her purse strap on her shoulder.

Kindra nearly bounced her latte out of the cup. "Earl wants you to buy a diamond necklace?" Her voice held a tone of glee.

"No, that's just an example." How could she explain this when she didn't understand it herself? Ginger crossed her arms. "I don't know what he wants."

The crowd pressed in tighter and jostled her slightly. Ginger smelled the cinnamon in Kindra's latte as she was squished against her.

Suzanne placed a protective hand over her stomach. "I don't know if this is the best place for a pregnant lady to be." She took a step back. "If it's all right with you ladies, I think I'll dip out of the crowd and come in after the rush."

"I'll go with you."

"No, Gin, you stay with Kindra. I need someone to grab me any 36 x 34 men's work pants and hold them until I can get inside."

Ginger gave Suzanne the thumbs-up. *For my friends, I will be supportive.*

People stepped to one side when Suzanne said "excuse me" and they noticed her large stomach. Suzanne disappeared into the crowd and then reappeared at the edge of the cluster of people with the other stragglers. A wave of sadness swept over Ginger. If Mary Margret were here, she would stand with Suzanne.

Four was just the right number for the Bargain Hunters Network.

"Everyone is so excited." Kindra tilted her head to see over the crowd, then looked back at Ginger, her smile fading. Her hand found Ginger's and squeezed. "I miss Mary Margret, too."

Ginger smiled. "Mind reader." She wrapped her arms around Kindra. "I'm glad I got you, kiddo."

A thin salesgirl came to the glass door with a key in her hand. The crowd compressed and gravitated toward the entrance. The doors of the department store swung open. Ginger and the others edged forward. Like a snake swallowing a frog, the crowd jostled and squeezed through the narrow entryway of the double doors. Kindra had been pushed forward several feet in front of Ginger. She turned slightly and offered Ginger an expression of excitement. As the crowd squeezed through the door, Ginger kept her eyes on the blond head.

Someone anxious to get to the sales racks bumped against her a little harder than was polite, even in a crowd. She glanced around. None of the men and women around her offered an apology. When Ginger looked ahead, she couldn't see Kindra. An odd panic exploded inside her. Losing sight of Kindra made her feel suddenly alone.

The emotion was irrational. She'd find Kindra in the store.

The vacuum of promised discounts sucked the crowd through the door, pressing them even closer together. A mixture of sweat, perfume, fabric softener, and garlic invaded Ginger's sense of smell.

Eight feet ahead, the door loomed in front of her. She could see the glossy floors, soft lights, and clearance signs. The proximity of people made breathing difficult. Almost there. Almost...there. Again, she felt a bump from behind. Turning around wasn't an option.

Something slammed into her ankle. She stumbled. Ginger's view changed from the back of people's heads, to a blurred picture of shoulders, to a kaleidoscope of colors. Legs, she saw lots of legs. She reached her hand forward touching nothing. Feet pounded very close to her ears. She held her breath and waited for the moment when her knees hit concrete.

A hand clamped around her forearm, pressing harder and harder, lifting her before she hit the concrete. She opened her mouth to say thank you, to turn and see who had helped her when a voice very close to her ear whispered, "Leave your dead friend alone or you'll lose another one." The hand let go of her, let her fall.

Her knees buckled, sending pain shooting up her legs. All the people around her seemed to be pulled back and away from her. The voice had been male. Seven or eight men populated the remains of the crowd behind her.

"Ginger, are you all right?" Suzanne's face was close to hers. Sweet Suzanne with her red cheeks and deep brown eyes framed by slightly crooked eyeliner. "Did you trip or something?"

"I–I–"

Suzanne placed her hand under Ginger's elbow. Ginger wobbled but righted herself. Stragglers milled past the two women, some staring, some of them offering condolences and queries of "are you okay?"

Ginger nodded, still not tracking with her surroundings. She looked again at Suzanne, whose gaze softened. The first time Ginger opened her mouth to speak, nothing but a strange moan came out. She was shaking, trembling.

Suzanne wrapped her arm around Ginger. The warmth of her friend's touch calmed her a bit. She patted Suzanne's hands. "I don't want to lose you too—"

Suzanne shook her head. "Lose me? What are you talking about?"

Ginger planted her feet, aware of the concrete beneath her shoes. Aware of the warm glow, scraping of hangers across iron bars, and excited chatter that spilled out of the store. A cool breeze soothed her, brought her fuzzy thoughts into focus.

"You and Kindra matter so much to me." She glanced into the store with its markdown signs. "None of this means anything without you."

"Ginger, what are you talking about?"

The expanse of the mall parking lot stretched out in front of her. Not far from them, a yellow car pulled into a parking place. The driver, a woman, got out, shut the door, and came around to the other side of vehicle. The yellow car was like the one that police lady drove.

Another car, a boatlike Buick, squealed to a stop twenty feet from Ginger and Suzanne. Arleta McQuire jumped out of the car, slammed her door, and shouted, "Ginger Salinski, I'm tired of living in the past. I'm here." She raised a fist to the air. "Let's go shopping."

Fifteen

Ginger swished the tea bag back and forth in her Styrofoam cup. A dollar twenty-five seemed pretty steep for an ordinary cup of tea. For a buck and a quarter, you'd think they would at least provide her with a nice mug. She always carried tea bags in her purse and just asked for hot water. But Arleta had offered to buy the drink, and Ginger didn't want to hurt her feelings.

At 12:45 a.m., the food court at the mall was abandoned except for the four women who sat around the table with her: Kindra, Suzanne, Arleta, and Officer Welstad.

Other shoppers still milled through the stores that were open, but the bulk of them had grabbed their goodies and gone home to bed. For the two times a year that the mall had midnight shopping, they stayed open until two in the morning, a tradition that had started twenty years ago when the mall was built.

Arleta leaned close. "Is that sweater keeping you warm?"

Ginger tugged at the collar of the cardigan Arleta had loaned her. "Yes, thank you."

Though it was a warm, summer night, the mall was kept at a comfortable temperature. But after that man had pushed her down and threatened to kill her friends, a chill she couldn't get rid of invaded her bones. The stress of it all had been too much. Already the shooting stars across her eyes and the feeling that her head was being squeezed tighter and tighter told her she had a couple of hours tops before her migraine became full-blown.

She'd dug through her purse for her medication the second the symptoms started. Maybe she'd caught this one in time and could ward it off. She needed to get home and take the nausea medication.

Tammy continued to talk, but Ginger could barely hear her above the voice that kept repeating in her head. *"Leave your dead friend alone or you'll lose another one."* She wouldn't risk losing the friends she still had to find Mary Margret's killer.

Arleta pushed her chair a little closer to Ginger's. What a horrible night the older woman had had. Ginger couldn't imagine having to listen to someone going through your personal papers. It seemed too coincidental that she and Kindra had been at Arleta's house, that Earl thought someone had been in their family room, and then an intruder had gone through Arleta's stuff all in the same night.

Ginger arranged the sugar packets into rows beside her cup. None of this speculation mattered. What would she do if she lost her bargain hunter friends? The quest for a good deal might have brought them together, but even if there was never another half price sale, she'd love these women until the end of time.

Kindra laid her hand over Ginger's. "What do you think of that?"

Kindra had on blue nail polish with little pink flowers painted on top. So pretty. Ginger reached over and squeezed the young woman's hand. "I'm sorry, I wasn't listening."

Tammy cleared her throat. "I know you're probably tired. I didn't mean for us to meet this late. The evening kind of got out of control for me."

"Someone pushed Ginger down in the parking lot when we were waiting to go into Macy's," Suzanne said. "Some people can just get so greedy that they throw manners out the window."

Ginger stacked the sugar packets one on top of another. She hadn't told Suzanne and Kindra about the man's threat. And she wasn't going to tell them. She didn't want them to worry.

"All I'm saying is that I think the investigation of your friend's death was swept under the carpet too quickly." Tammy leaned a little closer. "I can't afford to lose my job—I hope I haven't already lost it—but when I'm not on duty I will help you as much as I can. What matters here is that the right thing is done."

Kindra touched Ginger's shoulder. "That's good news, don't you think?"

"I don't see what good it will do. If someone powerful in the police department doesn't want us to get to the bottom of this, how are we going to find out anything?"

The furrows between Suzanne's eyebrows intensified. "What are you saying? We've worked so hard already."

Ginger tossed a sugar packet on the table. "And we've come up with nothing." She wrapped her arm around Arleta's bony shoulder. "This woman is obviously not a criminal. The stuff Mary Margret got from her is benign." Of course, she didn't believe that. The break-ins were probably connected, but she needed to protect Kindra and Suzanne.

Suzanne stirred her soft drink with a straw. "We still have to connect that shell box to someone."

"We need to catch Keaton Lustrum at home." Kindra bounced three times in her plastic seat. "I bet that box is worth a million dollars or something. Maybe it got sold by accident, like the fishing pole."

Ginger shook her head. If someone knew she was retracing Mary Margret's steps and that Kindra and Suzanne were her best friends, that meant someone had them under surveillance. What kind of power would a person have to have to find out that kind of stuff about you?

She stared at the store entrances that surrounded the food court, studying each loitering shopper. One of these people was probably watching them right now. A chill, like a million tiny spiders with frozen feet, ran down her spine. She gathered the collar of the cardigan up to her neck.

"The box isn't worth a million dollars. I think we should just forget the whole thing." Besides, just because three women could track down a good deal didn't mean they could take on a person who could track their every move. Maybe they should just pony up and hire a private detective.

"This isn't the best time to make a decision." Tammy took a sip of her Diet Coke. "Maybe you'll change your mind. I'll stay in touch."

Ginger wasn't so sure about Tammy's motive. First she said Mary Margret's death was an accident, and then she said it wasn't. Maybe she was a spy planted to watch them. She pressed the sugar packet between her fingers. She didn't know who to trust anymore.

"I just don't get you, Ginger." Kindra yawned, took the top off her latte cup, and peered inside.

Ginger had lost count of how many caffeinated beverages the nineteen-year-old had downed in the course of the evening. "It's late, kid. Why don't you come back to the house and spend the night. I just hate the thought of you walking through that dorm room parking lot and up that elevator by yourself."

And I just hate the thought of you getting an arrow through your back. Suzanne would be safe with Greg.

Kindra stared at her for a moment before answering. Ginger had never lied to her friends, never kept anything from them. This was worse than if one of her contacts at Dillard's told her about an upcoming sale and she hadn't told Kindra and Suzanne.

"Sure, Ginger. That might be easier than you taking me home." Kindra licked the foam off her coffee lid and continued to gaze at Ginger. The kid was no dummy; she knew something was up.

Tammy gathered her keys from the table. "Actually, I need to go back to your place. I left my son there with your husband."

"Oh, really?" Ginger rose to her feet. Tammy certainly was getting awful cozy with them very fast.

"Yes, your husband is quite a clever inventor. Trevor was pretty impressed."

Why was it that everybody else could know Earl for ten minutes and see him as a genius, and she had spent the last two years thinking he was "piddling" around his garage working on "contraptions"?

Ginger grabbed her purse. They headed toward the Macy's entrance where their cars were parked. Tammy waved good-bye and said she'd see them out at the house. When Ginger said good night to Suzanne, she held her an extra moment longer, squeezed her a little tighter. Suzanne smelled of cooking oil and baby lotion with the hint of her own floral perfume buried underneath.

She pulled free of the hug and held Ginger's hands. "Is everything okay?"

"Yes, it's just that I...I..." Ginger pulled her hands out of Suzanne's grasp.

Suzanne tilted her head and gazed at Ginger. The strong emotion she had not been able to keep out of her voice probably confused Suzanne. After all, she wasn't leaving to be a missionary in Antarctica.

"Ginger, is there something you're not telling us?"

"Yeah," added Kindra.

"No, it's just the fallout in the parking lot. It made me realize how much I care about you two."

"Kind of like a near-death experience."

Ginger nodded at Kindra. "Something like that, kiddo."

Satisfied with the answer, Suzanne lumbered toward the entrance. Even from the back, her duck walk gave away that she was pregnant.

Ginger unzipped her purse to pull out her keys. Inside were the three tea packets wrapped in cellophane that she always carried with her. She bought the tea in eighty-bag boxes at the Costco in a neighboring town. Such a deal. She pulled the bags out and turned them over in her hand.

"Kindra, why don't you go on up ahead. I'll meet you outside." Ginger took two steps and then turned back around. "Be careful."

"Yeah, sure." Kindra nodded, but her expression communicated confusion.

Ginger made her way back down to the food court. Arleta sat by herself sipping her dollar and a quarter tea. She smiled when she saw Ginger. The mall was almost completely abandoned, only a few stragglers left.

Ginger walked over to her table. "You must have had quite a scare. That man coming into your house and everything."

Arleta spoke rapidly, as though longing to talk to someone. "The police officer didn't believe me. But I am telling you that neighborhood is not safe anymore. I should just sell the place, but I can't think of where I would go."

"Must be hard to think about going back there tonight. Why don't you come and stay with me. I'll put Kindra on the couch, and you can have the guest bed. You can follow me out in your car."

SHARON DUNN

Arleta's mouth curled up and she nodded. "Thank you."

Should she share the financial benefits of carrying a tea bag in your purse instead of paying a buck twenty-five? Arleta had said she was on a fixed income, so she could probably use some money saving tips. Maybe she would save that little tidbit until they were better friends.

·······································

Suzanne crawled into bed beside her snoring husband and performed the twenty-minute procedure of trying to find a sleeping position that was within a couple miles of comfortable.

She was pretty sure she wouldn't ever get a good night's sleep until the last kid graduated from high school and left home. Who would have thought an ordinary thing like sleep would become such a precious commodity? Mattress commercials made her cry. All those people looked so comfortable, so relaxed. She pulled the body pillow a little closer.

Greg's voice, faint and groggy, floated across the bed. "Hey, how was midnight shopping? Did you have a nice time with the girls?"

Suzanne drew her legs a little closer to her body. The baby was doing karate in her tummy tonight. "We didn't get much shopping done. It was pretty exciting though. I'll tell you in the morning. Did the kids behave okay for you?"

Greg rolled over and touched her arm. "They were good. Except you need to have a talk with Emily about telling lies. She said there was a man with a price tag on his head looking for boxes in our house."

"She just has a good imagination, Greg."

"She made the dog bark, probably poking at him again, and I think she was trying to cover for that."

"A man with a price tag on his head."

"Weird, huh?" Greg's breathing intensified and then turned to snoring.

She stared at the ceiling, waiting for the heaviness of sleep to overtake the discomfort of being so huge.

A man with a price tag on his head. The thought of Emily telling the story while sucking on her fingers made Suzanne smile.

•••••••••••••••••••••••••••••••••••••

When she and Tammy entered Earl's shop, Ginger spotted two men whose welding helmets made them look like bugs. Earl and the teenager who must be Trevor were hunched in the corner of the shop.

The smaller bug placed the welding rod on one of the arms that came out of the Bobcat while the larger bug watched. From time to time, Earl jerked forward spastically as if he were about to grab the welding rod out of the kid's hands. But he stopped midspasm and continued to watch.

Tammy had arrived only a few minutes before them. She said she spent the time talking to her mother and calling work. Kindra had offered to get Arleta settled inside, an offer Ginger readily accepted. The aura with the bright lights floating across her field of vision had started. She was still hopeful that she had taken the medication soon enough to at least reduce the migraine's strength.

Tammy crossed her arms and shook her head, staring across the expanse of the shop; a faint smile formed on her lips. "I don't suppose there is any way we can get them to notice us."

Ginger wasn't sure what to make of this Officer Welstad. She had seemed compassionate that night she had to tell them about Mary Margret. But her actions after that had been contradictory. Maybe the police department really was trying to cover up something, and they had gotten tired of watching Ginger at a distance, so they sent in Tammy to buddy up to her.

And maybe the incident in the parking lot had made her paranoid.

The sparks stopped flying off of Trevor's welding rod. Both men tilted back their welder's hats. Trevor rose to his feet, set the rod down, and tore off his heavy welding gloves. "Cool, way cool. Mom, did you see? Mr. Salinski taught me how to weld."

Trevor continued to bounce around the shop; then he ran back to a corner and grabbed a skateboard, which had a motor mounted on it. He tilted it toward his mom. "Check it out. We used an old board that belonged to one of his sons, but I'm going to do the same to one of my boards."

"That's neat. Trev, we've got to go. It's late." Tammy offered Ginger a furtive glance. "We've used up enough of these people's time."

He dashed toward his mom. "Mr. Salinski is an inventor. Cool, way cool. Can you bring me out here again tomorrow? He's like a genius or something. He knows everything."

"Trev, that's up to him."

"Trevor is welcome anytime." Earl grinned as he wound up an electrical cord and placed it on a hook. "He's a good hand." He patted the boy on the back. "Come on, son, we need to put the tools away." They retreated to the far end of the shop where Earl held up each tool, handed it to Trevor, and pointed to where it needed to go.

Ginger's heart squeezed tight. Somehow, she had thought that she would be the one learning the names of tools and where they went. She could have alphabetized them.

Tammy put her hands over her mouth. Her voice wavered. "I know this won't make any sense to you, Mrs. Salinski, but your husband is an answer to prayer."

Ginger smiled. Whatever Tammy's motive was for staying close to them, she obviously loved her son.

Contradictory emotions swirled and chugged inside Ginger as she watched Earl give Trevor a friendly punch in the shoulder and hand him another tool. She was glad that Tammy's prayers about her son had been answered and happy that Trevor thought everything in Earl's workshop was cool, way cool. It was just that the night she had brought Earl his Stroganoff, she had pictured herself standing where Trevor was standing. Somehow, she thought she'd be the one wearing the extra welding cap and handing Earl his tools. Once she learned the names of them, of course.

Trevor bounded across the shop. Tammy put her arm around her son. "Come on, we better get home. I'll only be able to get in half a shift, if that." Worry colored her voice. "Grandma's waiting up for you." Trevor dashed out of the door carrying his new motorized skateboard.

Tammy stood in the doorway for a moment watching her son. "Maybe you will reconsider about your friend. I have a few things I can look into, visiting the place where her body was found for one." She looked Ginger in the eye. "But I sure would appreciate your help."

Ginger nodded. She was warming up to the idea that Tammy was the real deal. Most people didn't cry when they talked about prayer being answered if they were just pretending. Perhaps she should tell Tammy about the threat. It would be so nice not to have to keep it to herself.

Ginger pressed her lips together. "I wish I could give you my help, but I can't."

Tammy stared as if expecting more explanation.

Ginger was too tired to explain...too tired and too afraid.

The police lady left, closing the door behind her.

Earl continued to work, smiling and shaking his head. "That boy is something, huh?"

"He seems like a nice kid." Ginger's heart felt like it had been compressed to microscopic size.

"He's a quick learner. It's nice to have some help out here...and some company."

"I'm happy for both of you." Her voice lacked commitment. A pain she could not name welled up inside her. That coupled with an impending migraine meant it was going to be a doozy of a night.

Sixteen

Ginger's eyes shot open. She blinked several times. She rolled on her side to check the clock. Five-fifteen. She'd only had three hours sleep. No bright spots floated across her field of vision, but her temples throbbed and her forehead felt tight. She'd managed to reduce the full-blown migraine to a stress headache. A welcome exchange. She pulled the covers up to her chin and listened.

Earl snoring beside her drowned out the possibility of hearing anything else. The bed shook on his nasally exhale. An intruder could be in the house stomping around and listening to music, and she wouldn't hear it.

Earl must have slipped into bed after she'd fallen asleep. His schedule was so erratic, based only on the level of interest he had in the contraption—no, invention—he was working on. She'd seen him go twenty hours without sleep.

She turned over on her side. Earl had found his assistant, and it wasn't her. She squeezed her eyes shut. She ought to be exhausted. Her dreams had awakened her, and now she was hopelessly alert. After three more minutes of listening to Earl's impression of a motorboat, she sat up and threw off the covers.

His snoring subsided enough for her to hear a plastic something or other fall off the countertop. Just Phoebe, the monster cat. She played all night. This was how the cat amused herself when she wasn't sleeping on Ginger's head. She had

SHARON DUNN

grown used to the sound of things being pushed off counter-tops and display cases in the night. She had long since packed away the breakables.

Ginger rubbed her temples. Her dreams had been of someone watching her, following her in a brownish-gold car, looking at her through binoculars. And then when the man pulled the binoculars away from his eyes, he had no face.

Then she found herself at a dock by a lake. Kindra yelled for help, flailing in the water. Morning mist nearly obscured her from view. The panic in Kindra's voice had planted fear inside Ginger. The residue of the angst still paralyzed her even though she was awake and aware that it was a dream.

In the dream, Ginger stood on the dock and threw what she thought was a life jacket to her friend, but when she looked down through the clearing mist, she realized it was the vest Mary Margret had bought from Arleta. Kindra's screams and the splashing of water grew fainter and fainter. The dream had ended the moment she heard water lapping on the shore.

Ginger slipped into her bathrobe and headed toward the family room, where Kindra was sleeping. The nineteen-year-old lay on the couch, one leg stuck out from underneath a fleece blanket with kittens frolicking on it. Her blond hair covered most of her face. Moonlight washed over her pale skin.

She tiptoed across the family room and covered Kindra's exposed leg with the blanket. The dream didn't make any sense. Kindra was a wonderful swimmer. Yet Ginger could still feel the tightness in her chest the dream had caused. She listened to Kindra's soft breathing. Checking on the kid felt so natural. For years, she had gotten up in the night to check on her own four babies.

Phoebe knocked something heavy onto the kitchen floor. With a sigh, Ginger ambled into the kitchen. Her babies were gone, and now all she had was this mutant cat. The feline sat in the middle of the kitchen floor flicking her tail, chin in the air. Mary Margret's shell box lay on the floor with a few stray shells scattered around it.

Ginger picked up the box and turned it over in her hand before placing it back on the counter. She refolded the vest and flipped through the photo album, shaking her head with each passing photograph. She lingered for a moment by the photo of Arleta and David, arms around each other, surrounded by piles of rocks. They looked so happy.

She slammed the photo album shut. What in this pile of junk had caused Mary Margret to make that frantic phone call? Something horrible, something from the past.

David had been an archaeologist; his whole life had been about looking at the past. None of this made any sense. It was a puzzle with too many pieces missing. Yet Tammy felt strong enough about what she had seen at the police station to track Ginger down in the middle of the night.

She angled the photo of David surrounded by pine trees with the houses and radio tower on the edge. When she had first flipped through the album, this was the photo that struck her as familiar. Maybe it was a place she had visited.

Phoebe strutted to the door, sat back on her haunches, and stared at the doorknob.

"You want to go out, baby?"

Ginger stepped out onto the porch. There was just enough light to make out the silhouette of trees and Earl's workshop. Was someone watching her now? She zipped her bathrobe to the neck and shoved her hands in its plush pockets. The whispered threat about her friends ran through her brain on a loop.

Lord, what I am supposed to do?

SHARON DUNN

A few hours later, Ginger sat at her table watching Kindra dance around the kitchen while she talked on the phone to Tammy. Had she ever had that much energy? Her muscles were heavy from lack of sleep. Brain fog clouded her thoughts.

Kindra placed a hand over the phone. "Please, Ginger? You've got to take me to Suzanne's anyway. You might as well come out to the archery range." Kindra pointed the phone like it was a conductor's baton.

Arleta and Earl sat eating omelets Arleta had whipped up while she told stories of cooking over a fire for an entire archaeology crew. Earl's eyes were barely-open slits. So far his contribution to the conversation had been three groans and an "uh-huh." Ginger had learned early in their marriage the he wasn't technically human until his second cup of coffee.

"Tammy can go rooting around all she wants." Ginger pushed a piece of omelet across her plate. "I just don't think it's going to do any good for us to play Columbo."

Kindra spoke back into the phone. "Just a second, Tammy. Ginger's thinking about it."

Ginger put a hand on her hip. "That's not what I said, young lady."

"Just take me to Suzanne's. Even if you don't want to continue investigating, we do." She leaned forward and mouthed, "Pleasepleaseplease."

"Is Trevor coming with Tammy?" Earl took a bite of toast.

Ginger nearly jumped off her chair at the sound of Earl using actual words.

"I don't know. Let me ask." Kindra turned her attention back to the phone.

Arleta glanced at the clock on the wall. "I need to head home and get those shingles on my roof. I can take Kindra into town."

Kindra said good-bye and hung up the phone. She scooted in beside Ginger at the table. "Tammy says she can bring Trevor. So does that mean you're taking me, Earl, or is Arleta?" Kindra grabbed a slice of marmalade-slathered toast, tore off tiny pieces, and popped them in her mouth.

Earl rubbed his face and blinked several times. "Why don't I just take you straight to the archery range, and Suzanne can meet you there. I wouldn't mind talking to Trevor again."

Ginger sat up straight in her chair. "You want to talk to Trevor?"

"Yeah, he's got some good ideas." The glassiness cleared from his eyes. "He catches on quickly."

A twinge of jealousy pinched the back of Ginger's neck. The distance between her chair and Earl's felt like a million miles. She had good ideas, too.

If Kindra and Suzanne went to the range, they might be in danger. "You know, Kindra. I think I will go with you and Earl."

"Super-duper. I knew you'd change your mind." She patted Ginger's leg. "I'll call Tammy and Suzanne and have them meet us at the range."

....

"Tell me you found the name?" Tammy stood outside Deaver's house, which featured a fence made of old bicycles and several large antennae on the roof.

Bradley looked different without his white coat. The khakis and the *Star Trek* T-shirt made him look like a bald teenager. He waved a piece of paper in front of her. "It took some doing."

"How on earth did you track down the name of the hiker who found the Parker woman's body? Was it embedded on one of the hard drives? Did you piece together the report from the trash?"

"Actually, it was harder than that. I checked the newspaper story that came out a while after she was found." He handed her the paper. "The one that said it was an accident."

"Did you have to go to the library?" She had just swung by there with Trevor so he could check out books on engineering and electricity to show Earl.

"No, I save all the newspapers I subscribe to."

"All?" Tammy pictured a room stacked floor to ceiling with newspapers. Or worse, Bradley cutting out articles that had secret messages hinting of conspiracies and filing them in alphabetical order. She put the brakes on any kinds of thought connected with Deaver's personal life. She just didn't need to go there. Bradley was helping her, he could be trusted, and that was all that mattered.

She unfolded the piece of paper. "Remington Shaw. Sounds like a soap opera star."

"And get this." Deaver pulled another piece of paper out of his briefcase. "Remington is also a member at the archery range. Here's the entire list with phone numbers."

Ah, the legwork Officer Vicher was supposed to have done. She patted his shoulder. "Thanks, Bradley. Maybe I will call this Mr. Shaw and see if he can meet me up at the range."

Deaver grinned. "Already got it done for you."

"What would I do without you?"

Deaver zipped up his briefcase. "So what did Stenengarter say about your being late for your shift?"

She shrugged. "I have a meeting with him later today. I told him I had an emergency with my son, which was the truth." She kept her voice even, but the encroaching tension in her back betrayed her calm demeanor.

Deaver rubbed his nose and cracked his knuckles. "Hope it goes okay."

Tammy waved the membership list. "Thanks for doing all this for me." She stared at the list of members.

What was a hiker doing wandering around the woods in the middle of the night?

• •

The dirt road that led to the archery range wound around the mountain. The car jostled side to side as Earl drove the single lane.

Ginger stared into the evergreen forest. Mary Margret had died out there, somewhere between the time she made the last phone call close to noon and when her body had been found that night. What had she been doing all that time? Someone must have forced her to drive her car here. But why?

Ginger gripped the door handle. Mary Margret had hit four sales, gone to look at some property with another agent, and then gone to the library to look up information about twenty-year-old city commission meetings. Puzzle pieces that she couldn't form into a coherent picture.

Kindra sat in the backseat of the car. "Do you know if Mary Margret made the phone calls from the house or on her cell?"

Ginger picked at a loose thread in the seat cover. She really didn't want to discuss these things with Kindra, to encourage her. Someone might have seen them leave the house and head toward the archery range.

She feigned indifference about the question with a wave of her hand. "I assume the first one was out while she was still hitting the sales, so it was probably from her cell. And the other one was made from home. How else would her garage sale stuff be there?"

"Now that Tammy is working with us, we should see if she can get ahold of Mary Margret's phone records. That's what they always do on *Law & Order*."

Ginger turned around to look at Kindra's placid freckled face. "When do you find time to study?"

"I study and watch TV at the same time. We ADD people have to do that."

Ginger turned back around and continued to tug on the seat cover thread. It would only get harder to come up with excuses as to why they shouldn't look into Mary Margret's death. Kindra and Suzanne were determined to find out more. Should she just tell them about the threat?

When they pulled up to the archery range, Suzanne was already waiting for them, resting on a hay bale at the front of the range. She leaned back, supporting herself on her palms.

The range consisted of a gravel parking lot with a U-shaped building beside it. Targets were set up at two-hundred-yard intervals along the plowed dirt. Beyond that a berm of tarped hay bales lined the far end of the range. Pine trees framed the range to one side and behind the berm. Lodgepole pine, tall and growing close together, held a sort of foreboding. Ginger's chest tightened.

That must be where they found Mary Margret.

A stranger dressed in what looked like a burlap bag and frayed shorts stood in the gravel parking lot beside a battered Subaru. The man gripped a bow. Arrows held in some sort of carrier stuck up from one side of his shoulder. He was tall with a deep brown tan. His hair stuck out in funny sausage-like rolls. The first time Ginger had seen the hairstyle on a salesgirl, Kindra explained that it was called dreadlocks. Creating such a hairstyle involved not shampooing your hair for weeks on end.

Kindra piled out of the backseat. "Tammy must still be on her way. I wonder who that guy is."

"Tarzan," said Ginger.

Kindra giggled. "He's kind of cute."

In a sloppy, unkempt sort of way. Ginger may have come of age in the sixties, but she had been too square to embrace the idea of unwashed long hair as a style choice. While the rest of the world had been dropping acid and dropping out, she had been sitting in a Young Life meeting learning the real definition of free love—the love of Christ. The Young Life meetings had cushioned her against the chaos her mother created, and it was where she had met Earl.

Earl opened the driver's side door and stepped outside. Suzanne pushed herself off the hay bale and wobbled toward the other members of the BHN.

Tarzan sauntered toward the group. "I'm Remington Shaw. The guy who found your friend that Saturday night. Officer Welstad asked me to come here and show you guys where I found her. I'm real sorry about your friend."

They all nodded.

Remington yanked on the string of his bow and then narrowed his eyes at Kindra. "I know you. Calculus 102. You're the girl who threw off the curve." Mr. Shaw's bow looked very high-tech. Not like the simple things Ginger got for her grandkids. The front part of the bow was an arched piece of wood with what looked like pulleys on either end.

Color rose in Kindra's cheeks when she smiled at Remington. Ginger had to keep reminding herself that Kindra was one smart cookie. She never bragged about it. The blond hair and obsession with clothes tended to hide her super-brain attributes.

Kindra became fascinated with her shoes, and her cheeks grew even redder. "I'm sorry, I don't remember you, Remington."

"All my friends call me Rem. It's okay. I looked really different last semester: short hair and polo shirts. I sat behind you." He touched his dreadlocks. "I found my inner he-man last hunting season."

Inner he-man? Is that what that look was about? Maybe later on today Rem would find his inner bathtub and barber.

"What's with the bow and arrow?" Earl asked.

Rem touched one of the arrows attached to his bow. "Can you excuse me for a moment? I need to get something out of my car." He sauntered away.

When Rem was out of earshot, Suzanne scooted toward Kindra. "Nice muscles, huh?"

Kindra crossed her arms and rolled her eyes. "Oh, quit." Her cheeks, which had simmered down to a soft pink, turned red again.

Suzanne leaned close to Kindra's ear but spoke loud enough so Ginger could hear. "So, Kindra. I don't think I've seen tomatoes turn as red as you."

Kindra looked up at the sky. "Stop."

"He's cute, don't you think, Ginger?" Suzanne bumped Kindra's shoulder playfully.

If you want to date Neolithic man. "He's seems nice enough." His character was what really mattered. "I wonder if he's a Christian."

"He's cute, but I need to get through college before I can think about dating. I have a plan and I'm sticking to it." Kindra shrugged. "I might Google him later just for fun."

"Is that legal?" At the very least, it sounded painful. Ginger sat on a hay bale.

Suzanne sat beside her. Just standing had made Suzanne breathless. "That's where you type in someone's name on that Internet search engine." Sweat trickled down her face. "If he has ever been arrested or has a family website or has been in a newspaper or written something, it'll come up." Suzanne rested her hand on her stomach.

"That baby better be born soon or you're going to run out of lung capacity."

Suzanne tightened her lips and took a quick half breath. "Any day now."

Rem returned holding more arrows. "I thought these would work better." He plucked the string of his bow. "The lady cop thought that since I was an archer, I could help you figure out if a stray arrow from the range could have hit your friend."

Kindra rocked back and forth, casting furtive glances in Rem's direction. Somebody definitely had a little crush on Tarzan.

Tammy's yellow car appeared at the top of a hill and rolled into the gravel parking lot. Seconds after the car came to a stop, Trevor jumped out and raced toward the group. He sidled up beside Earl. "Hey, Mr. Salinski. Wait until you see the cool books I got from the library."

Earl slapped Trevor's back. "Sure."

Trevor bounced from foot to foot. "We can look at them right now."

Ginger felt that twinge in her chest as the men wandered back to the car. Her envy was silly, just silly. And really it wasn't about Trevor; it was about feeling so estranged from Earl.

Tammy came up beside them, nodding at the people she knew. She held out her hand. "You must be Remington."

Rem slung his bow over his shoulder, like a woman would a purse, and shook Tammy's hand. "I can tell you right now there is no way someone on the range could have shot your friend. Too far for the arrow to travel, and the angle isn't right. Lots of trees in the way. Not even a really bad shot would zigzag that way." Rem pointed with the bow. "Let me show you what I mean."

He pulled an arrow out of his quiver. Expertly, he placed it in the bow and pulled back on the string. The arrow flew through the air, falling short of the edge of the forest. "I get really good distance, probably one of the best in the club. And I can't even get it into the trees." He repeated the procedure from several places on the range.

Rem ambled back toward them. "If you ladies want to go down the hill, I can retrieve my arrows and show you where I found your friend." He gazed at Kindra when he talked.

Suzanne wiped sweat from the back of her neck. "I think I'll stay here and rest."

Ginger crossed her arms and tilted her head toward Suzanne, who had no color in her face.

"I'll be all right. The baby is not going to be born in the next ten minutes. I've done this three times before."

"Earl is just right over there if you need help." Ginger wrapped her arm around Kindra and strode down the hill behind Rem and Tammy.

Ginger glanced back at the range where Earl and Trevor stood by Tammy's car, flipping through a book, their heads close together. Suzanne, sitting on a hay bale, tilted her head back and closed her eyes. She already looked better.

Ahead of them, Rem stopped to pull an arrow out of the ground. On the edge of the forest, he yanked a second arrow out of a tree. Ginger and Kindra caught up with Tammy and Rem just as they stepped into the trees. The temperature dropped five degrees, and only a small amount of light filtered through the canopy of evergreens.

Ginger's feet treaded on the soft earth. "What were you doing out here hiking at night, Mr. Shaw?" Though she couldn't come up with a motive, Rem could have been the one who put the arrow through Mary Margret. He certainly had the means. He needed to be ruled out.

"I wasn't hiking. The paper said that for convenience, I guess. I was out testing some night-vision goggles. I cross-country ski in the winter, and sometimes I need to ski out after dark." Rem trudged ahead of the women. "I thought they might come in handy when I hunt, too."

"Night-vision goggles? Where do you get those?"

Rem turned to Ginger. "Sporting goods store in the mall sells them."

Hmm, who would have thought it? Earl sometimes didn't finish hunting until after dark. She'd have to get a pair for him. Maybe a gift that was about what he liked could open some discussion doors.

There was no obvious trail for them to walk on. They stepped into a clearing. Several fallen and rotting evergreens rested on the thick undergrowth. Toward the center of the clearing was a large white rock surrounded by smaller ones.

Ginger turned. The trees were thin enough that she could see the range, at least the parking lot and the U-shaped building.

"Just up here a ways." Rem directed them toward something that looked a little more like a trail.

She crossed her arms and slowed her pace. Did she really want to see this?

The narrowness of the path required them to walk single file with Rem in the lead. The trail curved and the others disappeared behind a clump of trees.

Ginger stopped. She could hear their voices and see flashes of color through the trees. She tilted her head, gazing at the tree-tops and clouds floating by, and tried not to think about Mary out here by herself with a killer. That hollow feeling invaded her heart. She wanted to run back to the car and drive for a very long time. Far away from this hole inside her that would not heal.

"Ginger?"

Kindra's voice sounded distant. Ginger waited for the trees around her to come into focus. She swiped the tears from her eyes and trudged forward. The others stood in a small clearing.

Rem turned a half circle. "The trees aren't that close together, but still, it's what we in the business call an impossible shot."

Tammy asked, "Could someone have been wandering around the forest with a bow and arrows?"

"Yeah, but look at your shot range: twenty feet at most, and unless it was pitch black, you'd be able to see a person. There is no way it could have been an accident. Arrows don't bounce off trees and into people." Rem tugged at the bandanna on his head. "Besides, why would you be practicing down here when the range is just up the hill?"

Ginger shivered. She must have made a small gasp because everyone turned and looked at her. She put her hand on her churning stomach.

Tammy cleared her throat. "Rem, that's probably enough details." She pulled a camera out of her purse and took several pictures. Ginger wondered what she was seeing but was afraid to ask. There were more white rocks in the clearing. Two with dark stains. It could be just moss. She didn't want to get close enough to find out.

Ginger closed her eyes and turned away. Kindra came and stood beside her. Whatever fear she had about her friends' safety, she needed to push through it. It wasn't right for Mary Margret to die this way and to receive no justice.

Ginger would find a way to protect Kindra and Suzanne and figure out who did this to Mary.

Kindra shook her head. "This isn't right. It just isn't right."

Ginger rubbed her goose-pimpled arms. "What else is around here anyway?"

"There are some luxury homes and a cabin or two. Not a lot. I already drove around to have a look," Tammy said. "There's a road not too far from here. Someone could have parked and come in."

"Basically, it's just forest," Rem added.

Tammy turned toward Ginger. "Was there any reason for Mary Margret to be up here?"

"If she had shown real estate in the area, she might know about it. But she wasn't an archer or a hiker." Ginger shook off the chill, the sensation of cold fingers tapping the back of her neck. Even more evidence that Mary had been taken up here against her will.

They made their way back up the hill in silence. At the range parking lot, Rem said good-bye, lingering beside Kindra. "Maybe I'll see you in class in the fall."

"Maybe." Kindra stared at her pink high-tops like they held the secrets of the universe. "Maybe, Rem."

He walked back to his car, waved, and opened the driver's side door.

Tammy kept her eyes on the Subaru as it headed down the mountain. "Sometimes the person who reports a crime is the person who perpetrated the crime, but I don't think Rem had anything to do with your friend's death."

"That's good news for Kindra." Suzanne rose from her hay bale to join the group.

Kindra groaned.

Tammy said good-bye, mentioning something about needing to talk to her boss. She and Trevor walked back to her car after Trevor made arrangements to come out to Earl's later. Suzanne wedged herself into her minivan. Kindra, Ginger, and Earl were the last to head down the mountain in the Pontiac.

Kindra gripped the back of the front seat. "If Mary Margret was kidnapped—which is what I think happened—we need to figure out why she was taken out here. There are lots of forested areas around Three Horses. Why out here? Why so close to the range?"

"I don't know. We need to retrace her steps, every step." It felt good to be doing something again to catch Mary Margret's murderer. "After she bought the four items, Mary said she was meeting one of the other agents. I think we should start by going back to the real estate office and talking to that other agent."

Earl drove the rest of the way down the winding road behind Suzanne.

Keaton Lustrum waited at the base of the mountain until the cars pulled out onto the main road. No need getting the Lexus all muddy and calling attention to himself by following them up the narrow road to the top of the mountain. This was where Renata said she had followed Mary Margret's blue Volkswagen that Saturday.

It had been easier than expected to follow the momof3 car. One of these women in one of the other cars had to be Ginger, holder of his seashell box. He had already let a yellow car whiz by, taking time to read the last digits of the license plate. The momof3 car edged past him. Then a Pontiac went by slowly enough that he saw a flash of brassy colored hair in the passenger seat.

He pulled out onto the road, lagging far enough behind so as not to call attention to himself.

Close to town, the right signal on the momof3 car flashed, and the car turned off the main road. Keaton followed the Pontiac.

Seventeen

Ginger hadn't noticed the light blue Lexus until Earl turned onto the gravel road that led to their home. She craned her neck. Unless some new construction she didn't know about was going on, there were no other residences beyond their property.

Earl glanced in the rearview mirror. "I see him, too." He braced his hands on the wheel, giving his biceps some extra definition.

Even the strength in Earl's voice made her feel safe. Almost two weeks ago, when she'd been nearly run off the road by the brownish-gold car, she'd never been more terrified in her life. But having Earl here made it less scary. She sure didn't want to lose that.

"Maybe we should drive past the house so he doesn't see where we live."

Earl hit the blinker. "He's not signaling." He turned onto their property. "We'll take our chances."

The blue car whizzed by.

Earl smiled at Ginger as he brought the car to a stop. "See, it was nothing. Think I'll go get to work. Tammy said she could drop Trevor off later today."

Trevor, Trevor, Trevor. Was that all he could talk about?

After dropping Kindra off on campus and making sure she was safe in her dorm room, Earl had talked almost nonstop about Trevor and the things they were planning on building. Ginger had listened, nodded, and smiled while her insides crumpled and compressed.

"Fine." Her word had bite to it. She hadn't been able to mask her frustration.

"Is something wrong, Ginger?"

Of course something was wrong. Didn't he see? She was trying so hard to be a part of his life. "I couldn't buy that full price dress because I was being trampled in the parking lot."

Ginger clenched her jaw. The words spilled out of her mouth. What an illogical leap. That wasn't at all what she intended to say. Why couldn't she talk about how she wanted to help him in the garage? She wanted Earl to talk about her the way he did Trevor. She wanted to be his assistant.

Earl's jaw dropped and his eyes glazed. "That's okay, honey." His words were slow and measured, and he had more wrinkles in his forehead than a linen pantsuit. "It was just an idea."

Ginger sat up a little straighter. Now he changed his mind again? The other night it had sounded so important. She was going to tell him that she felt jerked around by his constant and bizarre requests, that he needed to be clear on what he wanted.

Ginger twisted her purse strap around her wrist. She opened her mouth. "I need to go inside. The house is a mess." She sounded downright accusatory. "You need to invent something that reads my mind because I am tired of trying to explain my feelings to you, Earl Salinski."

Ginger cringed and pushed open the door. Oh, forget it. She'd never be able to say how she felt. Saying she wanted to be Trevor sounded stupid. She stomped to the house, leaving Earl in the car with his mouth open and his head shaking.

SHARON DUNN

Keaton drove down the road until he found a place to turn around. He'd had a moment of clarity right before he almost turned into that Ginger woman's property. If he knocked on the door and told Ginger he wanted the box, he would have way too many questions to answer. She was bound to think that something was suspicious about him tracking her down and going to all this trouble for a cheap shell box. If he offered her money, she might think something about the box was valuable, and then maybe she wouldn't give it to him at all.

No, he needed to devise a better plan, some sneaky way to enter the house and retrieve the box. He wouldn't try breaking and entering again. That was just way too risky. He had enough crime to try and cover up.

How do you get into a stranger's house without breaking the law? He shifted into gear as a plan formulated in his head. He might need Renata one more time before he put her and her sister on that boat.

••••••••••••••••••••••••••••••••••

Ginger laid the garage sale stuff out on the table—the vest, the photo album, the paper with six numbers on it, and the shell box. Through the window, she could see Earl still sitting in the car. Now he was just as confused as she was. Thinking about this mystery was easier than thinking about her lack of a relationship with Earl.

She flipped through all the photos, stopping to look at the one of Arleta's late husband standing by the tall, old Ponderosa pines with a radio tower and houses in the background. She pulled the photo out of the album and turned it over. All that was on there was the date 1986. Twenty years ago. Then she removed all the photos and checked the backs of them.

What had Mary Margret seen that alarmed her? Most of the photos only had dates on them; some listed people's first names. Ginger put her hands in the pockets inside of both covers. Empty. But maybe something had been there at one time. What if the thing that alarmed Mary Margret wasn't here anymore?

Someone had tried to run Ginger off the road and then tried to break in to her trunk; they had come into her house and probably searched Arleta's too. Whatever they were looking for, they hadn't found it yet.

Ginger picked up the shell box and viewed it at all angles. She opened it and touched the velvet lining. Could there have been something in the box, something Mary Margret put somewhere else? Maybe it was none of these things. Maybe the fishing pole she had given back to that Frank fellow was gold plated. Nah, she knew gold plating when she saw it.

Ginger paced the kitchen floor. The next step to putting together the sequence of events for Mary Margret's fatal Saturday was to talk to the people at Jackson-Wheeler Real Estate. She stood beside the window. Earl had gotten out of the car and was wandering around his Bobcat scratching his head. She touched the window.

She'd read about this kind of thing. A midlife crisis. Men bought sports cars, left their wives, and found girlfriends who were half their age. She took small comfort in knowing that Earl probably wouldn't find a girlfriend half his age. The man had a potbelly, and it wouldn't be long before he could join the comb-over club. But the rest could happen. He could just decide that Ginger was in the way.

SHARON DUNN

She paced the kitchen some more. If she was going to question Mary Margret's coworkers, a little help and company would be nice. She thought about calling Kindra or Suzanne but instead looked up Arleta's number in the phone book.

Arleta picked up on the first ring. "Hello."

"Listen, I have some things to look into with Mary Margret. Why don't you come along with me? I don't think your break-in was just because you are in a bad neighborhood."

The invitation solved two problems. Arleta wouldn't be alone thinking about the break-in, and she could pick Arleta's brain about how to make Earl a soul mate.

On the other end of the line, Arleta sighed. "That sounds wonderful."

"Gotcha, I'll be there in two shakes."

....

Tammy sighed. The chair in the captain's office pressed hard against her back. Paul Stenengarter had told her she was back on patrol and then proceeded to type on his laptop like she wasn't even in the room. The keys clicked for ten excruciating seconds while her teeth clenched tighter and tighter.

She'd come in on her day off, given up her precious free time with Trevor and her mom. "Is this because I've been hanging out with the Parker woman's friends?"

"I don't know what you're talking about." The way his fingers hovered momentarily over the keys told her he knew exactly what she was talking about. "You missed half your shift."

Tammy gripped the edge of the desk. "The second I knew I was going to be late, I phoned in—twice. I had a crisis with my son that threw off my schedule. Certainly you have other officers who have missed work for family reasons." She straightened her back and shifted in her chair.

Stenengarter's cheek twitched, but he kept his eyes on the computer screen. A photo of the captain with his wife and two girls sat on his desk. All four of them were smiling.

"Your daughters are teenagers now. When they have a crisis, I bet your wife handles it. I don't have that luxury."

He lifted his chin slightly. "Your choices were your choices, Welstad. You're back on patrol."

"Am I being held to the same standard as the other officers?" She leaned forward, resting her forearms on the desk. "Because I feel singled out. I've never missed a shift. I've never taken a personal day. I've never been late before. I work hard, and I don't expect special treatment because I'm female."

"You're back on patrol." He opened a drawer and pulled out a piece of blank paper. "If you push this issue, you'll be suspended."

Stenengarter spoke in code, but she knew the issue was her involvement with Mary Margret's friends. Of course, he would never admit that he was abusing his power. Other officers had done worse and not received such a severe reprimand. The threats were always veiled and indirect, but she got the message loud and clear. What she couldn't figure out was what he was covering up or who he was protecting.

While he'd always come across as a bit ivory tower, she had never known him to misuse the authority until the Parker death. Then again, he was from a political family; maybe he didn't view it as an abuse of power, just business as usual.

He stopped typing and finally met her gaze. He pushed his rimless glasses up on his nose. "You are dismissed."

Tammy stood. She pressed her feet hard against the floor. Her knees locked. Stenengarter just kept typing. She did not come in on her day off to be treated with so little respect. The demotion was embarrassment enough.

"Everything was given to you. Your family has pull and status in this town. You were the heir apparent for this job."

The keys clicked away.

She pounded her fist on the glossy wood desk. "You have no idea what it's like to fight and claw. To live paycheck to paycheck. Were you ever even on patrol?"

His fingers stopped, resting on the keyboard. Again, the twitch in his cheek.

"The men don't respect you."

He looked up at her. The rimless glasses hid as much as they revealed. At least he was paying attention.

"Maybe if you hit the streets yourself, put on a uniform, you'd understand better." Her throat tightened. "And you would know how it feels...to be busted down like this when you fought so hard to get the promotion."

He didn't take his eyes off her. At the same time, his expression gave nothing away. It was only his reluctance to break eye contact that suggested she might have hit a nerve, said something that made an impact.

Tammy tapped her hands on her thighs while her throat grew tight. "I'll be here for my shift tomorrow. I'll pick up my assignment. And I'll go out on patrol. I'm a good cop. I'll do what I'm told." She leaned toward him. "But I don't deserve this, and I know what it's really about."

Stenengarter rose to his feet. His Adam's apple moved up and down. A moment before his expression turned to granite, she thought she saw a flicker of something, maybe hurt. "You've got some nerve telling me that the men don't respect me." His voice was low, smoldering. "I will be checking to ensure that you make your shift."

Tammy nodded, then turned and strode toward the door. Ever hopeful that she had reached him with something she said, she glanced back. He squared his shoulders and lifted his chin.

Why did she allow herself to hope?

•••••••••••••••••••••••••••••••••••

Ginger drove into town. When she pulled up to Arleta's house, the older woman was waiting on the porch. Arleta's steel gray hair was pulled into a bun, and she wore slacks and a light blue button-down shirt. A sweater that looked like it had been in style during the Eisenhower administration was draped over her arm.

They drove to the Jackson-Wheeler Real Estate office. This time, the office was buzzing with activity. Several agents sat at desks flipping through piles of papers. Two agents dashed outside, cell phones and folders in hand.

A blond woman rose from her desk as Ginger and Arleta made their way down the center aisle. "I remember you. Mary Margret's friend, right?"

Ginger nodded. That whole day was a bit of blur, but she did remember this nice lady, whose name was Dana, Dana Jones. Arleta crossed her arms and wandered toward the wall of fame, where all the top sellers were pictured.

Ginger glanced over to where Mary Margret's desk had been. A redhead in a short skirt sat in the chair where Mary Margret used to sit. There was no evidence left that her friend had ever worked in this office.

Dana must have picked up on her sadness. "I miss her, too. She was a very kind person."

Ginger heard heavy footsteps behind her. She turned slowly. Mr. Wheeler, all six plus feet of him, loomed over her.

Just like the day of the funeral, he was dressed in jeans with a saucer-sized belt buckle, cowboy boots, a brown blazer, and Western cut shirt. He must have come out of the glass-walled office in the corner.

Arleta wandered toward Ginger. Some almost unde-tectable signal passed between Mr. Wheeler and Dana—a slight lifting of his chin sent her scurrying back to her desk.

"Ginger Salinski, right?" He held out a huge hand toward her.

Hmm. He remembered her name, too. "Yes." What was she? Some kind of celebrity?

Arleta whispered in Ginger's ear. "My goodness, you are popular."

After releasing Ginger's crushed fingers from a death grip of a handshake, Mr. Wheeler put his hands on his hips. "Have you changed your mind about setting up that fund for Mary Margret?"

"Actually, Mr. Wheeler, I'm trying to retrace Mary Margret's movements on the Saturday she died."

He cocked his head sideways, like he expected her to explain further. She didn't owe him an explanation. Behind Mr. Wheeler, she could see his office through the glass walls. The primary features were a huge desk that had only a telephone on it and some kind of dead wildlife mounted on the wall.

"She left a message on my machine saying that after she had hit a few garage sales, she would be meeting another agent at some property. I wonder if you know who that agent might have been and where the property was?"

Mr. Wheeler pulled a toothpick out of his chest pocket and placed it in his mouth. "Agents are always meeting other agents." He worked the toothpick back and forth with his teeth. "We wouldn't have a record of that. Sorry."

Dana jumped to her feet. "I might know who it was. Right before she died, Mary Margret was trying to get her sales up. Mr. Jackson was helping her by giving her some key listings and offering her some general advice on sales technique."

Mr. Wheeler yanked the toothpick out of his mouth and cleared his throat. "Well, there you have it. It most likely was Mr. Jackson himself. I'm sorry, he's not in the office."

"I know where he is." With a nervous glance toward Wheeler, Dana tugged on her shirt cuff. "Before Mr. Jackson left about thirty minutes ago, he said he was going to pop over to that restoration being done on the Wilson mansion."

Mr. Wheeler snapped the toothpick in half. "Thank you, Dana." He tossed it in the garbage can. "Maybe you should go back to your buy-sell agreement."

Dana lifted her chin and narrowed her eyes at Mr. Wheeler before turning to Ginger and Arleta. "It's over on Thomason in the nine hundred block."

She strutted back to her desk with a backward look at her boss. Wheeler returned to his office.

On their way out, Ginger noticed a photograph of Wheeler standing outside the office shaking hands with a slender dark-haired man.

Dana swiveled in her chair and offered an explanation. "That's the ribbon-cutting ceremony for when the Jackson-Wheeler office first opened twenty years ago."

Ginger rested a finger on the dark-haired man. "Who is that man with him?"

"That's Mr. Jackson. I guess he's gained quite a bit of weight over the years."

"Poor man." Ginger crossed her arms. "He must have gained 150 pounds. Does he have health issues that would make him gain weight?"

Dana shook her head. "He just likes pork chops and Twinkies."

....

Arleta and Ginger walked past two stone lions guarding the entrance to the Wilson mansion. Ginger was already breathless from trotting just to keep up with Arleta's huge stride. A hedge framed a huge expanse of lawn. A red Hummer was parked in the driveway. That car probably belonged to Mr. Jackson. All the other vehicles referred to some aspect of the construction trade on their doors.

They ascended a stone and brick staircase.

"I remember when this house was used by a fraternity," commented Arleta as they stood on the wraparound wooden porch. "It's gone through quite a few changes."

Inside, drop cloths covered the floor. A man in painter's pants and a mask worked on his knees spraying trim. The abrasive hum of power tools and the pounding of hammers echoed through the house.

Arleta took the lead as they walked down a dark hallway that led to a kitchen, where a man wedged a ceramic tile into place on the floor. The man rose to his feet and wiped his hands on a rag tucked in his back pocket. "Can I help you ladies?"

"We were told Mr. Jackson was here?"

The man pointed up. "Third floor. The servants' stairs behind me."

Arleta and Ginger made their way up two flights of narrow, winding stairs. Ginger's loafers with jewels on the toes made the floorboards creak with each step. The walls closed in on them in claustrophobic proportions. Servants' stairs indeed. She'd seen the huge sweeping staircase in the living room that the wealthy owner must have traversed at the turn of the century. The maid was the one who had to run the food and wine and candy up this scary contraption. The arrangement struck Ginger as very unfair.

The top of the stairs opened up into an expanse of room surrounded by windows. A billiard table occupied the center of the room. In the corner, Mr. Jackson sat at a card table, his lunch spread out before him. Ginger was pretty sure there was enough on the table to feed a small country—two sandwiches still wrapped in paper, a plastic bowl filled with salad, a Big Gulp, and several tacos completed the spread.

Mr. Jackson's eyes were visible above the sandwich he'd just brought up to his mouth. He bit into the sandwich, chewed for some time, took a moment to wipe his mouth with a paper napkin, and then sipped from his Big Gulp. "Can I help you, ladies? The house won't be on the market for another month."

Funny, Mr. Jackson didn't seem to remember her as well as Mr. Wheeler had. "We're not here to look at the house. I'm Ginger Salinski. Mary Margret's friend."

Mr. Jackson stood up, nearly knocking the table over. His head brushed against the slanted ceiling. He dropped his sandwich on the table. "Oh...yes."

"I'm trying to figure out what happened to my friend the day she died. I understand you saw her that Saturday morning."

Mr. Jackson ran his hands through his hair. He trudged to the billiard table and rolled a ball across it. "And you heard that from...?"

"Dana from your office."

Arleta crossed her arms and wandered to the window. Mr. Jackson rolled several more balls across the table before answering. "You know, that was almost two weeks ago. Mary Margret and I were getting together several times a week. I'd have to check my Day-Timer to see if we met that Saturday."

"So check it," said Arleta without turning around.

Mr. Jackson waddled back to the table and lifted a brief-case off the floor. He unzipped it and pulled out a burgundy leather-bound book. By the time he made his way back to Ginger, he was sweating and breathing heavily. "Let's see," he made a clicking noise as he flipped through the pages, "that would have been July."

Ginger stepped toward him. "Saturday, July 15."

He read and nodded at each entry as though it held a fond memory. In an effort to hurry him a little bit, Ginger peered over his shoulder. "Ah, here it is. Yes, she and I did a walk-through a house on Stalter Street."

"Did she seem upset?"

He shook his head for several seconds. "No, no." A stream of sweat trickled past his temple.

"Did she say anything about the garage sale stuff she had bought that morning?"

Mr. Jackson puckered up his bulbous lips and released them. "She said she was in a bit of a hurry because she was going to more sales after we were done. Oh wait, she mentioned a little fishing pole she'd gotten for her grandson, Donald Duck on it, I think."

"Mickey Mouse," said Arleta and Ginger in unison.

He pointed his puffy finger at her. "Right, Mickey Mouse."

"So she didn't seem agitated at all to you?"

Mr. Jackson shook his head, causing his second chin to wobble. The moments ticked by. One Mississippi. Two Mississippi.

Arleta turned to face Mr. Jackson. Her fists rested on her narrow hips. "How much does a house like this sell for?"

"When it's restored, it will be worth a couple million."

Arleta nodded. Ginger wasn't sure what had motivated Arleta to ask the question, but she was grateful for the participation. Frustration made Ginger's toes curl in her jeweled loafers. Mr. Jackson was hardly a hotbed of information. Both he and Mr. Wheeler had seemed reluctant to share information.

Arleta continued, "Did Mary Margret sell houses like this one?"

"I'm afraid a property like this is something a more successful agent like myself would take as a listing. Actually, I purchased this house because I knew it would be valuable when restored. Mary Margret tended to take on lower-end houses, fixer-uppers. She liked to help first-time home buyers. It was kind of her specialty."

Ginger shook her head. Once again, Mary Margret's heart had kept her from making the bigger money. She had loved it when she was able to help renters become homeowners.

Mr. Jackson removed his jacket, revealing huge sweat stains around his armpits. He tugged at his cartoon tie in primary colors. Bugs Bunny munched on carrots and ran from Elmer Fudd.

She stomped her foot lightly on the wooden floorboards. Mr. Jackson wasn't going to volunteer any information. She'd have to force it out of him. "Something sent Mary Margret to the library in a panic, and then she made a frantic phone call to me." She edged a little closer to him. "She must have said something to you."

"All of that must have happened after she talked to me. If you ladies will excuse me, I have a great deal of work to get done."

"Got to get back to laying that tile and sanding the banister?" Arleta said dryly.

Ginger had a hard time picturing Mr. Jackson doing anything physical without drowning in his own sweat. She appreciated Arleta's sharp wit. It was nice not to have to do this alone.

A nervous chuckle escaped through his lips. "I do have work to get done." He lumbered toward the stairs, not the servants' stairs, mind you, but those that the bigwigs of yesteryear used.

She listened to his footsteps pound on floorboards. Why had he left his fast-food banquet behind?

"He was kind of in a hurry to get out of here." Arleta patted her bun, tucking in a loose strand of hair. "He seemed nervous to me."

Ginger nodded. "I don't know. I think he sweats and breaths heavy all the time." She looped her arm through Arleta's. "Thanks for being my backup. How about I take you to lunch? I've got a two-for-one coupon for the Soup Bowl. If you're game, there's a shop downtown that sells the cutest velour jogging suits."

"Are you saying I need to update my wardrobe?" A faint smile graced her face.

"They would flatter your slender figure." Ginger's voice fluttered with excitement. "And they're on sale."

"I'm glad you offered to help. I've been thinking for some time that I needed new clothes. I just didn't know where to start."

They took the servants' stairs, walked through the now-vacant living room, and stepped outside. The summer sun lingered midway above the horizon, and the temperature was balmy.

Ginger stopped for a moment in the driveway staring at Mr. Jackson's red Hummer. Those cars had starting prices into five figures. A far cry from Mary Margret's ten-year-old Jetta.

"She didn't want the million-dollar properties, Arleta. She was having a hard time making ends meet, and she didn't want the bigger money properties."

"Your friend sounds like a wonderful person." Arleta rubbed Ginger's back. "I wish I could have known her."

"Me, too. You would have liked her." Ginger's eyes fell to the license plate on the Hummer. Something clicked in her brain. "Where have I seen those numbers before?"

Arleta shook her head. She stopped midshake. "They're the numbers David had written on that piece of paper." Arleta whistled. "What are the chances?"

Ginger glanced up at the third-floor window. Even though no one was there, she shivered. "Your husband has been dead how long?"

"Fifteen years."

"Did he know Mr. Jackson?"

"I think I would have remembered if he was one of David's acquaintances. Even if he was skinnier back then."

"What are the chances, indeed," said Ginger.

Eighteen

"I'm looking for night-vision goggles." Ginger stood in the middle of the sporting goods store, staring up at the tall salesman with snowy cotton ball hair and feeling very out of place. She had only been in the store two or three times to get Earl a gift.

"We have some nice Rigels we just got in. If you'll follow me." The salesman had an air of dignity in the way he carried himself, squared shoulders, chin up, even stride. His fingers drifted over several pairs of goggles displayed against a wall. "What are you going to use them for?"

Ginger suspected she wouldn't find a wrinkle on his striped button-down, even under a microscope. His khakis were pressed. His dress and manicured nails would have been better suited for a menswear store. The attention to detail with his appearance suggested a man who liked a high level of control in his life.

"They're for my husband when he goes hunting. Sometimes he's out after dark." The goggles were a last-ditch effort to connect with Earl. That Remington fellow had said that this was a good place to get them.

Ginger rocked on her feet, heel to toe. She didn't exactly feel at home here, too much of a guy place. In fact, when she glanced around at the other customers, they were all male.

On one side of the goggles and binoculars was a display of kayaks in lime green, orange, yellow, and red. On the other side was a locked display case with rifles and boxes of bullets.

"For hunting...hmm." He rubbed his chin staring at the choices in front of him. "You want something lightweight."

Judging from the age spots on his hands, the salesman must have been in his late sixties.

The man selected a pair off the rack and handed them to her. "These should do. I'll ring them up for you."

Ginger glanced down at the price. Her mouth went dry. Three hundred eighty-nine dollars. Yikes. "Ah, do you have any less expensive ones."

"The Rigels are at the lower end for price, still a good goggle though." The man laced his fingers together and leaned toward her. "We do have a payment plan."

"How about a catalog instead? I can ask my husband what he would like."

The man nodded and pulled catalogs from a shelf below the display. Ginger appreciated that he maintained decorum and didn't point out how incredibly cheap she was. Earl was right. She had some kind of disorder or syndrome. She'd buy an evening gown she didn't need because it was on sale, but she couldn't get her husband a nice gift that she knew he'd like because it wasn't on sale.

While the man handed her the catalogs and Ginger croaked out a "thank you," she wondered if there were support groups for the likes of her.

"Our goggles usually go on sale right before hunting season. Maybe that would be a good time for you to make a purchase."

She thought to ask how much of a markdown there would be but caught herself. "You've been very helpful." In more ways than one. "They should give you a promotion."

The man smiled, but his eyes remained placid. "Actually, I'm the owner." There was just a hint of venom in his comment.

"Oh, I didn't mean to insult you. Mr., ah..."

SHARON DUNN

"Stenengarter. Jeffrey Stenengarter." His fingers rested on his jaw. He tilted his head slightly. "I'm surprised you didn't recognize me. I was a state senator a few years ago."

Ginger shrugged. "I don't keep up with local politics." She held up the catalogs. "I might be back."

She wandered out of the store, looking forward to being in the more familiar parts of the mall and not having to think about what a tightwad she was.

• • • • • • • • • • •   •

"Connect the dots for me, ladies." From her porch, where she had spread out the garage sale items on the picnic table, Ginger sipped her mint tea. The sun warmed her skin as she leaned against the railing.

Trevor and Earl walked across the yard to the workshop. Earl slapped Trevor's back. This twinge of envy really wasn't about Trevor. Earl had done the same with their own sons, taught them about using tools and building things. No, the twinge was about the sense of separation she felt from her husband. It had probably been there all the time. She had just been too busy raising kids and practicing the art of being cheap to notice.

Kindra rose from the picnic table and stood beside her, close enough so their arms touched. It felt good to have all her friends where they were safe and she could protect them. So far, the whispering man had not made good on his threat. Maybe, hopefully, he wouldn't.

Suzanne and Arleta sat around the table. Ginger had lined up the scrap of paper on which David had written the six numbers, the photo album, the vest, and the shell box. The final item on the table was a piece of paper on which she had written Mr. Jackson's Hummer license plate number.

The same numbers as found in David's vest.

"Someone killed Mary Margret because of something here or something that was here and was taken out. Whoever did that didn't find what they were looking for because they tried to break into my car and searched my house, and they were probably at Arleta's for the same reason."

"Nothing connects to the shell box." Kindra set the box to one side.

"Unless whatever Mary's killer is looking for was in that box at one time." Ginger pushed it back into the circle.

Kindra tapped her chin with her index finger. "But they were looking for whatever at Arleta's house. So it must connect to Arleta's stuff. I say it was something of Arleta's that set Mary Margret into a panic, one of these photos maybe." Kindra scooted the box away from the other things.

"But Mary Margret put all the garage sale items in the basket."

"Maybe she was in a hurry and didn't have time to sort though it. You said yourself that this stuff was her note. Maybe whoever kidnapped her was coming through the door, and she needed to hide it quickly. She didn't have time to sort through it," Kindra said.

All four women nodded. Ginger had a feeling that none of them wanted to picture the details of what had happened to their friend. But they had to if they were going to get to the bottom of this mess.

Glints of sunlight danced through Suzanne's hair as she turned her glass of iced tea on the picnic table. "Arleta's husband and Mr. Jackson are connected by those six numbers. Mr. Jackson is involved. Tammy says this all somehow relates back to the police department not wanting an investigation."

Ginger paced the porch. "There is definitely more than one person involved here. We have Mr. Jackson and someone in the police department. Someone was chasing me down while someone else was taking Mary Margret up to the hills. That's at least two people."

"The numbers on the Hummer could be personalized. When I got my momof3 license, which I'm going to change to momof4—"

"Too bad momofmany won't fit." Kindra braided a strand of hair. "Then you wouldn't have to get a new one every two years." She elbowed Suzanne.

Suzanne cleared her throat and raised her eyebrows at Kindra. "As I was saying before I was so rudely interrupted, when I went to get my plate, the guy standing in front of me had the birth date of his dog on his license. Maybe those are Mr. Jackson's lucky lotto numbers or his birthday."

"So why would David have the same numbers? Unless—" Arleta shook her head. "David sometimes kept things from me if he thought they would worry me or make me sad. He was protective of my feelings. When he was turned down for a full professorship at the first college we were at, I didn't know about it until years later. Mr. Jackson must have crossed David's path for only a short period of time."

There was something sweet about David wanting to protect his wife. Sweet but not helpful at this point. Ginger took another sip of tea.

Kindra said, "You know there is a professor in the archaeology department who is older than dirt. Arleta, did your husband work with a Professor Chambers?"

"Oh yes, Lyndon Chambers. He and David were good friends." Arleta looked pretty in the purple velour sweat suit Ginger had bought for her at the sidewalk sale downtown. She was determined to gently bring Arleta's wardrobe out of the seventies.

"You and I could go talk to him. Maybe David told him something." Kindra lifted the shell box, turned it over, and then opened it.

"I haven't seen Lyndon in years. We older than dirt people should stay in touch." A smile brightened Arleta's face, and she leaned a little closer to Kindra.

Kindra continued to turn the box over in her hands.

"I thought we decided the box wasn't connected." Ginger placed her tea on the table. "What are you looking at, kiddo?"

"Do you have a ruler or tape measure?" She held the box at eye level. "I suspect that the dimensions on the outside of this box don't match those inside."

"I've got a ruler in my craft drawer." Ginger opened the sliding glass door by the deck while Arleta said something about putting her house on the market and maybe talking to the nice blond lady at Jackson-Wheeler Real Estate.

Ginger stepped into the cool kitchen just as Phoebe jumped off the counter. While she was rooting through her craft drawer, the doorbell rang. Who on earth? She opened the door.

Well, wire my jaw shut and call me Sally. Had she just stepped into a musical theater number? The two people in front of her looked absurd, like they were on their way to belt out a tune on a stage somewhere.

It took a moment, but she recognized the man as Keaton Lustrum. The lacquered Elvis-style hair threw her off. His shirt was buttoned up to his neck. He tucked his shirttail into polyester slacks pulled up past his belly button and cinched into place with a white belt. He looked substantially different than in his newspaper photograph. What on earth was he doing here in that getup?

The pretty lady beside him was dressed in an equally bizarre and dumpy outfit. Even the boxy denim jumper with

SHARON DUNN

embroidered puppies frolicking across her chest couldn't hide her perfect posture and skin. She looked like a model who was trying to appear plain.

When Keaton opened his mouth, he spoke with a Southern accent. "Excuse me, ma'am. We are from the Organized Bible Society."

The woman nodded, fidgeting with the handle of the tote bag she held up to her chest.

"The Organized Bible Society?" As opposed to the Unorganized Bible Society? This was getting weirder by the second.

Keaton turned his Bible so Ginger could see the cover. "Yes, if you would just allow us to come in and talk to you about the Lawd."

Ginger placed her hand on her hip. "The Lawd?"

"Yes, ma'am. If you would just welcome us into your lovely home."

Not too subtly the woman stood on tiptoe and looked over Ginger's shoulder. She suspected that the dumpy model was making an itemized list of the contents of her home. She was looking for something.

Ginger crossed her arms. "You want to come into my house?"

Keaton's lips tightened, suggesting impatience. "Do you have a personal relationship with Jesus?" He leaned toward her, spittle flying in her direction.

Ginger wiped her cheek. He had said her Savior's name like he was cracking a whip. "As matter of fact—"

The pretty woman in the dumpy outfit swung her tote bag in such a way that it was obviously empty. She leaned close to Ginger as if expressing a confidence. "Is the devil in your house? We get him out." The oversized cross the woman wore around her neck was big enough to knock out an elephant.

Kindra's voice rose from behind Ginger. "Oh please, give me a break."

The nineteen-year-old stood on the threshold between the family room and the kitchen. The shell box was tucked under her arm.

Keaton's mouth formed an oval shape. His hands twitched at his sides. He gazed at the shell box like it was a hot fudge sundae.

Kindra stomped across the kitchen floor and stood beside Ginger. "Where have you guys been shopping, the nerd factory? Christians don't act and dress like that. That cross could blind half of Africa if the sun hit it at the right angle. You've been watching too much network television."

The woman with the French accent lifted her chin and squared her shoulders. "Yes, that is correct. I watch the TV."

Kindra paced back and forth, gesturing by holding the box up and pointing with it while Keaton made odd noises and raised his hands toward the box. His head jerked in sync with Kindra's movement.

"I am so tired of these stupid stereotypes. I get this on campus all the time. Physicists are supposed to act and dress a certain way. Just because I'm blond and used to be a cheer-leader doesn't mean I'm dumb. People make assumptions about what I think because I'm a Christian."

Kindra grimaced at the French woman. "I would never dress like that. None of my friends dress like that. If you're going to pretend to be a Christian, at least do a little field research. Television is filled with lies when it comes to Christians."

"No." The French woman seemed to be having some sort of epileptic fit. She shook her head, blinked rapidly, and sucked in her collagen-enhanced lips so tightly they disappeared.

SHARON DUNN

Kindra stopped pacing and gazed down at the box. She lowered her voice. "We know who you really are, Mr. Lustrum."

The color drained from his face. He made a series of odd groans and squeaks. "You know my name?"

Kindra held up the box. "And I know this belongs to you."

Ginger did a double take toward Kindra. What had she figured out?

Keaton's fingers, stiff and splayed apart, reached toward the box.

"I am not stupid. I know not all is true." The French woman seemed to be on the verge of tears. "I just wanted to learn to be a good American." She dropped the tote bag on the floor.

Kindra shoved the box toward Keaton.

Ginger stepped back and watched the strange show taking place in her kitchen.

Keaton wrapped his arms around the box. He touched his stiff hair. "Thank you. It's a family heirloom."

Kindra rolled her eyes toward the ceiling and planted a fist on her hip. "Oh, cut the lies. You can get it in any ocean tourist shop in the world. You won't find what you're looking for in there."

The lawyer's eyes popped. He made his squeaking noises again.

Kindra pulled a pile of papers out of her back pocket. "I think this is what you want."

Keaton's jaw and the box dropped, clattering at their feet.

Nineteen

Earl stared out his workshop window at the Lexus in his driveway. Did they even know someone who drove a car like that?

"Is something wrong, Mr. Salinski?" Trevor's hands dripped with papier-mâché.

Earl pulled his drill off the elk antlers he'd been preparing to mount on his latest invention. "No, Trevor, why do you ask?"

"You been starin' out the window for five minutes, and you drilled three holes in that one antler." The boy ran his finger through curly brown hair. "I thought we just needed one."

"So I did. You caught me." Earl pulled his drill bit out of his drill. "I shouldn't be operating power tools when my mind is elsewhere." He handed the bit to Trevor.

The boy placed the bit back in its case. "Where is your mind?"

"Just on some adult things, marriage things." Earl's thoughts kept pace with the rapid winding of his drill cord. Would he and Ginger spend their remaining years operating in separate worlds? "You wouldn't understand."

Trevor shrugged. "Try me, Mr. S."

The innocence of his expression calmed Earl. What could it hurt to share? "Since Heidi left for the army, Ginger and I seem to be drifting apart." He placed his drill on a wall hook. "I thought once the kids were gone..." He shook his head. "Been reading all these books about relationships."

"Books? Books are just a bunch of words. What good will that do? When me and my buds have had some sort of rift, we just go skate together, no words, just silence. Pretty soon, we're having so much fun on our boards that we forget what we were mad about. We never read books about getting along."

Earl couldn't help but smile at the simplicity of Trevor's solution. "It's a little different with a wife than with a...a bud. Women are all about words. I know that much from the books. It's not that Ginger and I are angry at each other, and we already got way too much silence between us."

"But there is a rift?"

"I guess you could say that."

"So just hang together. Like we're doing. You know, hang."

"Just hang, huh?"

Trevor nodded. "And Mr. S.?"

"Yes."

"You need to make her your bud."

....

Seashells rattled and tinkled as they fell off the box and scattered across Ginger's floor. One of the hinges that secured the lid had broken, leaving the top of the box barely attached to the bottom.

Dowdy Woman gasped. "Now they know you are *hippo crit*, Keaton."

"The word is *hypocrite*, Renata. Learn the word. Hypocrite. You are the worst actress ever."

She opened and closed her mouth like a fish. "Do not blame me, Keaton."

"You're the one who saw people having a garage sale on TV and had to have one yourself. You are not in a movie. This is real life. It's my life." His voice cracked. "Now it's falling apart. As soon as I can book the flight, you and that annoying sister of yours will be back on a plane to France. You can watch all the Jerry Lewis you can stand."

"I knew that was your plan." The woman called Renata tilted her chin. "You think I am stupid. I have something on you now. So you cannot send me back."

"I will send you back, and you will keep your mouth shut." He stepped into Ginger's house, crunching seashells underfoot. "I'll take those papers, if you don't mind."

Ginger sidled toward Kindra and stared down at the documents. The paper on top was a title for a motorcycle.

Kindra held the papers to her chest. "I don't think so."

"Give them to me." Keaton lunged toward her.

Kindra gasped and stepped back. Ginger slipped in between Keaton and her friend.

The French woman grabbed Keaton's arm. "No assault. No assault."

Keaton pulled free of Renata's grasp. "No assault? You're the one who broke the law."

"I was trying to get your stupid box back. You broke the law, too."

Ginger's ears perked up. "What are you talking about?"

"The lady, Mary Margret, she give me her business card when she buy the box."

"She was a realtor. She gave everyone her business card," Kindra said.

"Keaton get all mad at me." The French woman paced in a two-foot line, bending her hands like she was doing bicep exercises. "He want his box back. So I go to her house."

SHARON DUNN

"We're not talking about that right now." Keaton's face was inches from Renata's. "These people don't need to know what you did." He gritted his teeth.

Ginger stepped away from Kindra. "Did you do something to Mary Margret?"

The woman raised an accusatory finger. "You did it, too." Her words oozed venom.

"You set me up." Keaton poked her shoulder. "You talked me into doing that."

"I broke the law; you broke the law. If you try to send me back to France, I will tell police all."

"You've said too much already, Renata. Just shut up." He whirled around and stalked toward Kindra. "Give me back my papers."

Ginger held up a hand to stop him. "Wait a second. I want to hear what Renata saw or did when she went to Mary Margret's house that day."

"Yeah, we want to know what happened." Kindra scooted close to Ginger and stood on tiptoe, looking over her shoulder and pressing against her back.

"None of that matters. Just give me my papers back."

Ginger walked backward as Keaton charged toward them. Clutching his shirttails, Renata leaned back in a squatting position, which slowed him down. For a moment, he ran in place like a hamster on a wheel.

"Look at them." Kindra slipped the documents over Ginger's shoulder. "Why has he gone to all this trouble for these?"

Ginger filed through the papers. They were all titles for motorcycles, ATVs, and snowmobiles. "You want to explain to me why a guy who doesn't want anyone else riding motorcycles and snowmobiles through the forest has a stack of titles for all kinds of motorized vehicles?" Ginger positioned the papers by her shoulder so Kindra could grab them.

"None of your business." He tore free of the French woman's grasp.

"Obviously, you went to great efforts to hide them and are willing to do this bizarre act to get them back." Ginger took three steps back. "But why?" On what planet did he think anyone would fall for his Organized Bible Society?

A vein popped out on Keaton's forehead. He curled his lip, revealing perfect white teeth. He dove toward them.

"Give them to me." He tried to push Ginger aside, but she planted her feet. If he thought he could hurt Kindra, he was mistaken. His fingers dug into Ginger's shoulder. Pain shot down her arm. She winced.

He angled around her and pulled at the lace collar on Kindra's blouse. Kindra screamed. Ginger screamed. The papers flew out of Kindra's hands. Titles rained down on them.

Keaton attempted to grab the documents as they floated to the floor. Ginger and Kindra stepped to one side. On hands and knees, he scrambled across the floor, gathering the titles into a chaotic, crooked pile. His hair had lost its gusto, probably from the amount of sweat he was producing. The top part of it had flopped over his forehead in one solid piece.

Renata stood in the kitchen, mouth open, head shaking,

"Why have you been keeping this a secret? So you own a few motorcycles."

"I counted twenty," said Kindra.

"Twenty." Ginger placed her hands on her hips. "Where do you keep all of them?"

"Eastern Montana, on his father's wrench."

"Shut up, Renata." Still on hands and knees, he spun around to face her. "And the word is *ranch*."

Sweat drizzled from Keaton's disintegrating dome head.

Ginger suddenly felt sorry for this pathetic man. "Mr. Lustrum, there is no crime in owning a motorcycle...or twenty. It's a little excessive, but it is not a crime."

Out of breath, Keaton clutched the piles of paper to his chest and sat up on his knees. "You don't understand. For the kind of people I represent, for the kind of speaking engagements I do, it is against the law—their law." He wiped his glistening forehead with a trembling hand. "If this ever comes out..."

"Why don't you just get different clients?" Kindra asked.

"I got my first case as a fluke. The money was so good. My whole career is based on these anti-motorized vehicles cases. I charge outrageous amounts for speaking engagements. Everything I own, the house, the Lexus, is because of the focus of my legal practice." He pointed to Renata. "Do you think *she* would stay around if I didn't have money?"

Some sort of transformation or realization seemed to be taking place in Renata. She shook her head and took a step backward, never taking her eyes off Keaton.

"Mr. Lustrum, all of that is just stuff. Certainly doing what you love, being true to yourself, matters more." Ginger picked up a wayward title and handed it to him. His thinking was so distorted. Was there no middle ground? He seemed to see everything in extremes. People weren't people; they were types. All environmentalists hated motorized vehicles. Christians wore denim jumpers and polyester suits, and French people loved Jerry Lewis.

"That is a fifty-thousand-dollar car out there." Keaton rose to his feet and placed the titles on Ginger's kitchen table. He attempted to run his hand through his hair, but it got stuck. "I grew up riding motorcycles and snowmobiling with my dad. Such good times."

Renata continued to shake her head. "You are shallower than me. True, I stay with you for the money, but you do not even believe in your cause."

"I love my motorcycles, but I—I could lose everything."

"It's just stuff." Kindra echoed Ginger's sentiment. Arleta and Suzanne had come to the open sliding door that led to the patio. They stood on the porch, watching the unfolding drama.

Keaton gazed at the women standing outside. Then he grabbed Ginger just above the elbow. "I just want to know that you are not going to the press with this."

Mr. Lustrum had an overrated sense of his importance. *Man admits to owning twenty motorcycles.* Would that even be a story? "What I don't understand is how you kept it a secret for this long." She didn't understand *why* either. But that was perhaps one for the psychiatrist to figure out.

Ginger filed through the stack of titles on the table. "Certainly someone at the DMV would have squealed on you by now. You being a local celebrity and all."

"How I keep it a secret is none of your business." Keaton wrung his hands. "So you ladies aren't going to blab about this?"

Ginger had a feeling that Renata, judging from the scowl and stiff posture, would do the blabbing or use the secret to leverage staying in the United States.

"Your girlfriend is right; you are a *hippo crit*," Kindra said.

"I might be a hypocrite, but I'm a rich hypocrite." He gathered up his titles, tapping them on the table to straighten them before turning back toward Ginger. "So I have your word that you won't let this leak? I can write you a check right now. Just name the amount."

"I don't want your money, Mr. Lustrum." Ginger was confident that the French woman would do any dirty work required.

Keaton squared his shoulders and tucked his shirt back in his pants. His attempt at regaining some level of dignity backfired. The follicle explosion on his head made that impossible. The polyester pants cinched up to his pectorals didn't help either. "What do you want?"

"Your girlfriend has to tell us what she knows about Mary Margret."

Renata glued her eyes to Keaton and made a sound that resembled hissing. He shot her a threat-filled look, eyebrows drawn together, head shaking.

"Did you...did you hurt my friend?"

"Keaton said I could not tell. He said people would find out about the box. I not thinking; I not mean to do it. I only try to get his box back."

"I think we should go." He grabbed Renata's wrist and waved the titles in the air. "A word of this to anyone, and I can find a legal way to make your life miserable."

Renata turned back around and opened her mouth as if to say something.

Ginger stood, unable to speak, processing what Keaton had said. No one had ever threatened her in that way.

Pressing the titles against his chest, Keaton yanked Renata toward the door. She neglected to close the door behind her, which afforded all of them the bonus feature of watching her break free of Keaton's grasp and yell at him in French. Ginger didn't speak a word of French, but she was pretty sure Renata wasn't paying him any compliments. They both got into the Lexus, car doors slamming.

Suzanne spoke through the screen door. "Just like the nonsugar babies."

"The what?" asked Kindra.

"I have friends who don't feed their kids any sugar. So when the kids get around sugar and away from the parents..."

Suzanne mimed stuffing her mouth. "Maybe if Keaton had just taken a moderate position and given himself permission to buy one aboveboard motorcycle, he wouldn't think he had to have twenty hidden ones. He's out of control. What did he think he was doing threatening Ginger like that?"

Outside, Keaton gunned the engine of the Lexus and performed a turn that sprayed gravel across the yard.

Stunned, Ginger continued to shake her head. She picked up the tote bag Renata had dropped. Empty. They must have thought they would locate the box and simply shovel it in the bag while Keaton distracted her with the life-changing message of the Organized Bible Society.

Arleta came and stood beside Ginger. "Do you think his threat was real?"

"I think he has an exaggerated view of how much power he has," Suzanne said.

"They both know something about Mary Margret. We have to find a way to make them talk." She massaged her temples. "I just don't know how."

Ginger picked up the broken shell box and tossed it in the garbage.

• •

Ginger sat in Earl's easy chair wearing her fuzzy slippers and a large purring cat on her thighs. She had spent the day and into the evening thinking about Keaton. If they confronted him, he would just make more threats. She could threaten him with blowing his cover about the motorcycles. That might be the leverage she needed. She had no idea how to threaten someone to get them to talk. Maybe Tammy could help in an unofficial capacity.

From where she sat, she could see the night-vision goggle catalogs she'd gotten for Earl sitting on her desk.

Her tingling leg threatened to fall asleep from the weight of Phoebe's body. "Come on, baby, get off Mama's lap. You're cutting off all the circulation."

In an effort to remove Phoebe from her thigh, she turned her head sideways. The chair smelled like Earl, the faint scent of musk and sweat and just plain Earl. She buried her face even deeper in the chair.

"Hey." Earl stood in the doorway dressed in the Carhartt overalls she'd given him for Christmas. The ranch supply place had had a sale in July. The thought deflated her. She had never paid full price for a gift. Not even for Earl.

He rubbed his head. "I didn't know you were still up."

The cat jumped off Ginger's lap, sauntered over to Earl, and rubbed against his leg.

Ginger jerked her head away from the chair. Had he seen her bury her face just so she could smell his scent? "I've just been up thinking."

She wanted to tell him he had been right about how it would be good for her to buy a dress at full price, to quit being so cheap 'cause it hurt his feelings. Instead, she said, "Your dinner is in the refrigerator." She leaned forward. "I can get it for you if you like." She slipped back into domestic busy mode, the safe place. That's not what Earl wanted. That's not what she wanted. It wasn't what soul mates did.

Earl held up his hand, indicating she didn't need to. He tilted his head sideways. "Penny for your thoughts?"

Ginger crossed her legs at the ankle. "I charge full price now."

She was stalling. She didn't think she could even put her thoughts into words. Despite the slight paunch and thinning hair, Earl's strong features were still handsome. The way the chair smelled like him, the thought of him, flooded her system with emotion. The power and the smoothness of his voice made her heart beat faster.

"I picked up some catalogs for night-vision goggles for you." She pointed toward the desk. How trivial. That's not what she wanted to talk about.

Earl walked the few feet to her desk and picked up one of the catalogs. He flipped through it. Ginger couldn't gauge his reaction. His expression hadn't changed. She wanted him to know she was thinking of him, of what he liked to do.

"I thought maybe I could get some for you, for when you go hunting, but I—" She wrapped the belt of her bathrobe around her hand. "They cost a little more than I expected." *And I was too tightfisted to get them for you.*

"Oh." He nodded and smiled. "Nice. For hunting."

Not exactly the over-the-top reaction she'd hoped for. Of course he probably would have jumped a little higher if she had put the actual goggles in his hand.

Earl dug into his overalls pocket. He walked the few feet to where Ginger lounged, grabbed her hand, held it open, and pressed a quarter into it. "Full price, for you." His hand encompassed hers, warming it.

"I—I—don't know if I can say what I need to say." The longed-for conversation lay just beneath the surface of their words.

"Why don't you come out and give me a hand with some stuff I've been working on? Don't worry about talking; we'll just, you know, hang."

Memories of the previous disaster made Ginger's chest tight, and she wasn't sure if she knew how to *hang*. "Oh, Earl, I don't think... Didn't Trevor help you today?"

He leaned close and squeezed her hand even tighter. "Trevor isn't my wife."

　　　　　　　　　　　　SHARON DUNN

Ginger sank deeper into the chair and relished the touch of his hand on hers. With all the mean things she had said to him, he hadn't given up on her. "Oh, Earl."

He winked at her. "Come on, take those fuzzy slippers off and get out of that bathrobe. Come see what I've been working on."

Ten minutes later, Ginger found herself dressed and outside in the evergreens that surrounded their property. Being outside was a little less foreign than going into his shop...and he had said such sweet things.

Earl chattered as he walked through the trees. "Since I'm a hunter, I've been thinking that my inventions should have something to do with hunting. So I've been working on a couple things." He held up one of the night-vision goggle catalogs. "That's why I thought it was funny that you were thinking about my hunting, too."

So that's what that neutral expression had meant.

"We're thinking along the same lines." Earl grabbed her hands. "It's because we know each other, Ginger."

She felt light-headed. "Is that what it is, Earl? Is it really?"

They came to a small clearing where something was hidden under a blanket. The blanket was one of their good ones from the house. She hadn't said he could take that outside and get it all dirty. She was here to be with him, 'to hang' as he put it.

She exhaled slowly. It was just stuff. *Let it go. Just let it go.* "What's under the blanket?"

Earl waved his arms and annunciated as if he were presenting to the board of directors at Microsoft. Had he been waiting to share with her, planning a little presentation? "I was looking through one of my books on past patented inventions. And there was this guy who invented a decoy cow that you hid in until wildlife came close enough. Then you burst out of the cow and shot the wildlife. So I thought to myself, a cow? You don't use a decoy beaver to attract ducks to a body of water. So here's what Trevor and I came up with."

He lifted the nice blanket and threw it on the ground, getting dirt and pine needles on it. Ginger trapped accusatory words by clenching her teeth. She was here to *be* with him, not clean up and alphabetize his life. In front of her stood what resembled a cross between a moose and an elk made out of leather, papier-mâché, and chicken wire. Earl had mounted some real elk antlers on the animal.

Ginger swallowed and tried to think of something supportive to say.

"Now this is just a prototype. It still needs work." Earl mimed holding a rifle. "It's designed so your shotgun goes up into the head. And come around this way." She tiptoed to where Earl was pointing. "See, there's a door so you can crawl in easily. What do you think? Very realistic, huh?"

"I don't think most elk have doors, Earl."

He dismissed her comment with a wave. "The elk never sees the door." The hatch creaked when he opened it. "Try 'er out."

Ginger stepped toward the beast. Earl tapped her shoulder before she slid all the way in. "Oh, and I got a gift for you, too."

A gift? He had been thinking about her?

Right before the door squeaked shut, Earl said, "If you look out through her neck, there's a 180-degree view."

Earl's voice was muffled. Being surrounded by chicken wire and plaster reduced sound. She sat on the chair inside the elk, which she noticed was their brocade footstool from the house.

"Pretty comfortable in there, huh?" Yes, she had always thought the brocade footstool was comfortable...for her feet. Ginger sighed. It was just stuff.

"Can you see?"

She leaned forward toward the elk's neck. A colossal view of Earl's eyes and nose caused her to jump.

"I installed the same kind of glass they use in spotting scopes. It enlarges everything. Works good, huh?"

Enlarges indeed. Earl's pores looked like moon craters. She made a mental note to encourage him to wash his face with something other than Ivory soap.

"The gift is under the footstool."

Ginger felt around and pulled up what looked like an ordinary leather purse. Her expression was probably just as blank as Earl's had been earlier.

"It's a travel purse," Earl shouted into the elk. "It's got a secret pocket for traveler's checks and stuff. For our life of adventure. We are going to go places and do things."

Ginger may as well have been holding gold and diamonds. The gift was that precious to her. "Yes, Earl, for our life of adventure...together."

She decided then and there that she would go to the mall and pay full price for a dress to show Earl that she could be adventurous. Maybe she'd get him those night-vision goggles, too. No. Scratch that idea. She'd have to work up to that.

"Let's pretend like you see an elk, and he is close enough for you to shoot. See that button on the side by his upper thigh?"

"I see it."

"Push it."

She pressed the button and was treated to a sudden abundance of light and wind and sensory information.

Earl shoved his hands in his pockets and rocked back and forth. "See, the head opens up, and you got your meat for the winter." He grinned, looking at her in hopeful expectation.

"It's really nice, Earl. Really." She stepped out of the elk to stand beside him. "Well thought out."

He rubbed his hands together. "This might be the one I get the patent on."

His excitement about the future prospects for his invention, not the invention itself, made her laugh. "That would be so wonderful." Honestly, she wasn't that enthused about a papier-mâché elk, but his joy was infectious.

"I got something else to show you. Look inside the purse in the secret compartment."

She stared at the inside of the purse. In the dim evening light, she had to study the lining for a long time to see that what she thought was a seam wasn't a seam but a tiny hidden zipper. She unzipped the pocket and pulled out what looked like an ordinary flashlight with a spray nozzle on one end.

"When you hunt, you want things that are lightweight and multipurpose. One end is a light." He pointed to a small button on the device. "And the other end contains pepper spray. In case you encounter a bear."

"Or a creepy guy in a dark parking lot." She turned it over in her hand. "Women would love something like this."

"I hadn't even thought of that." He leaned a little closer to her face. "You're good at the marketing end of things."

"You just need a clever name."

"We'll work on that together."

Work on that together. She liked the ring of that. She put the pepper spray/flashlight back in her purse.

"I have one more thing to show you." He pulled two silver squares out of his pocket. The metal was only slightly larger than a credit card. "I'm still working the bugs out of this one." He placed one in her hand.

"What is it?"

SHARON DUNN

"A lightweight long-distance walkie-talkie. Sometimes when you're hunting with a partner, you need to let him know the herd is headed his way. Cell phones aren't reliable in the mountains, and walkie-talkies are too bulky."

She stared down at the tiny silver box. "That's a really good idea." Way better than the elk and almost as clever as the pepper spray/flashlight. "You built this?"

"It's still got some problems. Want to test it?"

He was like a little boy showing off his new toy. "Sure." She giggled.

He held her hand in his. "This is your antenna. This is where you talk, and here is your on-off switch. Press it down when you want to talk. Let up when you want to listen."

Ginger smiled at the truth of what Earl had said. "I let up when I want to hear you." True, in more ways than one.

"Yes, that's correct." He stroked the back of her hand. His touch electrified her skin. "Walk that way into the trees, and listen for a clicking sound."

After slinging her new purse over her shoulder, Ginger trudged on the thick undergrowth, holding Earl's invention and enjoying the coolness of the summer night air. She looked behind her. Earl had disappeared. Branches shook where he must have gone. She kept walking. They had bought five acres with the house. Most of it was still forest, so she would have to walk a long time before she came to the end of their property line.

The silver card made a glitchy noise, and then she heard Earl's voice. "Ginger, are you there? Over."

"I can hear you, honey. It's a little fuzzy." She lifted her finger from the button.

Silence.

She pressed the button. "Earl?" She let up.

"You forgot to say *over*. Say *over* when you're done."

"Oh, sorry." She walked without looking up, focusing on pushing the right buttons at the right time. "Still fuzzy, but I can hear you...over."

"Keep walking. Over."

When she gazed upward, the sky had turned from light gray to charcoal. She pulled Earl's clever flashlight out of the purse and clicked it on. The trees took on a dark shadowlike quality. Branches creaked. She shone the light on the walkie-talkie to see the buttons. "Earl, are you there?" She walked a few more steps. Oops. "Earl, are you there? Over."

Nothing.

She stopped in the middle of a large clearing. "Earl, can you hear me at all? Over." She walked a little faster. *Come on, Earl, say something.* Maybe this was one of the bugs he was trying to work out. It only worked for a couple of transmissions. She trudged through the trees. A branch brushed her face. She drew a protective hand up to the stinging scratch on her cheek.

She entered a meadow that sloped down. The sky had darkened in the ten minutes she had been walking. The flashlight only provided a small radius of illumination. She stopped and then turned in a slow half circle.

A bud of panic blossomed inside her. Trees stood motionless. Silence made her heart beat faster. Was someone watching her? Just like they had when she'd gone to Arleta's? When she'd been with Suzanne and Kindra? Had Keaton come back to do more than threaten her? Ginger took in a ragged breath.

Again she pressed the button. "Earl, are you there? Over." Her voice quivered. Static came across that may have had a voice hidden in it. She waited for the noise to stop.

"I can't hear you. All fuzzy. Over." Goose bumps formed on her bare arms. She hadn't brought a jacket. "I need to hear you," she whispered.

She turned in the direction she thought was home. This forest wasn't that big.

"Ginger, are you there?" His voice was faint. "Over."

She felt a sense of relief that was bigger than the event seemed to warrant. It wasn't like she had been lost in the woods for days, but her joy at hearing his voice made it seem as if she had.

She spoke into her husband's invention. "I can hear you. I can hear you." She gripped the walkie-talkie even tighter. "Oh, sorry. I can hear you. Over."

"Tell me when your reception clears up. Over."

"I can hear you, but I'm still losing words. Static too. Over." She strode forward focused on the conversation. "Earl, say something. Over."

"Beautiful night, isn't it? Over."

"Yes." She glanced up at the twinkling stars.

"We used to stargaze a lot before we had kids, remember? Over."

She gave a little laugh. "Yeah, I remember. Long nights, staying up late. Over."

"That's for sure. Over."

"You're starting to clear up. Reception is good. Over." She brought the tiny device close to her lips.

"That's good. Over."

"Oh, now you are just clear as a bell. I hear you really well. Over."

"That's cause I'm standing right next to you, hon."

Ginger looked up. There was her husband of thirty-eight years. Evening light gave his skin a soft glow. His intense brown eyes studied her. Her heart pounded but not from fear. "Oh." She laughed and waved the walkie-talkie. "Silly me."

"You walked in a circle." He stroked her bare arm just above the elbow. His touch sent a tingle up her arm and into her racing heart. He pulled the walkie-talkie and pepper spray/flashlight out of her hand, slipping them both into her purse.

"I just got so caught up in the conversation." His proximity made her dizzy.

"So did I." Earl wrapped his arms around her waist and pulled her toward him. He bent close and kissed her.

Ginger's toes curled in her cross-trainers. Warmth flooded through her despite the night chill.

Twenty

Ginger slipped her Pontiac into a parking space by the mall just as her cell phone rang. "Hello."

"It's an MLS number."

She recognized Arleta's voice. "What's an MLS number?" She slung the travel purse Earl had given her over her shoulder. Just carrying it made her smile.

"The numbers that David had in his pocket and the numbers on Mr. Jackson's license plate. I told you I was thinking about putting my house on the market."

With the phone pressed against her ear, Ginger pushed the car door open. "Oh, Arleta, that's a wonderful idea."

"I need to let this place go, start another chapter of my life. Anyway, I am sitting here in the Little Bear Real Estate office with a lovely agent named Dana. She left Jackson-Wheeler two days ago. She said there has always been tension between Mr. Jackson and Mr. Wheeler, but it seems to be getting worse."

"Arleta, the MLS number?"

"Turns out when they list a house or a piece of land, they assign numbers to it. Those six numbers must be a piece of property Mr. Jackson was fond of to put it on his car like that."

Ginger walked through the mall parking lot, which was about half full. A white car drove by her and wedged into a parking space.

"I hear traffic. Where are you?"

"I'm at the mall." She slowed her pace. "I am going to buy a dress at full price."

"Why?"

"I have to prove something to my husband—that I can be adventurous—and buy what I really want, not just what's on sale."

"I don't understand. But it's your life."

Ginger stopped about thirty yards from the Macy's entrance. Her heart froze as she looked up over the roof.

"Listen, I gave Kindra a call. I really like her. She and I are going on campus to talk to David's friend in the archaeology department, Lyndon Chambers."

Ginger walked backward still looking up. Behind her, a car honked. She stepped to one side but continued to back up.

"Ginger, are you still there?"

"I'm here."

"Oh, you sound kind of far away, like you're thinking about something. We still need to figure out what we're going to do about Keaton and his girlfriend."

"I know." She kind of doubted that Renata was even his girlfriend anymore. Maybe that was the answer. Keaton wasn't about to talk, but maybe if they could get Renata alone...

"It all fits together somehow." Arleta's voice was strong and clear. "I'll let you know what we find on campus. Bye."

"Bye, Arleta." Ginger said after Arleta hung up. She tilted her head back. The radio tower was just visible over the high slanted roof. She shook her head. A lot could change in twenty years. Most of the surrounding neighborhood was different. The trees were gone. She was 90 percent sure that where the mall stood now was the same place David had stood and leaned against the pine tree in the photograph. The MLS number

SHARON DUNN

had to be for this property. Twenty years ago, Mr. Jackson had sold this land, owned it, or developed it. Maybe all three. It had to have been a huge moneymaker for him.

Mary Margret must have recognized the picture. She made the connection between the number in David's vest and the one on Jackson's license plate. That really wasn't enough of a revelation to kill someone over. David had had his picture taken on the property that later became the mall, and he had written down the property listing number.

Ginger walked a little faster to the entrance. She really wanted to show Earl that she could buy a dress at full price, but this new discovery distracted her. While she stood in the polished aisles of Macy's, she dialed Suzanne's number. Her throat went dry as she walked past the clearance racks. By the time she passed the 25 percent off section, her chest was tight. Her hand lifted toward the sales racks. Maybe she would just peek at the sales items...and then she would go buy her full price dress.

Suzanne picked up on the third ring. Ginger could hear children screaming and laughing in the background. "Hello?"

"It's Ginger. Can you do me a favor and go back to the courthouse to find out about the city commission meetings twenty years ago? But this time, see if you can find anything about the mall being built. Was there any kind of controversy, any conflict over the land? Look to see if David McQuire was involved or the college. I would go, but I have to pay full price for a dress."

Suzanne gasped. "Get out of town."

"It's the beginning of an adventure for me and Earl, and it's cheaper than his and hers Harleys, so I'm still saving money." That thought made her feel a little better about the task before her.

Suzanne snorted. "Three years ago, I used to pay full price for everything, all those designer labels for my kids just to make myself feel like a good mom. I had credit card debt out the kazoo. Everyone at church kept saying, 'You have to talk to Ginger. She'll get you on a budget. Talk to Ginger. Talk to Ginger.'"

"I was glad to help you." Ginger smiled at the memory of meeting Suzanne in the church foyer. Three years ago, the first unofficial member of the Bargain Hunters Network had had two children and one on the way.

"What you do, how you help people with their spending, is almost like a ministry, you know."

Ginger brushed her foot across the store floor. She'd never thought of what she did as being that important. "I don't know if it's a ministry. It's just that my mom never taught me sensible spending. I guess I don't like the idea of people having to figure it out alone like I had to."

She stood in front of the full price rack while her heart pounded and the inside of her elbows grew sticky with sweat. "You know, though, you should always buy what you truly want, not just because it's a good deal. It's just as bad to be a tightwad as it is to live beyond the money God provides." She touched a rayon blend dress that she'd admired when it was first put out on the floor.

"That's the hard part, isn't it? Figuring out what you really want, not just what fills an emotional hole." Suzanne's voice faded. Judging from the muffled tone, she had pulled the phone away and was saying something to one of her children. She came back on the line. "Before you helped me, I used to have clothes in the closet with the price tags still on them. I bought for the thrill of the purchase, the rush. Don't buy it if you aren't going to use it; that's my number one rule."

SHARON DUNN

"Like evening gowns you never wear?"

"What are you talking about?" On Suzanne's end of the conversation, gleeful screams and giggles of children threaded through sharp yips of a dog.

"Long story." Ginger touched cool rayon fabric. The dress had a pretty, subtle daisy print with a blue background. "Suzanne, this is the hardest thing I've ever done. My hand felt hot when I walked past the clearance rack. There is some sort of magnetic pull or something." She grabbed the tag on one of the full price dresses. Her vision blurred. All the air left her lungs. She'd never paid that much for a dress in her life. "I don't know if I can do this."

"Sure you can. I'll pray for you while I drive across town to the courthouse. I'll let you know what I find out."

Ginger hung up, slipped the phone into her travel purse, and pulled a different size 12 dress off the rack. She had tried this one on when it was first put out on the floor. It had fit her, but as always, she was waiting for it to be marked down.

She pressed the dress against her chest. *I will not look at the price tag. I will not look at the price tag.* She may as well have been walking through mud to get to the cashier. She glanced around, wondering if anyone was watching her haul this full price dress to the counter. Of course, she didn't see anyone she knew. All her friends hung out at the clearance rack.

The cashier, an indifferent-looking girl about Kindra's age, stared alternately at her fingernails and at the laughing woman behind the makeup counter.

Ginger felt like she was drowning in sweat. *This is for you, Earl.* She saw white dots. The room spun and the floor undulated, but this wasn't a migraine. This was something different. Invisible weight pressed on her chest, and she couldn't catch her breath. Maybe she wasn't meant to pay full price.

Cheaper than two Harleys. Cheaper than two Harleys. Let the adventure begin. Her vision narrowed; a black circle closed in around the salesgirl. *Focus, Ginger, focus. You can do this. Almost there.*

Laughter rose up from somewhere in the store. Ginger glanced around. The women at the 50 percent off rack were having such fun. She longed to join them.

She gripped the dress. Her body swayed slightly.

●●●●●●●●●●●●●●●●●●●●●●●●●●●●●●●●●●●●●●●

Kindra had a hard time keeping up with Arleta's long strides. With her arms swinging, the older woman booked across campus. Montavo Hall, a three-story brick building with small windows, was situated in the older part of campus surrounded by high cottonwoods. Even on a sunny day like today, the building was covered in shadows because of the trees.

Arleta patted her heart with an open hand. "My goodness, I haven't been on campus in years. Used to come up here all the time to eat lunch with David."

Kindra pushed open the door. "Third floor. I took a class from Professor Chambers freshman year, Intro to Anthropology."

The building had a musty smell. Ornate wooden railings stood in sharp contrast to the concrete stairs. Arleta took the lead up the stairs. "When David was teaching, the department was over in Lewis Hall."

"Lewis Hall? I don't think I've heard of it."

Only a few sputtering fluorescent lights illuminated the hallway.

"Some of the classes he taught were here in Montavo Hall." Arleta stopped on the stairs, gripping the railing, not even breathing heavy. "Lots of memories." She waved both hands as though trying to keep mosquitoes away. "But that's not where I live anymore."

Kindra was grateful Arleta had stopped for a moment, so she could catch her breath. "Nothing wrong with good memories," she panted.

Arleta burst up the remainder of the stairs. She stopped and turned to look at Kindra. "True, but you shouldn't make them your permanent address." She opened the door that led to the second floor.

Kindra was too out of breath to respond.

"Speaking of starting over, what do you think of my outfit? Ginger's been helping me pick out some new things."

The older woman looked hip in her animal print T-shirt with coordinated capris and white sneakers. "Ginger's good at that."

"Only twenty dollars for the entire outfit." Arleta did a half twirl. "She's a very smart shopper."

"That's how I met Ginger—shopping." Kindra shifted her weight from one foot to the other, wondering if she needed to share the whole story. "Sort of."

They traipsed across the earth-toned carpet. "What do you mean, sort of?"

"It was about a year ago. I had just started college, and I was getting a lot of pressure from my parents to do well in school. I found this underhanded way to rebel and deal with the stress: I shoplifted."

This story is about who I used to be. I'm different now. She took a deep breath and plowed forward. "Ginger caught me stuffing a blouse in my tote bag."

The older woman stopped walking and turned to face her. Kindra waited for that flash of judgment she so often got when she shared this story. The kindness in Arleta's expression gave Kindra the courage to continue.

"Ginger came over and told me there was a better way. I knew she was a Christian from overhearing her conversation with the woman she was with, who turned out to be Mary Margret. So when she said there was a better way, I thought she was going to whip out her Bible and scream 'repent.' Instead, she made me put the blouse back and took me to a different shop that had close to the same blouse for a lot less. When I told her I didn't have any money, she bought the blouse for me."

"So you haven't always been a Christian?"

"It's been not quite a year for me. Ginger kept taking me shopping with her, teaching me how to get nice clothes for cheap. I came from a family where you only felt loved if you got A's on your report card. When Ginger bought that blouse for me, after she knew I was a shoplifter...it was one of the kindest things anybody had ever done for me. I deserved to be turned in. After she did that, I understood God's mercy."

Arleta studied her for a moment. "I guess I never thought about the existence of God, let alone His mercy. David and I were so busy." Arleta put a fist on her narrow hip. "Isn't that funny? To be this old and never to have thought about God."

Kindra shrugged. "It happens when it needs to happen."

Arleta nodded. "You might be right. I never felt empty until I lost my David."

Kindra faced the older woman and rested her palm on her own heart. "I'm no expert or anything. But I think this empty place is where God fits."

"I'll have to think about that." She touched Kindra's elbow. "Let's go find Professor Chambers."

They took the last flight of stairs and entered a hallway with worn, nearly black carpet. Kindra theorized that at one time the carpet had been classified as dark blue, but now it was anyone's guess. "He's on the end." She walked past several gray-blue doors.

"Chambers's office used to be in Lewis Hall." Arleta peeked through an open door and glanced up and down the hallway. Kindra suspected that Arleta was making note of the changes since she had been there. "Lewis Hall is quite a unique building. I'll show it to you if we have time."

"That sounds like fun," Kindra said. "Chambers only teaches that one freshman class. Like I said, he's older than dirt." She winked at Arleta.

Arleta shook her head and rolled her eyes.

At the end of the windowless hallway, a blue-gray door with the word *Chambers* on the placard was slightly ajar. Kindra tapped and the door swung open.

The man sitting at the desk resembled Einstein having a bad hair day, if that was possible. His hair stood up like Einstein's, but it was wiry and stringy instead of fuzzy. The office was a conglomerate of books, rocks, bone fragments, and boxes of Bazooka bubble gum. Professor Chambers leaned over a stack of papers, blew a bubble, and popped it. He wore Dockers and a pressed oxford shirt.

When she had taken his class, Kindra's first impression of him was that there had been some sort of bizarre accident at the plastic surgeon's office. Chambers's face was wrinkled and old, but his body was that of a man thirty years younger, not muscular but lean, without a tummy paunch or bent shoulders.

Arleta leaned into the office. "Lyndon?"

The professor raised his head. Dark brown eyes stood out against chalky skin. Recognition spread across his face.

"Well I'll be. Arleta McQuire."

Arleta giggled like a teenager. "You remember me."

"How could I forget David's lovely bride."

He turned toward Kindra. "And I remember this one, too. Argued with me about evolution."

"I always waited until after class." Kindra brought her heels together and stood up a little straighter, leaning back. *I need not to bounce three times. People are going to start calling me Tigger.* "I didn't want to disrespect you."

"You were a pleasure to have in class. I like thinkers." Lyndon rose to his feet. He grabbed a box of bubble gum off the shelf and offered them some. Both Kindra and Arleta grabbed a piece.

"What on earth brings you two over to the dark side of campus?"

"Actually, Professor Chambers—" Kindra peeled the wrapper off her gum—"we have some questions to ask you about David, about something that happened twenty years ago."

"Twenty years ago, huh? I still got it up here." He pointed to his head. "Quiz me."

"It would have been about five years before David died." Arleta took a step into the office. "Do you remember what he was working on then? I have the feeling he kept something from me. We think it had to do with the city commission."

"Twenty years ago. 1986. City commission." He stood nodding for a moment; then he pulled a leather-bound notebook off his shelf and flipped through it. He touched an entry with his finger. "I was working on the dig in eastern Montana, which would mean that David..." Light flashed in his eyes and then his expression flattened. "David was working on the Indian ruins outside of town."

"Indians ruins outside of Three Horses? Why don't I remember that?"

Lyndon gazed at Arleta. "I've got some hot water. Would you like a cup of tea, Arleta? How about you, Ms. Hall?"

Arleta put a hand on her hip. "Lyndon, you are stalling."

"David wanted to protect you." He leafed through the papers he had been reading. "That's why he didn't tell you."

"He should have known he could share anything with me."

"This was heartbreaking to him. Twenty years ago, David thought he had found a place where Shoshone may have camped before Three Horses was even a trading center. The Ponderosa pines had cultural scarring on them."

Before the question had time to form in Kindra's mind, Arleta answered it. "Some tribes used to peel the bark off of trees where they camped; the cambium layer underneath is sweet and good to eat. It left scars hundreds of years old on the trees and usually meant artifacts were in the surrounding ground."

Lyndon unwrapped a piece of bubble gum for himself. "You should have been an associate professor yourself, Arleta. Sharp as a tack."

"I was always happy helping David with his work."

"That photo in your album. With David and the trees. The one you couldn't place." Kindra leaned against the door frame. Professor Chambers's office smelled like old books.

Arleta nodded.

Lyndon put the gum in his mouth and chewed for a moment. "They were all ready to break ground on the property for the mall, cut down the trees. David had to go before the city commission to prove that the land had historical significance. The findings were just preliminary, but he thought he put together a pretty good argument, at least for stalling development and letting him dig around."

Chambers shook his head and pressed his lips together. "He was trying to change things in the eleventh hour. There are all kinds of federal regulations protecting areas of historical significance, especially Native American sites.

If the site was suspected of having historical importance, they stood to lose a ton of money if they couldn't build there." Lyndon pushed a chair out from the wall and motioned for Arleta to sit down. "David was the only one who noticed the trees."

"That was my David." Arleta slumped into the chair. "What happened?"

"He lost. The development went through. It devastated him, Arleta. He was getting toward the end of the active part of his career. Every archaeologist wants to have that one big discovery on their résumé."

Arleta swiveled in the chair. Her hands rested on her flat stomach, and the sparkle had gone out her eyes. "Everything David worked on was important."

"I don't remember the exact sequence of events, but David began to think that some bribery of city commissioners took place on the part of the developer. He started to ask around."

"Did he find out anything?"

"All of this was right before he died, so that colors my memory. He was my friend, my good friend." Chambers chewed his gum. "It seems as though one of the commissioners came to him. He was dying or moving to Florida, I can't remember, but I do remember that David said something about getting a written confession."

· ·

"Ma'am, you've dropped a dress on the floor. Ma'am?"

The twentysomething store clerk leaned over the counter and pointed. Ginger didn't know it was possible to scrunch up your face like that. Irritation tainted the clerk's voice. So much for those customer service seminars.

Ginger leaned over to pick up the dress. "I'm sorry." She expelled a nervous laugh. "I must have been having a hot flash or something." She knew full well it wasn't a hot flash. The thought of having to pay full price for something had made her dizzy. As she picked up the dress, she caught a glimpse of the price tag.

"Ma'am, are you all right? You look like you're about to throw up."

Her eyes remained glued to the price tag. Her breathing was shallow.

"Do you need to sit down or something?" the girl snapped.

She couldn't do it. She couldn't pay full price. She just plain wasn't that adventurous. "I think I'll be okay once I put this back on the rack."

Ginger trudged back to the full price rack and hung up the dress, averting her eyes so she wouldn't have to look at the price tag again. On what planet could she ever bring herself to pay more for a dress than she had paid for the down payment on her first car?

Not on this one, that's for sure. Sorry, Earl.

Maybe what she needed was a latte. Kindra said the drink helped her focus. A few minutes to clear her head and work up the strength to buy that dress might help. Ginger wandered out into the mall toward the coffee shop. After she ordered her drink, she sat in a booth. When she checked her messages, there were none. It was nearly five; Suzanne must have made it to the courthouse by now.

· ·

The government employee behind the counter stared at Suzanne. She was a fiftyish woman with a hairstyle similar to the original Betty Crocker and too much rouge on her cheeks.

The woman did a head-to-toe inspection of Suzanne. Apparently, she had never seen a pregnant lady before.

Suzanne repeated her request. "The transcripts of the city commission meetings aren't where they were the last time I was here. The ones from twenty years ago."

Prior to Suzanne interrupting her, the woman had been stamping a pile of papers with insane efficiency. Her slowness in responding to Suzanne suggested that the interruption was an incredible inconvenience. Heaven forbid that a citizen would expect help from a government employee.

The clerk continued to stare at her. All she needed were some old city commission records. This wasn't a problem that required bringing in Mensa for a consultation. Suzanne touched her stomach. She really needed to sit down. The baby was kicking like a Rockette at Christmastime. Her forehead and cheeks pulsed with fever. Having to stand while Betty Crocker composed an answer only made her feel sicker.

Finally, the clerk opened her mouth to speak. "Records that old have been moved up to the top floor. They are being computerized."

Oh great, another flight of stairs. Suzanne consoled herself with the thought that she'd get this done and then go home and catch a nap. Greg had taken the kids to the park, so the house would be quiet.

"It's just around the corner and up the stairs. The intern will direct you to the file or recording you need."

Suzanne wobbled out the door, across the marble floor, and past the display that featured Lewis and Clark artifacts. The glass cases were filled with bones and fur and yellow documents. She gripped the railing and pushed herself up the stairs. Yep, that nap was going to feel good.

There was only one office on the fourth floor. Suzanne leaned against the doorway and sighed heavily. A man with a boyish face sat behind a metal desk piled high with papers. He jumped when he saw her.

"Oh, are you lost?"

The man looked like he was twelve. His reading material consisted of a comic book, which only added to the impression that he wasn't eligible to vote yet. He was probably a college student doing an internship, but the pudgy cheeks and fat fingers made him appear much younger.

"No, I'm not lost." Suzanne's forehead burned. He must not get too many people wanting to examine old records. "I'm looking for information on city commission meetings twenty years ago. I don't know if you have an indexing system or what. I need to find out about the building of the mall, a real estate agent named Jackson, and an archaeology professor named David McQuire."

The child clerk stood up, scraping his chair across linoleum. "We organize things by years." He moved toward a computer that rested on a separate waist-high counter. "They hired me to get everything in order up here. If the funding comes through," he pointed to the rows of file cabinets, "all of this will be put on CDs and logged into a computer so you can access it from our website. Right now, we have written transcripts and recordings."

The tightening ache in her calves almost overwhelmed her. "Wow, that sounds like an impressive project."

Apparently happy with her response, the clerk nodded and tapped a few keys on the computer. "I remember seeing something about the mall." He slipped past her nearly to the end of the file cabinets and opened a drawer. "It seems like it was sometime in the summer of '86."

Suzanne felt suddenly light-headed. "You know what? I really need to sit down."

"Oh, oh, sorry." The man moved toward her and pulled his chair out from around the other side of the desk. "Please forgive my inconsideration." He placed the file on the desks. "Can I get you anything? Glass of water?"

Suzanne lowered herself into the chair. "I just need to sit down. Those stairs took a lot out of me. What is your name anyway?"

"Todd Enger."

"Well, Todd, I'm Suzanne Thomas. I appreciate your helping me with this."

"It's my job." He fanned out the files. "Each file has a month of meetings. There is an agenda at the beginning of each meeting, so you know what was covered."

She grabbed two of the files, and he worked his way through the other set of three.

After a few minutes of reading, he said, "Here it is." He flipped through the file. "Looks like it was on the agenda for three meetings. At one point David McQuire testified that the mall property might have archaeological significance based on what he had found on some trees on the site. The city commission voted three to two to let the development go through. And you're right. Mr. Jackson was the owner and developer of the land."

Suzanne grabbed a piece of notebook paper out of her purse. "A three to two vote?"

"There are five commissioners. In order for the city to approve a subdivision or even someone adding on to their garage in a way that goes against city standards, at least three commissioners have to vote yes. Some of it is routine, just a matter of jumping through the right hoops, and some of it is very controversial."

Suzanne leaned forward in her chair. She was having a hard time getting a deep breath. "So maybe I should write down the names of the city commissioners."

"Sure." He flipped through the pages again. "I'll read them to you." He glanced up at her. "Are you sure you're all right? You look really pale."

She poised her pen over the notebook page. "I just need a nap. Give me the names," she panted.

"In 1986, the commissioners were Jennifer Mack-Olsen, Jeffrey Stenengarter—"

"Stenengarter. What a weird name." She leaned toward Todd to check the spelling. Her stomach muscles tightened.

"The Stenengarter family has been in Montana politics forever." Todd continued to read. "Elias Holms, Keith Wheeler—"

"Wheeler really? As in Jackson-Wheeler Real Estate?"

Todd shrugged. "Could be."

Suzanne wrote down the name. Her hands were moist. Ginger could figure out what the connection was. "And the last guy?"

Todd chuckled "You are going to love this. The last city commissioner is named Joe Smith."

Suzanne finished writing and looked up. "Todd, you have been very helpful. Could you do one more thing for me?"

"Sure, Mrs. Thomas. What is it?"

"Could you call an ambulance? I think I am having my baby right now."

Twenty-One

"There it is, Lewis Hall." Arleta pointed to a two-story boxy building masked by the taller surrounding structures.

"I didn't know this even existed." Kindra peeked around the trunk of a large oak. "Do they hold classes here?"

Walking across campus with Arleta was like having a private tour guide. The sky had turned a dusky gray by the time Arleta had given Kindra a history of almost every building on campus along with personal stories.

Outside of Lewis Hall, Arleta gazed up at the tall trees. "I didn't go back and get the key from Professor Chambers to show you the classrooms." A subtle smile enhanced the brightness of her features.

They walked arm in arm down the stone walkway. The canopy of trees made things even darker. Branches creaked and flapped in the wind. Leaves shook like cheerleaders' pom-poms. An image from a children's book flashed through Kindra's head. Hansel and Gretel being lured to the witch's house with the enticement of candy. What a weird thing to think about.

"Do you think Professor Chambers was right about David getting a written confession from one of the city commissioners?" Kindra asked.

"I just can't believe David kept it from me. For the last five years of his life, it seemed like the wind went out of his sail, like he lost his passion for his work. I just thought it was because he was close to retirement."

They walked up the wide stairs. The building looked like a house that had been converted to a lecture hall. The only distinct exterior feature was two large bay windows on either side of the stairs.

"The confession sure isn't with anything Ginger has. She went all through that photo album and vest, and it obviously wasn't in that shell box."

"Maybe that's why they were looking in my house." Arleta put the key in the keyhole. "Maybe they thought Ginger had given it back to me after they searched her house and couldn't find it." Arleta pushed the door open.

The entryway featured mosaic tile that led to a spiral staircase done in a dark wood. Kindra's nose wrinkled at the dusty smell. On the main floor were doors, two on each side. Probably classrooms.

The huge chandelier hanging from the eighteen-foot ceiling caught Kindra's attention. Their footsteps echoed on the floor.

"This was one of the first buildings constructed when the college was established at the turn of the century. I think it was a residence before that. When David first got his teaching appointment, his office was upstairs. Come on, I'll show you."

Arleta swept up the stairs. Kindra followed. Would she forever be racing breathlessly up stairs chasing the athletic older woman? Arleta reached the top and disappeared around a corner.

Kindra looked down at the empty entryway before following. They'd left the door slightly open. A slim sliver of light cast a geometric shadow on the floor below.

Arleta had gone into a room that was piled high with boxes, which she had already started to move. A patina of dust on the floor suggested that the room hadn't been used in a while.

"We were like schoolkids when we were first married." Arleta set an opened box on the floor.

Kindra peered into the box. Sweatshirts with the college logo, of all things. The next box contained a stack of papers. Kindra picked a paper off the top. Three stapled pages for English 221, spring semester 1985. She read the name at the top. "I wonder if Kevin Gage wonders why he never got his paper back. He got a B-plus."

"Here it is." Arleta's voice skipped up half an octave. In the wall, the words *David loves Arleta* were carved. "How junior high, huh?"

"I think it's neat. You guys loved each other enough to be so silly."

Arleta laced her fingers together and gazed at the ceiling. "Kindra, this trip across campus has been therapeutic for me." She stood up straight. "Meeting you and Ginger and Suzanne has been good for me."

"Glad we could be of help. You must miss David very much."

"Less each day." Arleta raised a fist in the air. "I am back in the land of the living."

"How did he die?"

Arleta got a faraway look in her eyes, as if a scene were playing out before her. "He was killed in a car accident."

Downstairs, the door slammed shut. Heavy footsteps pounded across tile and up the stairs. Some sort of physiological security system activated an instinctual tightening in Kindra's rib cage. It was too late in the day for classes. "Who could be—?"

Ginger pushed her fourth latte aside and rested her head on the table. Who was she kidding? No amount of caffeine was going to give her the fortitude to pay full price for anything. She'd just have to tell Earl she couldn't do it. Maybe there was some other way she could start her life of adventure, something easier, like nailing oatmeal to the wall.

Shoulders drooping, Ginger gathered up her purse and trudged through the mall. On a whim, she stopped at a phone booth and looked up Keaton Lustrum's phone number. It surprised her that it was listed. She wrote down the number. If Renata was the weak link, maybe she could call and hope the woman answered.

Outside, the sky had turned gray. The mall parking lot was nearly empty. As she walked to her car, Ginger pulled her phone out of her purse and glanced at the number she had written down.

"Hey, I remember you."

Beside her car was a truck that said *The Housewife's Helper* on the side. A man and a woman in matching blue and red checked shorts stood with their arms around each other. It wasn't their faces that triggered Ginger's memory. The truck, with its reference to a business, was what she connected with that day shortly after Mary Margret's death.

"Frank and Beth?" asked Ginger. Bobbleheads and a Mickey Mouse fishing pole.

"Hey, you remembered. I'm glad we ran into you." Frank stepped forward. He still had a full head of black hair and the farmer's tan, but something was different. Maybe he had lost weight.

Beth sidled up beside her husband and grabbed Ginger's hand. "We owe you such an apology for the way we acted that day in front of you and your friend." Her appearance had changed, too. Had they both been on a fitness kick or something?

Frank wrapped his arm around his wife's waist. "That day was a turning point for us. We were fighting about stuff all the time, for most of our marriage." He leaned closer to Ginger as though sharing a confidence. "I got rid of all my deer antlers."

"We did mean things to each other with stuff. Frank would buy an expensive piece of electronics without talking to me, so I would go out and buy a pair of three-hundred-dollar shoes just to get even." Still shaking Ginger's hand, Beth leaned a little closer. "When I threw his bobbleheads out, I was trying to hurt him. Very passive-aggressive."

While Frank and Beth plowed through a dialogue that belonged on *Dr. Phil*, Ginger tried to grasp the concept of paying three hundred dollars for a pair of shoes.

"It was all this private little war, until that day you and your friend saw how ugly we had become to each other." Frank leaned against the tailgate of his truck. "You do things in private, but when someone else sees it..."

Beth finally let go of Ginger's hand. "Now we talk about purchases and agree on what we'll buy. We're a team."

"It's all just stuff anyway." Frank held up his hands for emphasis. "My wife is more important."

"We decluttered our lives like we've been trying to do for years." Beth smiled.

Frank grinned and nodded, looking a great deal like the bobbleheads he'd recently parted with.

That was what was different. Her memory of them that day was of two people with tight fists and tight faces. None of that tension was in their expressions or body language.

"Matter of fact." Frank leaned into the truck bed and grabbed something from underneath a tarp. "We got a load ready to take to the dump. I don't need this fishing pole anymore. It hasn't worked right since I took it back anyway. The line keeps jamming, never used to do that." Frank placed the pole into Ginger's hand. "Beth said your friend bought it for her grandson. I hope he gets some use out of it."

Ginger's lips parted, but she couldn't think of anything to say.

Beth and Frank got into his truck. Frank rolled down the window as they drove past Ginger. "Thanks for everything."

After a long moment of still trying to fathom how anyone could pay three hundred dollars for a pair of shoes, Ginger closed her mouth and shook her head.

She pressed in Keaton's phone number on her cell. *Please let Renata answer, please.* The phone rang three times.

"Allo."

Ginger's heart jumped. "Is this Renata?"

Long silence. "Yes."

"Don't hang up. This is Ginger. You were at my house yesterday."

"Keaton would not want me to talk to you."

Ginger bit her lip. She needed to choose her words carefully. "But you want to talk to me. You're not happy with Keaton."

"I am object to him. Like his Lexus or his vacation condo. Now he want me to go back to France so he can get a new object."

"Did you...did you see my friend Mary Margret?"

Renata took in a deep breath. "Keaton said I break the law. He said I would get in trouble and be sent back to France. So I am silent. I am not dumb. I see that he is thinking of sending me back to France anyway. So I make him do the same. We are even. I break and enter. He break and enter. "

"My friend, what happened with my friend?" She had tried to purge her voice of any impatience.

Again, there was a long pause. "You want to know. I tell you. I want Keaton to hurt, like he hurt me. I have Mary Margret's card, right?"

Ginger tapped her fist on the trunk. "Right."

"I go to Mary Margret's house to get the box. She race out in her blue car with a man. Keaton put much pressure on me to get the box back so I follow, thinking I will ask her. They drive long time. At first, they get out of the car, he push her around, I see she is in danger so I follow to help. They go to his fancy house in the forest. I break and enter to help her. I hide. They did not see me. She escape in her car. He follow in his. I call Keaton. He say, 'Get out, get out, you break the law.' He is worried not about me, but his reputation."

Ginger couldn't believe what she was hearing. "Renata, could you identify the man if you saw him?"

"Maybe. I see him only short time. He big. Big belt buckle. Big cowboy hat."

That was half the men in Three Horses. "How about the house—could you identify the house?"

"Will this hurt Keaton? You know, he has been giving friend at DMV money for silence about the motorbikes."

Ginger rolled her eyes. Keaton thought everyone could be bought. Unfortunately, most people could be. "We will find a way to make all of this hurt him."

"The house was up winding roads and dark, but I think I could find it."

Ginger picked up the fishing pole Frank had given her and fiddled with it. "I'm at the mall right now, Renata. Can you get here and take me to the house?"

"*Bon*, my sister come with me."

The reel on the fishing pole rattled. "I will be waiting in the corner by the car wash, sitting on my car trunk. It's an older Pontiac."

"I be there."

Ginger hung up. She sat on the trunk of her car while the sky grew darker and the last few cars pulled out of the front lot. She had to tell somebody the news.

She leaned the pole against the bumper of her car and checked her cell phone. Still no message from Suzanne. She tried Kindra's cell. Nothing. No one was answering at Arleta's either. Hmmm. The law of averages dictated she should be able to reach at least one of them. She hopped off the trunk.

With the phone still in her hand and her purse strap resting in the crook of her elbow, she lifted the fishing pole to put it in the trunk. The reel was really loose. She shook it. Maybe that was why it hadn't worked for Frank. She set her purse and phone on the trunk. It probably just screwed back on. She twisted it. The reel fell into two parts in her hand. Earl would be on her case for that one. She couldn't even remember the lefty loosy, righty tighty rule.

When she stared inside the reel, a piece of paper slightly larger than a postage stamp was wedged around the spool of fishing line. She maneuvered it out. New creases in the older brittle paper made it fragile. Once she'd unfolded it, her eyes went to the signature at the bottom: Joe Smith. That had to be a made-up name. The date at the top read June 15, 1991.

To whom it may concern:

 I am writing this letter because I am not in good health and desire to be free of the guilt that has weighed me down for five years. I sought out Professor David McQuire because he sensed five years ago that the city

commission's decision not to allow him to investigate
the possibility of the archaeological significance at the
mall property site was not right.

The developer and owner of the property, Mr. Jackson,
offered me, Keith Wheeler, and Jeffrey Stenengarter a
substantial amount of money to push the mall develop-
ment through without delay. I always saw myself as an
honest man, but even I had a price tag on my soul.
Because death is just around the corner for me, I don't
want this on my conscience. I can only hope that justice
will result from this confession. If the site did have histor-
ical significance, that has been lost forever.

Joe Smith

Ginger looked up from the letter. Renata should have gotten here by now. Was this confession what her friend had been
killed for? It seemed like there would be some kind of statute
of limitations on bribery. Mary Margret had put the fishing
pole on top of the basket to call attention to it. Ginger hadn't
figured out that part of her friend's "note." But who thinks to
take a fishing pole apart?

She could only guess at the sequence of events, the order in
which Mary Margret had connected the dots. Had she found the
handwritten MLS number and recognized it as the one on
Jackson's license plate? She probably knew it was the MLS number for the mall property. Maybe she had mentioned that to
Jackson, not realizing the significance of what she was saying until
she found the confession. The confession had probably been
stuffed in one of the pockets of the photo album, or it could have
been in one of the vest pockets. Mary Margret wouldn't have been
foolish enough to ask Mr. Jackson directly if the confession was
true. Something she said or did must have clued him in.

SHARON DUNN

A slight breeze ruffled the paper in her hand. She gripped it tighter. The police. She needed to call the police. She stared at the phone. Tammy had said that this somehow connected back to the police department. She didn't know Tammy's home number or how she would reach her directly if she was working.

The sky darkened. *Renata better hurry up and get here.*

If Wheeler wanted to cover up the bribery and save his business reputation, he had motive, too. Certainly the law couldn't go after them after twenty years. She shook her head. It still didn't seem like reason enough to kill Mary Margret.

Ginger slipped the confession into the secret compartment of her travel purse. She needed to call Earl first, to hear his voice. She dialed and waited. The phone rang two, three, four times. Of course he was in the shop. The message clicked on. After listening to her own voice she said, "Earl, I found something. I think it connects to Mary Margret's murder. I am waiting here in the mall parking lot. The French woman knows the house where Mary Margret was taken. I'm—"

A hand squeezed Ginger's shoulder, and her phone was yanked out of her hand. "Why don't you show me what you found?" Ginger turned around slowly. Keith Wheeler, dressed in his usual cowboy boots, Levi's, and Western shirt, grinned. He was minus a hat, but Wheeler had to be the big man Renata had made reference to. Wheeler turned the phone off.

"Nothing. I didn't find anything." She could barely croak out the words. "It's just a...game my husband and I play."

"Ah, Mrs. Salinski, you are not a good liar. I heard what you just said. Is it in the purse? I saw you put something in there." His eyes rested on the fishing pole. "Is that where she hid it? Your friend glanced back at the basket right before we left. I started to get a feeling, so I sent.... Then you had to go and take the stuff. Mary Margret told me she had hidden it on her garage sale route." His face muscles tensed. "She spent half the day leading me on a wild-goose chase."

If he was with Mary Margret, Wheeler couldn't have been the one who chased her that Saturday. "And then you killed her."

Wheeler raised an eyebrow but did not respond.

Anger like she had never known flared through her muscles. Mr. Jackson *and* Mr. Wheeler were involved in Mary Margret's death. And maybe the other city commissioner, what was his name? Stenengarter. Where had she heard that name before? Wheeler stood close enough to grab her if she tried to run.

He snatched the broken fishing pole. "This wasn't with the stuff when we finally found the garage sale things."

There was that "we" again. *Found the garage sale things* must have been his euphemism for breaking and entering. They must have broken in a second time. The first time the garage sale stuff had been with her. Ginger straightened her back. A lucky accident or God's protection?

After he peered inside the broken reel, he tossed the pole. "What did you do with it?" He grabbed the purse from her and rifled through her stuff, dropping her compact and her coupon envelope on the asphalt. His face scrunched when he pulled out the flashlight/pepper spray, but he put it back. "You will tell me what you've done with the confession."

He shoved the purse back toward her. "I'm not going to let that letter slip through my hands again. It opens a Pandora's box, and I have my business to think about. How about we go up to my office while I have someone search your car? The mall is closed. There won't be anyone to hear you scream."

Ginger crossed her arms. "Excuse me, I'm not going." Her voice trembled. She glanced around the parking lot hopeful that she would see Renata.

He opened the flap of his blazer. The handle of a knife stuck out of an inside pocket. He yanked her arm, twisted it behind her, and pressed upward.

Ginger gasped. "Maybe I will go with you." She clutched her purse to her chest with her free hand.

The closest person was a man way across the lot. With the wind blowing, he probably wouldn't even hear her yell for help. Ginger listened to the sound of her own footsteps clicking on concrete and tried to think of what to do next.

Twenty-Two

Suzanne lay in her hospital bed and counted holes in the ceiling tiles. How much time would pass before Greg processed her request?

"You want what?" His voice floated to her in rippling waves.

"I said I want my cell phone, Greg."

"Suz, you're in labor."

"I have an important call to make. And I need to make it—" Radiating pain, starting in her uterus, spiraled through her body. "Now, Greg!"

He ran over to the pile of stuff that had been brought in with Suzanne. He pulled her cell out of the purse, dropped and picked it up twice, and trotted back to her. "Here, honey, here."

She held her hand up, indicating that he would have to wait a moment. She breathed through the contraction. *Find your happy place. There it is. A store where everything is 90 percent off retail.* The pain subsided.

She lay her head back down on the hospital pillow, turning slightly to enjoy the clean smell. "How far apart are the contractions?"

Greg checked his stopwatch. "Ten minutes." He handed her the cell.

Ten minutes. She had ten minutes to call Ginger and let her know what she had found at the courthouse. Suzanne held the phone above her and pushed buttons. Ginger wasn't

SHARON DUNN

answering her cell. No one picked up at home either. She tried Kindra. No answer. Even Arleta wasn't picking up.

"Honey, will you find me a phone book? Look up Tammy Welstad for me."

"Sure. Can I get you anything? Water? Cold cloth for your head? A sandwich?" Greg smoothed the sheets around her and patted her pillow.

Suzanne wasn't sure why Greg was so nervous. They had been through this three times before. She spoke in a measured fashion, enunciating each word, the same technique she used with her five-year-old. "I don't want a sandwich. I'm in labor. You know the drill. Before you look up the number, can you look in my purse for a list of names I wrote down on notebook paper? It should be on top."

After rooting through her purse, he extended the paper toward her. She grabbed his hand and pulled him close to her face. "It's gonna be okay. Can you relax?"

He grinned a silly half smile. "I'm never gonna get used to this part."

She touched his cheek. "I think this should be the last one. I love my babies, but I'm tired."

"You say that every time, Suz."

"This time I mean it."

Greg grabbed the phone book on the nightstand and flipped through it. He rattled off the numbers while Suzanne pressed them in. Tammy picked up right away. Suzanne explained why she was calling her and not Ginger and then read off a list of names and explained the mall connection.

"Stenengarter." Tammy repeated. "He used to be a city commissioner? Twenty years ago he would have been barely out of his teens. What is the first name?"

"Jeffrey."

"Oh, his dad. Business owner. Former state senator, thinking about running again."

"I'd love to chat, Tammy." She lifted her head slightly from the hospital bed. An intense twisting heat whirled in her abdomen, threatening to become a full-blown tornado. "But I have to have a baby right now."

She hung up just as the pain folded into a tight knot and exploded through her.

....

"Please, you're hurting me." Searing white stabs penetrated Ginger's arm.

Wheeler pushed up even harder on her elbow. He had directed her to the back of the mall, where there were fewer streetlights. Without turning her head, she surveyed the parking lot. Nobody, not a single person, moved through the lot. But there were still a few cars. If she walked slowly, maybe a clerk or a store manager who had stayed late would come out of one of the back doors. And maybe they wouldn't think she was nuts if she screamed for help.

"So do you manage the mall? Is that why you have an office?"

"I own the mall." He pulled the knife, still in its sheath, out of his inside pocket. An action she ironically welcomed because it meant that he let up on her arm. Her triceps and shoulder burned.

Wheeler was probably Mary Margret's killer. If time had run out on the bribery, maybe the discovery of the confession made them fear that something else would surface. Wheeler had said it opened a Pandora's box. But what? From Earl's episodes of *The Rockford Files*, she remembered that the only crime that time didn't run out on was murder.

Ginger assessed the possibilities for cover if she made a run for it. The only option was a Dumpster about forty yards away. Not close enough. Wheeler was probably not only stronger than her but faster. "I thought Mr. Jackson owned the mall."

"Did you learn all that by reading the confession you say you don't have?" His hot breath stained her cheek.

Even in the dim light, his eyes held a flash of intensity that suggested the level of violence he might be capable of. How had Mr. Wheeler ended up with the mall if it had been Mr. Jackson's investment? "I think I read it in a newspaper. The same one Mary Margret was looking at."

"Your friend was quite the little Miss Marple." He released her from his grip and pushed her toward a door that said Employees Only.

His cell phone rang. Before answering the phone, he unsheathed the knife, backed her up against the door, and held the knife an inch from her stomach. "'Lo." He kept his eyes on her, twirling the knife. "You what?" He spat the words out. His cheeks and nose crimsoned. "You were just supposed to follow them and watch. I've got the one who has it."

The voice on the other end of the line was frantic enough for Ginger to hear but not discern words.

"You messed up again. We can't let them go. The trail has to be wiped out." Wheeler pressed his lips together. "You tell me. All of this would have died if it hadn't been for your big mistake fifteen years ago." He pressed the end button and shook his head.

"Who can't you let go?" Judging from the vein popping out on Wheeler's forehead, something had gone wrong.

"Change of plans. We are not going to my office until I can put this fire out." His snarled as he punched in another number. "Are you in the shop? I have someone who needs to be babysat." He hung up.

He shoved a key card into her hand. Its sharp edge sliced across her palm. "Open the door and step inside; then go two doors down." Wheeler raised the knife a little higher.

Ginger swiped the key. He wasn't going to put that knife down anytime soon. "I thought arrows were your weapon of choice."

"You talk too much." He grabbed the key card out of her hand. "Now open the door and go inside."

Ginger pushed down on the cold steel handle, eased open the door, and stared into blackness. She bent across the threshold but couldn't see a thing.

He leaned inside and clicked on a light, revealing metal shelves stacked with boxes reaching to the ceiling.

Wheeler pushed her inside. "Are you waiting for an invitation?"

"Are you coming with me?" Not that she wanted to pick out curtains with him or anything.

He pressed the tip of the knife into her upper back. The nerve endings in her neck flared. "Go on, hurry." As if he couldn't cause her more pain, he pressed the knife harder. Not enough to break the skin, just enough to remind her who had the upper hand. "What's the holdup? Are you having a hot flash or something?"

In addition to being a criminal, Mr. Wheeler was rude. No manners at all. "I am only a few years older than you, so I suggest you quit making insulting references to my age." Rude, rude, rude.

"All you got to do is tell me where that confession is, and you can go." He lowered his voice. "I have to deal with this problem Jackson has created."

He led her past the tall metal shelves. One of the boxes was labeled "basketballs," and a kayak sat on a lower shelf. This had to be the storage room for the sporting goods store. That's where she had heard the name. The Stenengarter who owned this store must have been the other city commissioner. So they had both gotten a piece of the mall. Wheeler just got a bigger piece.

He pushed her through the storage room until they came to a door that said Big Sky Sporting Goods. This time he swiped the key card himself and shoved Ginger into the well-lit store.

Mr. Suave, Jeffrey Stenengarter, leaned against the checkout counter. His white hair looked less than perfect, flatter. Sallowness had permeated his sixtysomething skin.

"Just got back to the shop. I had to have a little—" he coughed and cleared his throat—"talk with my son."

"Jackson has gone and done it again." Wheeler's voice was low and smoldering, like a rottweiler's growl.

Stenengarter picked up a nail file and proceeded to clean and buff his nails. "Why should I be surprised? He was jumpy from the beginning." A crooked smile crossed the older man's face. "He didn't know what he was dealing with when he came to us."

Wheeler pushed Ginger toward Stenengarter. She still clutched her purse to her chest, which was a good place for it. Her heart was thudding so intensely that the pulsations were probably visible through her shirt.

"Keep an eye on her. I'm sure she'll feel like talking when I get back."

Stenengarter swung an arm around to the inside of the checkout counter. His actions caused the jail bar sliding door that led out to the rest of the mall to open. Wheeler stepped through. Stenengarter repeated the same action. The door eased across a railing and clicked shut.

Stenengarter smiled a politician's plastic smile. "That door is locked." He strode across the linoleum. "And I'm about to lock the door you just came through. You might as well get comfortable because you are not going anywhere."

SHARON DUNN

From the booth in the coffee shop where she sat, Tammy heard the voice behind her. Bradley Deaver's words beat on her back like a hard rain.

"They're on to you."

On a piece of scratch paper she'd pulled from her purse, she'd written the names Jeffrey Stenengarter, Paul Stenengarter, Keith Wheeler, and Evan Jackson. Then on the opposite side of the paper, she'd written *mall dev.* and drawn a line from those words to all four of the names. The older Stenengarter had been a city commissioner. The captain had to be protecting his father, covering up something.

Tammy closed her eyes and leaned her head against the booth. Deaver had a habit of sneaking up on people that was almost creepy. Only a few patrons mingled around the coffee shop this time of night. And yet she hadn't heard his footsteps.

"How on to me? And how did you find me?"

"They've seen you with those other women since you went back to patrol. Stenengarter got a visit from his father about an hour ago." Deaver slid into the opposite side of the booth. "And to answer your second question, I called your home. Your mom said you go here when you need to think."

She did need to think. Like Ginger had said, she needed to put the puzzle pieces together. How had Bradley been alerted to what was going on with Stenengarter? If he knew the conversation was sensitive, the captain would have closed the door to his office. "How do you know what they said?"

"I have my ways."

Tammy couldn't imagine what sort of elaborate eavesdropping devices Deaver had rigged up, electronic or otherwise.

As if Bradley had read her mind, he added. "He left his office door open. I don't think he realized they were going to raise their voices or that anyone was close to the office. Anyway, Stenengarter Junior was quite upset." Deaver imitated Stenengarter's wispy low voice. "'Everything is out of control, Dad. This has gone too far.'" He watched her with a steady gaze as if gauging her reaction. "Then Junior said he wasn't going to do it anymore."

"By 'do it,' he probably meant threaten me and lose evidence." Tammy crossed her arms. Interesting. Sounded like something was about to explode, or had already.

"Then Senior blamed everything on that 'stupid woman cop.'"

"Guess that would be me."

Deaver wore a T-shirt that made reference to a comic book convention. His bald head glistened beneath the lights. "Considering there are no other women in the department, you get to play the part of stupid woman cop."

Tammy laced her hands together. "What I can't figure out is what they are so worried about. What one or all of them might have killed that Parker woman over." She summarized the link to the city commission of 1986 for Bradley.

He touched his bald spot. "I don't know if this helps, but out of curiosity, I looked up the records of David McQuire's death to see if there were any leads."

"And?" For all his eccentricities, Deaver had good instincts. Tammy had only casually mentioned that Arleta was a widow and had had her house broken into.

"He died in a single-car accident. But I didn't find that out from the police report. There was no autopsy, only a death certificate. No paper trail, not even an accident report. I found that out from the July 23, 1991, newspaper. No, I don't have that issue at my house. But it's amazing what you can find at your local library."

"Thanks for the public service announcement." Tammy tapped her nearly empty paper cup on the table. "You think there was something suspicious about his death?"

"Do you have any idea how weird police departments are about paper trails in the age of lawsuits? There is nothing on this guy."

"But why would they need to kill him? The vote was three to two in favor of the mall development, and he died five years after the vote. Sometimes an accident is just an accident."

"Maybe so. Maybe so. In light of the department having a bead on you, what are you going to do?"

Tammy took the last sip of her Chai. "Act natural, but be superalert." She held up the piece of paper she'd been writing on. "Destroy all evidence."

"I can shred that for you if you like. Shredding documents is fun."

Everybody needed a hobby. Deaver's was shredding paper. "In the meantime, I'm going to head out to Ginger's because I have to pick up my son. I can ask Ginger if she knows anything." She flipped the paper over before handing it to Bradley. It was the list of archery club members. Remington Shaw's name was underlined. "Is this the only archery club in town?" She glanced over the list. No Wheeler. No Jackson. No Stenengarter.

"There might be other clubs. What are you thinking?"

"Some archers don't belong to clubs. The weirdest thing about this case is that she died in a place she had no reason to be in and she was killed with an odd murder weapon."

Deaver nodded, eyebrows arching, and shook a finger at her. "Unless you were an archer and had those weapons in your car. Not premeditated. It was convenient to kill her that way. The weapon was at hand."

"People tend to gravitate toward places they are familiar with. I bet you anything that either Mr. Jackson, Mr. Wheeler, or Stenengarter Senior has a home out there."

"Or one of the real estate agents listed a house out there." He dragged her piece of paper across the table. "I can find out for you."

"Call me as soon as you find out anything. And act natural." Deaver was putting substantial effort into concealing the contents of the scratch paper by holding it against his chest. Acting natural was kind of a tall order for Bradley Deaver.

She scooted to the edge of the booth and stepped out. "In the meantime, I gotta go get my kid."

....

Stenengarter leaned his back against the counter, crossed his legs at the ankle, and continued with his manicure. The swishing grind of the file across his nails was oppressive.

This was a sporting goods store. Certainly there was something she could use to escape. She took a few steps then gauged Stenengarter's reaction. He brought his curled fingers to his lips and blew on them.

She stopped at the archery display.

"Don't even think about it."

Her back was to the main corridor of the mall. She touched one of the arrows. "Did you kill my friend with one of these?"

He only chuckled. Rage smoldered through Ginger's body. How could he laugh about her friend's death? She kept her

SHARON DUNN

voice even. "The bribery was twenty years ago. You wouldn't go to jail for that."

Again he chuckled. "I am a politician. I can't have skeletons in my closet."

"So you helped kill my friend." She spun around, ready to stomp toward him, but movement in her peripheral vision stopped her in her tracks. What she saw on the far side of the mall corridor caused all the air to leave her lungs.

Her heart stopped. Kindra and Arleta, heads hanging, shoulders slumped, trudged forward. Mr. Jackson waddled after them holding a small pistol. Wheeler strode behind. The stiffness of his stride suggested extreme irritation. This had to have been what the phone call was about.

Her own breathing surrounded her, the rhythm of her inhale and exhale, like a dirge. Kindra and Arleta slipped around a corner, leaving Ginger's field of vision. She took a few steps toward the jail bar doors.

"Not a step farther," Stenengarter barked.

Ginger stared out into the dimly lit mall corridor. Empty, the mall was empty. And her friends were being taken...somewhere. But why? She was the one who had what they wanted. Jackson must have gotten impatient and gone after Kindra and Arleta. What had Wheeler said in the phone conversation? That they couldn't let them go. Her breath caught in her throat. They were going to kill her friends.

She squeezed her eyes shut to block out the pictures that entered her mind. No. She wouldn't think of the bad things that might be happening to her friends. The images would only cause panic. And panic caused stress, which triggered a migraine. She had to keep control if she was going to help them.

She studied the room without turning her head. What weapon was available? The light switch five feet from her caught her eye. A moment of darkness would buy her time enough to grab a weapon. Most of the knives were under a glass display case except for a set of collector knives on the counter not far from the light switch. She could make it there before Stenengarter fumbled toward the light switch.

Could she actually slice something other than a tomato? And then she thought of Arleta and Kindra. All she needed to do was threaten him with it and get him to open the jail bar door.

Ginger took a breath filled with prayer and dashed toward the light. The store went black. Stenengarter cursed. She stumbled in the direction of the knives. She slammed into something. She stretched her hands out in front of her, expecting to touch glass. Nothing. Oh no. The darkness had disoriented her.

She wasn't surprised when she heard footsteps on the linoleum, but it still made her heart beat faster. A sliding sound and curses replaced the footsteps. Something rolled across the floor. Whatever she had run into had spilled across the floor and caused Stenengarter to stumble.

The delay bought her some time. Ginger crouched on the floor swinging her hand out in front of her. She worked her way toward what she thought was the far wall hoping it would hide her...temporarily.

All she had to do when the lights went on was get to the switch behind the counter, open the jail bar door, and race out to save her friends. Provided she became Wonder Woman in the next twenty seconds, that would be easy.

....

"Mom, that guy is tailing us."

Tammy checked her rearview mirror. Through the smear created by pelting rain, a set of headlights glared at her. "I see

SHARON DUNN

him, but let's not jump to conclusions." The comment was meant to calm Trevor. In light of hearing Ginger's message when she got out to Earl's, there was good reason to jump to conclusions. In the dark, she couldn't make out the model of the vehicle. The headlights were up high enough to suggest it was a larger car.

In her rearview mirror, Tammy could see Trevor rub his hands together. "You might have to drive like they taught you in cop school, huh?" His voice had just a smidgen too much glee in it.

From the passenger seat, Earl craned his neck. "It does seem like he's been behind us for a long time." Judging from the way Earl had his hand braced against the front dash, he was one of those people who didn't like riding in a car unless he was driving.

Tammy hit her turn signal and pulled out onto the road that led back into town. Earl had nothing to worry about; she had been driving since she was fifteen and had never had an accident. "Let's just focus on getting to the mall and finding your wife first."

Earl's jaw slackened. His face drooped. "That message scared me. Even Ginger can't shop this long. The mall closed two hours ago."

"He turned when we turned." Trevor reported from the backseat. "He's following us."

Again, she glanced in her rearview mirror. "Thanks for the update." Tammy sped down the two-lane. The increasing tension between her shoulder blades signaled that her attempt at nonchalance wasn't working. She hit her blinker again.

Trevor leaned forward. "What are you doing?"

Drops of rain pinged on the metal of her car. Her wipers cleared a quarter-circle view for her.

Tammy turned onto a dirt road that dead-ended at the back side of the city dump. "Settling this once and for all. I am not a multitasker. I need to focus on finding Ginger."

Trevor slid back on the seat and glued his face to the back window. "No lights."

"I didn't see any lights whiz by either," said Earl.

Tammy slowed the car. Gravel crunched beneath her tires.

"There, a car just went by." Trevor wiggled in his seat.

"Trev, I can't see anything in my mirror with your head in the way."

Her son groaned with the drama only a teenager could manufacture. The noise suggested inconvenience of the highest level. "I'm looking for you."

"Shouldn't we get turned around and find my wife?" Earl's hand lifted from the dashboard with a jerk. His arm was ramrod straight, muscles tensed and hard.

She swallowed, hoping to wash down the comment to Trevor about how his paranoia had cost them time. Constantly placing blame on your child was at the top of the to-do list for bad parenting. She'd managed to suppress the observation, but it had flicked across her brain. "Sorry, Mr. Salinski. I know you're worried. So am I. There's a place at the edge of the chain-link fence where we can get turned around."

Trevor slammed his body against the backseat and crossed his arms. "Sorry, Mr. Salinski."

Tammy caught a glimpse of her son, his head turned sideways. She smiled. It had been a long time since he had apologized without being prompted and prodded into it. "Sorry I snapped at you, too."

"It's all right." Trev shifted in his seat so the reflection of his sweet face was visible in the mirror.

SHARON DUNN

Tammy turned her attention to the windshield and the smeared view in front of her. "Oh, no." She braked. "My wipers stopped working. I can't see anything." She shifted the car into neutral.

"I can get it," said Earl.

Tammy opened her door. "That's all right. It does this all the time." Rain jabbed her skin the second she stepped out onto the gravel. Her cotton T-shirt soaked up the moisture like a sponge. She could have taken two seconds to grab her Windbreaker off the headrest of the driver's seat. But no. Sometimes being in a hurry cost more time than it saved. She shivered. It certainly lowered your core body temp. Droplets trailed down her face. Rain fell hard and fast enough for her to wonder if it wasn't being poured from buckets. God was draining the pool. Her mother used to tell her that.

She leaned across the windshield, cupped the wiper, and flattened the rubbery thing that had wound up into a ball. She had to get that thing fixed the next time she went in for an oil change. She only thought about it when it was raining. That was the problem.

Her cell phone rang. Maybe, hopefully, it was Ginger. "Hello."

"Tammy." Deaver's nasally voice vibrated across the line.

"This better be good. I'm standing in the rain."

"Wheeler was on his college archery team, and Stenengarter Senior was his coach. And get this, Wheeler has a home not too far from the range."

"That was worth getting soaking wet for."

"One more thing. When I traced back Jackson to his college days, he was never on the archery team, but he did work as a car mechanic. I got that little tidbit from an aunt of his. People will tell you anything if you're nice enough."

"You're the best, Bradley. I owe you." Tammy stood in the light created by her headlights, conical intersecting bands of illumination.

"Like a millions bucks, right?"

"Or at least a cup of coffee."

"It's a deal." He chuckled. "So are you glad I believe in conspiracies?"

"More than you know." They hung up at the same time.

She folded her phone shut. Headlights revealed the gravel road they had just come down...and the silhouette of a man. Breath caught in Tammy's throat. Even though he was mostly in shadow, Tammy could make out the outline of a gun in a holster on his belt.

The man walked toward her car.

Twenty-Four

Stenengarter's footsteps tapped across the linoleum of the dark sporting goods store. Ginger prayed her irrational prayer. *Please, God, make me invisible.* She pressed her back against the wall. He was the God of the impossible. *Please, please, please.* Feet passed by with only a clothing rack between her and Stenengarter.

More footsteps, moving away from her. One by one, the fluorescent lights all the way across the store buzzed to life. Stenengarter checked the clothing rack close to her. Hangers scraped across metal.

She drew her knees up to her chest and pressed even harder against the wall. He'd find her for sure now. This was too obvious a hiding place.

The man walked away from the rack. *Thank You, Lord.*

Taking care not to bump anything, she crawled the four feet to the clothing rack that Stenengarter had just checked. Men's coveralls surrounded her and draped to the floor. Now she could see the shoes of her pursuer, polished oxfords. Through a coverall-framed window, the counter and the promise of escape shone like a beacon.

She clutched her purse to her chest. The older man paced around the store. Feet came into view from around the archery display, then disappeared. She leaned back. Dumb move. Like that was going to make her less visible.

Her legs cramped. Calf muscles hardened and stretched. This was no way for a grandmother to sit, all scrunched up like this.

The polished oxfords came closer and checked the display ten feet from her. One step. Two steps. She scooted to the back of the rack. Rough canvas fabric of the coveralls rubbed against the back of her head.

Her pulse, rapid and intense, drummed in her ears. The shoes came one step closer. She could almost reach out and touch his pant leg. Her breath hitched.

The shoes turned slightly, then tapped on the linoleum, growing fainter.

One by one, the lights went off again.

What was he doing? Had he left by some unknown exit?

She listened until she could separate the buzzing of the mall lights from a low electrical hum. Listening. Waiting. Listening. Waiting.

Arleta and Kindra were in danger. Stenengarter must be gone. Might as well find the switch that opens the main door and bolt for the entrance.

She pushed the coveralls aside and crawled out of her hiding place. She rose to her feet, pivoted one way and then the other, tracing the outline of the racks and displays, looking for any movement. Too dark to see anything.

She reached into her purse and pulled out Earl's pepper spray/flashlight. She felt for the flashlight end and clicked it on just long enough to locate the counter.

Then she bolted toward the counter, placing her hand in the same spot she had seen Stenengarter touch. She smacked the surface until her fingers touched what felt like a switch.

The abrasive rattle of metal broke the quiet. She ran toward the opening door. Something whizzed past her ear.

The sting of warm blood alerted her to a cut on her earlobe. What was that?

She cupped her hand over her ear and looked up into a dummy dressed in camouflage hunting gear. An arrow stuck out of the canvas bag he had slung over his shoulder. The arrow probably had her blood on it.

She turned slowly to find the source of the arrow. Her breathing provided a backbeat to the next few seconds of her life, which seemed to last forever. All her senses clicked into overdrive.

The moment froze, and her mind took a picture of a tall man wearing night-vision goggles and placing an arrow into a bow. The man slipped behind the display of snowboards. She'd seen him long enough to register that white hair.

Stenengarter had nearly put an arrow through her neck—and he was about to take a second shot.

The man disappeared into shadow. Footsteps. The door reversed order in its tracks threatening to lock Ginger in her prison.

The electric door had maybe four feet left to go before it closed completely. It squeaked and rattled. With only a glance at the arrow and the maimed mannequin, she dashed toward the diminishing store entrance.

She leaned forward, half leaping, half crawling, stretching through. Her knees hit the carpet. She slid. Metal scraped against metal, and the door moved in its track. She pulled her legs through, but lost one of her leather ballet flats in the process. The door locked in place with a click.

Ginger pulled herself to her feet, stumbled and swaggered. Bleeding ear, one shoe, rug burns on her forearms and knees—wasn't she just the picture of pretty? It took her only a nanosecond to register who she was and what she was doing. Then she saw the arrow on the carpet.

He'd actually taken another shot at her.

When she looked back into the dark store, Stenengarter had disappeared. He didn't have to chase her. He could just call Jackson or Wheeler and alert them to her location.

Really, this was not fair. Three against one, and they had the keys to all the doors.

Arleta and Kindra. She had to find Arleta and Kindra. She had to get hold of the police, of Tammy, of Earl, the SWAT team, the FBI, somebody with firepower.

She stumbled in the direction Mr. Jackson had taken her friends, toward the far end of the mall and around a corner that held specialty shops. She ran past a maternity shop. Sort of ran. Having only one shoe created a big stride, drag foot, little stride effect. She'd really liked those shoes, too. So comfortable and you could dress them up or down.

The industrial carpet was roughly the equivalent of sandpaper on the bottom of her foot. She ran past the remainder of the shops, which were locked and dark. Far as she could see, Arleta and Kindra were not in any of them. Where else could Jackson have taken them?

She rushed toward the exit. The first set of doors opened, but the second, the one that would have allowed her to get outside and find some help, was dead bolted. Ginger stepped back from the locked door and rested her palm against her forehead.

Despair encroached on her thoughts, but she pushed it away. No escape. Think. She had to think. She was not dead yet. There was still hope.

If he was going to come after her, Stenengarter would be delayed a few minutes by having to unlock the metal door. She pushed back through the first set of doors. A different door with nothing written on it caught her attention. When she tried the knob, it turned.

SHARON DUNN

This was the only place on this side of the mall that Jackson could have taken her friends.

Ginger's ear stung from where the arrow had nicked it. Her elbows and knees flared with rug burn pain. When she looked down at her hands, they were trembling. No. Scratch that. She'd been mistaken. Her entire body was shaking, a delayed reaction to the trauma she'd just been through.

Oddly, despite the level of stress, she didn't have any migraine symptoms. *Thank You, God, for that little gift. Please help me find Arleta and Kindra and a way out of this mall that has become a prison.*

She pushed open the unlocked door.

Twenty-Five

Even though she had no weapon to defend herself, Tammy's hand automatically touched her hip. Rain spattered across her face. The man with the gun on his belt gravitated toward her. She tensed but kept her feet planted. He took another step. Her mind whirled, assessing possibilities for escape and defense. She had two people in the car who needed protection.

The silhouette of his vehicle was barely visible beyond the illumination created by her headlights. Could she get back behind the steering wheel before he drew his weapon?

The man with the gun stepped into the light.

"Captain Stenengarter, what are you doing here in uniform?" Friend or foe? Friend or foe?

"I was out on patrol. I saw your car pull out and followed it." He touched his uniform. "I was trying to earn the respect of my men...and of my one female police officer. But I'm afraid it's too late. I'll have to resign for what I've done."

Tammy shook her head.

"Twenty years ago my father was involved in a bribery scam as a city commissioner. Mary Margret Parker figured it out. Dad wants to run for office again. He asked me to bury this scandal."

Stenengarter pulled his rimless glasses off and stood close enough so she could see his face. "My father's money can buy a great deal. But it cannot buy respect."

SHARON DUNN

"Where is your father now?"

"He said he has some stuff to finish up at the shop."

"The shop?"

"The sporting goods shop in the mall."

"We have to get out there! That was the last place my wife went. She called and said she had found something connected with the murder. Something has happened to her."

Tammy had been so focused on Stenengarter that she hadn't heard Earl get out of the car. He stood by the open door, rain pelting his straw hat and soaking his shoulders.

She had a few questions for her boss. What was the extent of Stenengarter Senior's level of involvement? Had he been the one to put the arrow into Mary Margret? Or had he simply used his son to bury the twenty-year-old secret that would ruin him politically? "We need to get out to the mall." She had a lot of questions, but no time to ask them.

Stenengarter turned toward his car. "I'll meet you there. I'll call this in to the station so we can get backup if we need it."

．．．．．．．．．．．．．．．．．．．．．．．．．．．．．

Ginger hadn't realized how hard she had been running until she stepped inside the dark room. Her side hurt. She made a mental note that maybe she needed to work out at the pool six times a week instead of four. She felt along the wall for a light switch.

When she turned to assess her surroundings, a blitz of color and sparkle filled her field of vision. Five fully decorated artificial Christmas trees took up one side of the room to her right. Boxes with garlands and shining things heaping out of them lined the wall to her left. Santa's cardboard workshop and velvet couch occupied the rest of the room. In addition to the neon 3-D deer and a Merry Christmas sign, the wall opposite her featured a blue door. But no Arleta or Kindra.

Ginger collapsed on the Santa couch and tried to shake off the hopelessness. What now? Her foot was freezing and sore.

The door she had just come through remained closed. For whatever reason, Stenengarter wasn't coming after her. She had zigzagged and he moved a lot slower than her, but if he was coming after her, he should have been here by now. Maybe something had distracted him.

Her shoulders drooped. He probably knew this was a dead end, that she was trapped. She rested her head in her hands. If she was to find Arleta and Kindra, she had to go back out there—and be target practice for the archer and the gunmen. She was outnumbered and outgunned. *A little help would be nice here please, God.*

She lifted her cold foot and warmed it in her hands. This concrete floor may as well have been a sheet of ice. After rummaging through several boxes, she located a pair of elf shoes with bells on the end of the long curled toes. Charming. Oh well. Beggars can't be choosers.

She stood up on her feet and rocked heel to toe. The shoes were surprisingly comfortable, kind of spongy. Of course someone who was on his or her feet all day lifting heavy children into Santa's lap would wear supportive shoes. The bells jingled when she turned her foot sideways. Bouncing some more on the shoes cheered her. Good-fitting shoes were better than a prescription for Prozac. Her head cleared and a plan formed.

She pulled the bells off. Better to be silent than musical. Hope was not completely lost. She had one more door to open before she ran out of options, and then she would gather the strength to go back out into the mall.

Enjoying the cushioning in her shoes, she strode toward the blue door, twisted the knob, and pushed it open. She stood on the threshold of a small concrete room.

Other than having no windows, the main feature of the room was a series of monitors showing different parts of the mall. A worn office chair with a massaging pad was turned away from the monitors, facing the door. The room smelled of mildew and cigarettes. It seemed odd that there was no phone, but maybe the security guy carried a cell with him. Though she couldn't pinpoint the source, water dripped somewhere, making a *plonk-plonk-plonk* sound. She'd heard it in the other room, too.

Wheeler must have either bribed or bullied the security guard to leave when he decided to make the mall his private torture chamber.

Most of the screens covered the common areas of the mall, the entrances and the long corridors. The larger stores also had their own monitors. She couldn't see any of her three pursuers.

There were buttons beneath the monitors. Since only parts of the store were visible, the button must switch to a different camera within the stores. She clicked through the Macy's men's department, housewares, women's apparel. Oh, they were having a sale on decorative T-shirts. She pressed the button again.

Movement by the makeup counter caught her eye. She leaned closer. A black-and- white image in a dimly lit store was hardly high resolution. But she'd bet her AARP discount that somebody was hiding around the counter. She studied every inch of the monitor. There it was again. Just the hint of motion. A flutter of a hand...or maybe a head.

Gradually, she separated shadow from substance. It was like studying one of those pictures where if you looked long enough, you could see two separate pictures—a very young lady and a very old lady—on the same canvas.

In this case, one old lady. Arleta's pale skin slowly separated from the shadow of the counter and displays. The camera was positioned so it revealed the interior of the counter. No doubt designed to keep an eye on shoplifting employees. Most of Arleta was still in shadow, but her pale hands had slowly materialized.

She clicked through the buttons again, hoping to spot Kindra. Instead, she saw Jackson still holding the gun, swaying through the children's section of Macy's, glancing side to side.

The pace of her heart kicked up a notch. Her hands curled into fists. She had to get to Arleta before Jackson did. She unzipped the purse and wrapped her hands around Earl's pepper spray-flashlight. Not much of a defense against a gun, but maybe she could find something on the way. It was a long trot from this side of the mall to Macy's on the other end.

As she strode through the Christmas room, visions of being in one of her grandkid's video games, where she dodged arrows and bullets, played inside her brain.

....

Arleta thought that for a woman of seventy-five she was pretty darn flexible. With minimal rearranging, she'd managed to scrunch herself into the cupboard beneath the makeup counter. Mr. Jackson's heavy footsteps grew louder. It had been a risk to hide instead of keep running. The outside entrances were locked. There was no way out of the mall. She'd have to wait it out until morning.

Then, when the salesgirls came in the morning to open up—surprise! She would jump out and get them to call the police.

If she could keep her legs from cramping, she'd be safe and sound by sunrise.

The footsteps stopped.

Then she heard shuffling, a moving back and forth. Arleta pulled her knees up to her chest. Of course, there was only one hitch to her brilliant plan. She didn't know where Kindra was. When they'd gotten away from Mr. Jackson, they had run in different directions. They had bolted when he turned his back to look for rope to tie them up with. Mr. Jackson had a gun, but he was unbelievably slow when it came to running.

The stink of perfume in the cupboard gave her a headache. She'd never liked the stuff. She wished right now that she had Annie. Then she would show Mr. Jackson who was the marksman. When he had found them in Lewis Hall, he'd grabbed their purses and dumped the contents on the ground screaming, "Where is it? Where is it?" Naturally she had thought he was talking about Annie.

Jackson had acted touched in the head, really frantic.

As he ranted and raved with sweat pouring off his face, it became obvious that the gun was not what he was talking about. Mr. Jackson was convinced that they had the confession they'd just learned about hours earlier from Lyndon Chambers. Since her husband had worked in Lewis Hall, Jackson insisted that they had gone there to hide it, that she must know a secret hiding place.

Until Mr. Jackson mentioned it, they hadn't heard the name Joe Smith.

Arleta pushed something out of her way that was digging into her hip. She ran her hand over it. Round flat disks, probably compacts. How had Mr. Jackson known where her husband's office had been fifteen years ago?

If it stayed quiet long enough, she'd spell herself by sticking her legs out of the cupboard to stretch them. She listened to the sound of her own breathing. It only took a few minutes for her to realize that her greatest enemy was not going to be leg cramps; boredom got the top spot. There wasn't even any decent reading material in here, let alone some light. Her mind kept wandering to Kindra. Was she safe?

If only Mr. Jackson hadn't taken her purse. She always kept a paperback in there and a miniflashlight. Even if she could find one of those light-up mirrors, she was sure reading about the latest shade of rouge would be a real yawner. Ho hum. Who would've thought that fighting for your life would be so tedious?

She couldn't hear footsteps anymore. No noise at all. She leaned a little closer to the cupboard door. With nothing to read or occupy her thoughts, Arleta thought about something she hadn't thought about in fifteen years—the night David died.

• •

Ginger leaned around the corner that led to the main drag of the mall. She studied the shops and corridors. No sign of anyone. She couldn't be so lucky as to hope that they had decided to call the whole thing off and go out for pie instead. Something must have required their attention.

Still watching, she edged along the wall.

She slipped into a kiosk that sold sunglasses and goggles and peered above the counter to see if she could see anything.

Nothing.

As she was straightening, she caught a glimpse of herself in a mirror that was set up next to a display of sunglasses. Bloody ear, armed with pepper spray, and stylish travel purse. *Dirty Ginger to the rescue. Do you feel lucky?*

She glanced at her elf shoes. Her heart fluttered. She put a palm on her chest. Who was she kidding? She was terrified. Scared she'd never get out of here. Afraid that something had happened to her friends. Afraid that the early morning mall walkers would find her body stuffed in a trash can.

The mall PA system made a scratching noise, and then she heard the voice that cut through to her marrow.

Twenty-Six

After David died, Arleta's grief had overtaken her with the force of a tornado. She had functioned in the rubble that remained of her life, reminding herself that she needed to eat, to keep breathing. Thinking about David's death would have interfered with that. She hadn't reviewed the specifics of that night until now, when she faced her own possible demise.

David had called her before he left Lewis Hall to say that he was going for a drive to think and that he had something important to tell her when he got home.

At the time, she had assumed that his news had something to do with a decision about a sabbatical they had been discussing. But now, with her feet pressed up against the latest lipstick colors, she remembered the hollow tone that had threaded through his voice.

He must have been coming home to tell her about the confession and everything connected with it. He had to have hidden the confession either in the vest or the photo album. The secret had remained hidden until Mary Margret found it.

Arleta closed her eyes. She could still see the young police officer standing at her door that night fifteen years ago. Single-car accident, he had said.

She pushed aside some tubes that dug into her thigh and twisted at the waist to try and get comfortable. David had been a good driver. It hadn't been raining that night.

Arleta gripped a lipstick tube. Jackson had known that David worked at Lewis Hall because he had either tampered with the car or followed David from Lewis Hall and caused the accident. Somehow, Mr. Jackson had gotten rid of the only man who would reveal his crime—her David.

The footsteps returned, circling the makeup counter. She recognized the slow motion drag of his steps. A thudding noise above her. His hand on the counter? No, too heavy for that.

His breathing was raspy. She'd given her husband's killer quite a workout. Anger, fifteen years in the making, made every muscle in Arleta's body tense up.

Jackson's breathing irritated her. She grabbed the first thing her fingers touched, stuck her feet out of the cupboard, and pushed herself out onto the floor. She was on her feet before Jackson, standing eight feet away with a counter between them, could react.

His mouth formed a misshapen oval. He was sweating so much he glistened.

Simultaneously, she threw the thing in her hand and screamed, "You killed my David!"

Moments before his face disappeared in a red dust cloud, she saw the light come into his eyes and his mouth grew even wider and more distorted. Coughing rose out of the cloud.

The thud she had heard was his gun being put on the counter.

When the whirlwind of loose powdered rouge settled, Jackson's face, neck, and chins were red. The powder had glued to his sweat. He stuck his tongue out, making puffing noises and finally resorted to wiping it with his hand. He dug at his eyes.

Arleta reached for the gun but stumbled on makeup and boxes she had pushed out during her exit from the cupboard.

She fell forward. Her outstretched hand brushed against the gun and sent it spinning off the counter to the floor.

She leaned over the counter, her face about a foot from David's killer. "Why?"

His eyes watered from the amount of powder in them. "At first it was about getting rich." His blubbery lips quivered. "This property was supposed to set me up, my first really big deal."

"Didn't it?"

"Wheeler has been blackmailing me about the murder for fifteen years. He has everything." His looked down and spoke to Daffy Duck on his tie. "I only have the appearance of wealth."

"Why kill my husband?"

"He was going to bring it out in the open. I didn't want to lose everything. Didn't want to go to jail. I didn't mean for Mary Margret to die. This greed, it just keeps compounding on itself." His shoulders drooped even more.

Arleta's jaw was clenched so tight she was in danger of breaking a tooth. She could barely see Jackson's pudgy face through the smear of tears. She fixated on his tie and those stupid, stupid cartoon characters laughing and dancing.

Her words came out slowly with measured control. "You killed the love of my life for money."

She crawled over the top of the counter, grabbed his tie, and yanked it tighter.

Jackson leaned forward but didn't resist. He spoke in a staccato rhythm punctuated with choking, gasping sounds. "I'll turn myself in. I'm so tired. I've been Wheeler's prisoner for fifteen years anyway."

Arleta lifted her head and let up on the tie, when the mall's PA system made a scratching noise.

SHARON DUNN

"Attention mall shoppers, especially Ginger Salinski. I think I have something you want. And I think you have something I want. We should make a trade. One bouncing blond coed for one tiny piece of paper. Such a good deal." Even filtered through speakers, Wheeler's voice shook Ginger to the core.

After tossing the pepper spray back in her purse, she bolted out to the middle of the mall. So that's why they hadn't come after her: They'd been chasing down Kindra. Ginger ran, staring into the dark and dimly lit stores. For the love of Pete, she didn't know where the PA system was housed, probably in the mall office, but where was that? All these years of coming to the mall and she never had a reason to locate the office; there was never anything on sale in there.

Walls closed in on her. She darted back and forth trying to think. Would it be on the main floor? Off in a side corridor? She'd never seen a sign. She trotted down the main corridor of the mall. Looking...looking.

As she neared the fountain in the center of the mall, she slowed. The fountain was turned off, but someone was tied to the stem that jutted out of the fountain's bowl-like base. She saw the delicate hands with rope wrapped around them, the purple nail polish and the fingers with blood on them.

Ginger circled around. She was out of breath from running. Her heart ku-thudded in her chest. Her skin tingled; an odd numbness blanketed her arms, her legs, her rib cage. She stepped slowly around. The paralysis, in response to what she saw, made her feel as though someone else was telling her to put one foot in front of the other to keep moving.

"Hey, kiddo." Ginger raised a hand toward her friend.

Kindra lifted her head and forced a smile. "Nice getup. Tell me you didn't pay full price for those shoes."

"It w-was the b-best I could do on such short n-notice." She let out a quivering breath when Kindra turned her head and she saw the gash across the kid's cheek. "Oh, honey." She strode toward her friend.

"I wouldn't go any closer if I were you." Wheeler's gruff voice pelted her back.

Ginger whirled around to face Wheeler. Stenengarter stood beside him with a gun aimed at her. But of course, Mr. Sporting Goods had an endless supply of weapons. She made no effort to hide her anger.

He stood about twenty feet away. "I wouldn't try to get your friend untied." He tilted his head toward Stenengarter. "My friend here will put a bullet through both of you."

Ginger's hands balled into fists. Boy, did she want to pummel him for what he had done to Kindra. Instead, she planted her feet and pressed her lips together really tight. The last thing she needed was to lose control.

"Now, I think we have a trade to make. You give me that piece of paper. I'll let you untie your friend and you can go."

This was of course the biggest lie of the evening. Wheeler was going to kill them. All part of covering up the trail that was on his to-do list.

Ginger played along in his little game of pretend. She had no other option, and this bought her some time to try and come up with a plan. Unless she came up with a brilliant idea, she and Kindra were going to die. And Arleta, too, if it hadn't happened already.

Ginger closed the distance between her and her assailants. She positioned her hand on top of her purse.

The gun in Stenengarter's hand jerked.

"The confession is in here." Ginger's heart galloped at Kentucky Derby speed. *Please, please don't shoot me.*

"I looked in there," barked Wheeler.

"It's a travel purse, dummy. It has a hidden compartment." Her hand brushed over Earl's pepper spray/flashlight before inching up to the zipper for the hidden compartment.

"Bring it over here."

She walked slower than molasses pours. Surveying the area around her and thinking-thinking-thinking. "The bribery crime is old. If you hadn't killed my friend, you wouldn't have gone to jail."

"My reputation was on the line. Nobody buys houses from someone connected with a scam like that, proven or unproven." Wheeler pouted.

"Nobody buys houses from someone who commits murder either." A light patina of sweat formed on Ginger's brow.

"Shut up and give me the paper." His expression would have put him in the running for sourpuss of the month. "Your friend drove me to it. She led me on all day and then tried to escape from my house."

That was it. She was looking at Mary Margret's killer. Renata had said that Wheeler chased after Mary. He must have had archery equipment in his car. This whole bribery coverup had smoldered for twenty years and turned to burning rage.

Ginger's hand hovered over the open purse. If she grabbed the pepper spray, she'd have time to disable Stenengarter but not Wheeler. Maybe she could get to the gun before Wheeler could.

"Hurry." Stenengarter raised the gun a little higher.

Wheeler leaned toward her. "The man said hurry."

"Sorry, I've been running quite a bit." Ginger fanned herself. "I'm just so old and menopausal."

Wheeler narrowed his bloodshot eyes at her. "Oh, please."

Ginger cut her glance toward Kindra, who lifted her head. All of this was a gamble. She was risking both their lives. But what other choice did she have?

Her hand slipped into her purse, and she wrapped trembling fingers around the pepper spray. "Okay, I'll give you what you need." She placed her thumb on the disperse button.

Stenengarter adjusted his grip on the gun, but his finger rested over the trigger, not on it. She was maybe three feet from him, and Wheeler was behind him four feet away.

Her heartbeat drummed in her ears.

Stenengarter's cheek twitched.

This had to work or they were all dead. Her mouth went dry. *Please, God, help me. Please let Earl's invention work.*

Wheeler curled his lip. "Give it to me."

That was it. She'd had enough of these guys. She lifted the spray out of the purse, aimed it at Stenengarter, and pressed the button.

Stenengarter moaned, dropped the gun, and clutched his face. His eyes watered. He gasped for air. He bent over, face in his hands.

Ginger dove for the gun. Wheeler pushed her away. She saw a flash of an image. His hand placed over the top of the gun.

A boom of energy like nothing she had ever heard before filled the space around her. Wheeler still on his knees put both hands in the air. The gun remained on the floor.

"There is more where that came from. That was a warning shot. The next one goes straight through your heart."

Ginger would recognize that voice in the darkest cave. Arleta. Wheeler continued to hold his hands in the air. Ginger picked the gun up off the carpet and turned around.

Arleta stood with the pistol held in steady hands. "This thing doesn't shoot like my Annie."

Jackson thudded toward them. A bubble of panic tightened Ginger's throat. "Arleta, Jackson is—"

"Don't worry about him. Remember that picture we saw of a skinny Jackson in his office? He's eaten his weight in guilt over the last fifteen years for what he did..." Her voice faltered. "...To me. He's ready to turn everyone in."

Wheeler shouted a curse at Jackson. Stenengarter dropped to the floor still clawing his face. He wheezed. His chest labored up and down.

Kindra let out a small whimper. "Go, Arleta, go."

Ginger raced over to untie her. Through blurred vision, she struggled with the ropes. The knot had been tied tightly. She dug her fingers between the ropes. Once she got them loose, they were easy to undo. Ginger unwound the rope from Kindra's narrow wrist.

The younger woman wrapped her arms around Ginger. "Thank you." Kindra's voice wavered. Ginger supported her friend while she stepped out of the fountain and onto solid ground. Arleta continued to hold her gun on Wheeler. Stenengarter struggled to his feet but gave up midway, collapsing on the floor and clutching his chest.

Movement down the main corridor of the mall caught Ginger's eye. Tammy and a tall man dressed in a policeman's uniform rounded the corner by the sporting goods store. Trevor trailed behind them.

Ginger ran toward them. Now that she was safe, the full force of what she had been through hit her. She wanted her husband, to be held by him. "How did you get in? The place was locked."

Tammy held up her hands. "Misspent youth. It took us quite a while, but I picked the lock to a back door. A little trick my ex-husband taught me." She turned toward the tall man with rimless glasses. "Ginger, this is my boss, Paul Stenengarter."

The man in the uniform touched the gun on his belt. "If I'm still her boss. I'm afraid I abused my power." He tilted his head toward the man writhing on the floor. "A practice I learned from my father."

Ginger's purse made an electronic scratching noise.

"We can help you mop up this mess. We've got patrol cars outside." Tammy placed a hand on Ginger's shoulder. "Suzanne will have some news for you tomorrow."

Ginger pulled the walkie-talkie out of her purse and pressed the transmit button. "Hello."

"Hey, I was worried about you."

Earl's voice made her warm all over. "Me?" She walked a distance from the others so she could hear more clearly. "Are you still back at the shop? Does this thing work that good?"

A static-filled chuckle came across the line. "It looks like you can handle yourself just fine. You are quite adventurous."

Ginger surveyed the length of the mall. He was here somewhere. A calm surrounded her like a down blanket on a winter's day. Her Earl was here. "You forgot to say *over*."

Earl stepped out from behind a kiosk that sold jewelry and waved. He pulled the walkie-talkie away from his mouth and said, "It'll never be over." His gaze dropped to her feet. "That's quite a pair of shoes you got there."

Ginger put her hands on her hips and sauntered toward him. She did a pinup girl pose, placing one hand on the back of her neck and the other on her hip. "Thanks, I've been getting comments about them all night."

He gathered her into his arms.

She held up the pepper spray/flashlight. "I hope you don't mind. I field-tested your invention."

"And?" He held her close, swaying from side to side.

She tilted her head toward the writhing Stenengarter Senior, who was brought to his feet and handcuffed by his son. "It stops the bears in their tracks."

She tossed her purse and wrapped both arms around his shoulders. "This should be the one you get the patent on. I'll help you come up with a name and market it."

"Thanks for being my cheerleader."

She stared into the brown eyes she had fallen in love with thirty-eight years ago, the eyes that would remain the same no matter how old they both got. "Earl Salinski, you are one clever fellow."

"I have good taste in women, too." He leaned in to kiss her.

Ginger glanced over at Kindra, who stood at the entrance of Macy's. Kindra bounced three times and waved. "Looks like my support is in place at checkpoint one."

"You can do this, honey." Earl offered her a salute from the bench outside the store. Tammy sat beside him. "If you can track down three criminals." He held up the newspaper. The front page featured a picture of Ginger and a very somber-looking Keith Wheeler. He pointed to a smaller article on the bottom of page one. "And see to it that Keaton Lustrum never works as a lawyer again."

"Renata did that. The last straw was when he wouldn't let her show me Wheeler's house. She squealed to the paper about his illegal activities and hypocrisy."

"What she saw and heard will be invaluable at Wheeler's trial," Tammy added. "Paul's dad confessed to chasing you down in his car."

Earl tossed the paper on the bench and leaned back. "After what you did five nights ago, this will be a piece of cake."

Ginger's stomach tightened. "I don't know. Buying a dress at full price is a lot harder."

He slipped the walkie-talkie into her hand. "You've got your support team in place, and I'll talk you through it."

Ginger took the walkie-talkie and sauntered the thirty feet to the store entrance.

SHARON DUNN

Kindra gave her the thumbs-up. "Go for it, Ginger. Full price, you can do it."

She spoke into the walkie-talkie. "I'm at checkpoint one."

Earl's voice came through loud and clear. "Looking good, hon."

Ginger adjusted her purse strap on her forearm. "To think I spent all this time teaching other people to buy stuff on sale."

"Some of us needed to learn that, but you need to learn to treat yourself once in a while. You are so worth it." Kindra pointed toward the rack of beautiful summer dresses. "Suzanne is waiting for you at the next checkpoint."

Suzanne, with a baby sling cutting a diagonal across her torso, twisted and swayed. She tilted her head toward the rack. "I think the pink ones look pretty."

Ginger touched the sling, feeling the warm, still body beneath the fabric. "How is little Natasha?"

"She is enjoying her first shopping excursion." Suzanne folded back the sling, revealing a fuzzy black head. "This is the last baby."

"You say that every time."

"Yes, but I mean it this time." Suzanne had pulled her hair up. Wispy brown curls framed her face. Her cheeks flushed a soft shade of pink. She looked pretty, serene. "I'm not getting another license plate."

Shaking her head, Ginger pulled a dress with a floral print off the rack.

"Remember, you can't look at the price tag."

"I know the deal." Her heart beat a little faster at the thought of holding a dress that had to be priced through the roof. "None of this means I am cheap, you know."

Suzanne nodded. "Arleta is waiting for you at the checkout."

Ginger spoke into the walkie-talkie. "I've just left the second checkpoint. Over." Earl offered her more affirmation.

"We're all behind you." Tammy chimed in.

Ginger turned back toward Suzanne. "'Course someone who wasn't cheap wouldn't need a whole support team just to pay full price for a dress." Ginger put her hand on her hip. "I am a tightwad, aren't I?"

"You are the only person I know who uses paper towels twice and washes dental floss."

"Cheap comes in handy once in a while."

"I wouldn't have a zero balance on my credit card if it wasn't for your cheap skills." Suzanne twisted side to side. "Now get on up to the checkout counter."

Ginger lifted the dress, touching the cool fabric. She fanned herself. "I only feel a little dizzy." She lay a hand over her churning stomach. "I feel like a teenager right before her prom date shows up, excited and a little scared."

"Go." Suzanne pressed Ginger's shoulder and waved her forward.

The distance from the full price rack to the checkout was approximately a million miles. Arleta, with her coat folded over her arms, stood straight as a metal pole at the cashier counter.

Ginger's pace slowed from a brisk walk to a trudge. *This isn't for Earl. It's for me. I have something to prove to myself.* She was about twenty feet from the checkout. Her feet dragged.

Arleta offered Ginger a reassuring smile. Yup, this was for her. It was about letting go of irrational fear that if she paid full price for something, there wouldn't be money for food. She was about three feet from the checkout. The saleswoman wasn't the same pouty girl who had been there before. This one had a soft smile.

Small talk would keep her mind off of what she was doing. "You know what I've been thinking?"

"What's that?" Arleta adjusted the moss green moleskin jacket on her arm. Ginger had helped her pick that out, along with the matching pants.

"I've been thinking that if you keep your fist closed too tight, God can't put the good things in it that He wants to give you. You have to live life with open hands, let Him control the money."

Arleta turned so she stood shoulder to shoulder with Ginger. "I've been thinking about that God fellow quite a bit myself. Even old women can change their habits."

Ginger smiled at her new friend. She hadn't even talked about her faith. Who would've thought that coupons and half price sales would bring someone closer to the Savior? "You got that right." She placed the full price dress on the counter. "Arleta, there have always been four of us in the Bargain Hunters Network."

"Where is the membership application?"

"It's a little less formal than that." Ginger raised a warning finger. "But if you see a sale and don't tell us, we'll write you up a citation."

The saleswoman flipped the dress over to find the price tag. Ginger turned sideways so she wouldn't have to look. The woman scanned the bar code. Ginger winced.

She stared at the ceiling and took several deep breaths. *Breathe in. Breathe out.*

The saleswoman chirped, "That'll be eighty—"

Arleta made a shushing noise. Then she waved her hands, crisscrossing them in front of her. "We are not to know the price."

The woman behind the counter let out a perplexed, "Oh."

Sweat droplets formed on Ginger's forehead. She swung around to face the salesclerk. "Eighty what?"

"Ginger, just hand her the credit card."

Her heart squeezed. "Eighty what?" she squeaked.

Arleta steadied Ginger's trembling hand with her own. "Stick to the plan. Just hand the lady your credit card."

In between pulling her credit card from her pocket book and handing it to the saleswoman, Ginger dropped the card twice.

The woman stared at the credit card.

"Is something wrong?"

She waved the card. "It's just that it's kind of wet from sweat."

Ginger peered into her purse. "Maybe I should give you a different one."

"No!" Four voices, one male and three female, spoke in unison behind her. Her support team had closed in. They knew her too well.

Ginger tilted her head coyly. "Guess I better just use that one." She giggled. "After all, it's just money. There are more important things."

The clerk wiped the card on her sleeve and swiped it. Ginger touched her palm to her chest. Earl's hand rested on the middle of her back.

The clerk handed the card back, put the eighty-plus-dollar dress into a bag, and pushed the bag across the counter.

"You did it." Kindra clapped her hands together and bounced three times.

Ginger turned around to face her support team—the BHN, Tammy, and Earl. Arleta squeezed her shoulder.

Earl tilted his hat. "To our life of adventure."

"To our life of adventure, good friends, and good deals." Ginger lifted her bag. "And all that God provides."

SHARON DUNN

Don't miss the next
Bargain Hunters mystery
coming January 2008

About the Author

Sharon Dunn can't recall ever paying full price for anything. She inherited all her bargain hunting skills from her mom, whose most famous purchase was three grocery bags of cheese because "it was on sale." Mom froze the cheese. Thawed cheese crumbles and tastes, well...previously frozen. Like Ginger, Sharon had to learn that God was a better financial manager then she was. Giving Him control of the checkbook allows her to operate from a place of gratitude instead of fear. Sharon clips coupons and haunts the clearance racks, where she buys things for her three children and very tall husband. She would love to hear from readers—visit her at www.sharondunnbooks.com. It won't cost a dime. Such a deal.